THE
GIRL
IN THE
PICTURE

BOOKS BY MELISSA WIESNER

Her Family Secret

Melissa Wiesner

THE
GIRL
IN THE
PICTURE

bookouture

Published by Bookouture in 2021

An imprint of Storyfire Ltd.
Carmelite House
50 Victoria Embankment
London EC4Y 0DZ

www.bookouture.com

ISBN: 978-1-80019-559-2
eBook ISBN: 978-1-80019-558-5

For Sid. I am so lucky to be on this adventure with you.

PROLOGUE

"Tegan, come on!" Jamie's voice rippled across the hollow like the creek he was traversing, his feet hopping from one stone to the next as the water flowed past. "I'll hold your hand, you won't fall in."

I eyed the bubbling creek with suspicion. Did it have the power to sweep me away? I'd spent eight years of my life in apartments in the city, and had never learned to swim. Neither had Jamie, but at thirteen, he might be tall enough to stand on the rocky bottom. Besides, Jamie was the strongest, toughest kid I knew. Jamie would *never* fall in.

Hopping back to the stone closest to me, he scrubbed a grimy hand on his equally dirty cut-off jeans and held it out to me. "I promise you'll be okay."

I leaned over the water and grabbed his outstretched palm without hesitation. There wasn't much I could count on in this world except for my big brother's word. If Jamie promised, I knew without a doubt he'd keep me safe. Just like he always had.

I inched my toes toward the edge of the creek bank. "Ready?" Jamie asked, bracing himself on the narrow stone. "One… two… three…"

I squeezed my eyes shut and jumped. When they popped open again, I found the sandstone sturdy beneath my feet, and Jamie's proud smile warming me like the sun slanting through the sugar maple overhead. Hand in hand, we turned and leaped from stone to stone until we landed together on the opposite bank of the creek. From there, we scurried up the hill through the brush, crawling over fallen logs and pulling ourselves up on monkey vines when the incline grew too steep.

Finally, we reached a clearing covered in knee-high grasses swaying in the breeze and dotted with wild daisy and black-eyed Susan. Jamie lifted the bottom strand of a barbed-wire fence for me to crawl under, and I hesitated again. What if there were *cows* in there? Before we'd come to West Virginia to stay with Grandma, I'd never seen such a huge animal in all my life. Back home in the city, the only animals we had to dodge were the pit bulls that strained on their chains to bark at us as we walked through back alleys.

Jamie's gentle nudge propelled me forward, and soon we were under the fence and running across the field toward an old, crumbling stone wall surrounding a stand of pine trees. Jamie sat on the wall, swinging his sneakered feet while he waited for me to catch up. For the first time, I noticed the soles of those old shoes were hanging on by a thread. As I sank down next to him, he waved a hand at the view.

The West Virginia hills stretched out in all directions, a patchwork of colors like the quilt on Grandma's bed. Beneath us, the trees shimmered in every color of green as the wind teased the leaves on their branches. Somewhere down in those woods wound the creek that fed into a pond, sparkling jewel-like in the valley. Beyond that, dusty brown roads criss-crossed through pastures spotted with cows so tiny they looked like they'd fit in my pocket.

An old silver pick-up truck puttered along in miniature, and the dirt rose behind it into the air like steam from the kettle. "Maybe that's Grandma on her way home," I mused.

She'd had a doctor's appointment in town that morning. We'd only been staying with Grandma for a few months, but we could tell from her hushed late-night phone calls that these appointments were important. Jamie said Grandma was sick, and he was willing to bet we'd have to go back to living in the city with Daddy. Jamie was never wrong, but I hoped this would be the exception.

"Look, Tegan." Jamie grabbed my arm. "Over there. That's the one."

My gaze swung out across the valley in the direction of Jamie's pointed finger, to an expanse of green so pure it could have been plucked from my Crayola box. At the very top of the hill stood an old white farmhouse with its tin roof glinting in the sunshine. A wraparound porch encircled the home, and I thought I could make out flower boxes on the windows and a swing swaying in the breeze, or maybe my imagination simply conjured them up. To the left of the house, a tractor idled under two enormous oak trees, and a lane wound down the hill to a faded red barn.

"Oh." I breathed out the word like a sigh. "Oh, it's perfect."

Jamie and I had studied every rambling little farm we'd encountered since we hopped on the Greyhound bus that had brought us to this strange and wonderful world away from the gritty Pittsburgh neighborhood where we'd lived with Daddy. If Jamie's instincts about Grandma were right, we wouldn't be there much longer. So, we were on the lookout for the perfect country house, the perfect small town where we could live far away from the danger, the pollution... the memories... of our life of shuffling from rundown apartment to rundown apartment in the city.

When Jamie turned fifteen, he was going to get a job working construction. He'd save every penny, and I'd get a job too, as soon as I was old enough. We weren't fancy, and we didn't need much. Just a small house on a little bit of land with neighbors who'd stop by to say hello, and a sturdy wooden porch where I could sit and write my books.

"We're gonna find it, Tegan. You and me, we'll find our place, and we'll make it a real home."

A real home. I could hardly imagine it. "Do you really think we will, someday?"

Jamie gave my hand a squeeze. "I promise."

And that's when I knew. There wasn't much I could count on in this world except my big brother's word. If Jamie promised, he'd make it happen. Just like he always had.

CHAPTER ONE

Tegan

As the ballpoint of Tegan Walker's pen stabbed the truck driver's thigh with a meaty *thunk*, he let out a scream so piercing she expected the windshield to shatter. He reared back, clutching his leg. Tegan threw her shoulder against the door on her side, yanking the handle with one hand and grabbing her backpack with the other. The door flew open and she lurched out of the cab, falling into the dirt on the side of the road.

Her left knee cracked on the ground and her right hand scraped across the pavement, but she couldn't stop to wipe the blood from her leg or pull the gravel from her palm.

"You bitch!"

The desert dust billowed around as she crawled across the roadside berm to where her backpack had landed a few feet away. Ignoring her burning hand, she threw the strap over her shoulder and pushed herself to her feet. A short distance away, the truck driver's door screeched open, and her heart rate doubled.

She had to get away from this scumbag. *But, where am I?*

Tegan stumbled into the road, her gaze following the broken white line down the center until it disappeared in a shimmering haze of dust over the horizon. She swung her head wildly to the left, and then right. There was nothing. Not a car, or building, or even a damn cactus for as far as she could see.

Her backpack slapped against her arm as she whirled around, scanning the opposite horizon, but she shouldn't have bothered. Reddish brown dirt stretched for miles, punctuated only by an occasional scrubby bush not even big enough to hide behind.

Her heart played a staccato bass line against her ribcage.

"Don't panic, don't panic, don't panic," she mumbled like a mantra.

Somewhere behind her, a pair of sneakers slapped against the pavement. She swung back around and, less than twenty feet away, stood the truck driver, his face as red and angry as the blood seeping through the hole in the thigh of his faded jeans. Before she could stop to think about it, she twisted her arm through the other strap of her bag, yanked it onto her back, and took off down the embankment.

Barreling across the dune, her feet churned up dust and sent a couple of prairie dogs scurrying out of her path. Her sneakers snagged on the twisty little bushes that managed to survive in the parched landscape, but she pushed on, silently willing her legs to move faster. She picked up the pace, gasping for air as she raced to the top of the ridge and back down the other side.

She kept running, her desire to escape eclipsing the protests from her burning muscles. But, eventually, she staggered to a stop, bending at the waist and propping her hands on her thighs to suck more air into her lungs. She watched as rivulets of sweat and blood formed a Jackson Pollock painting as they trailed down her legs through patches of grime and dozens of tiny scratches.

Something scraped in the dirt behind her, and she whirled around as an enormous red-tailed hawk took off into the sky with a field mouse in its claws.

If that wasn't a metaphor for her situation, she didn't know what was.

The road and the truck were nowhere in sight, and there was no way that pot-bellied trucker could have chased her across the desert, especially with a stab wound in his thigh. But a guy who thought it was okay to stick his hand up a woman's shirt while she was sleeping was probably the kind of guy who'd be pissed off when she'd fought back. What if he'd radioed his trucker friends to come out there and help him find her?

The sun blazed overhead, broiling her bare shoulders and her scalp where her hair parted. It would be about five minutes before the freckles multiplied on her nose, but that was the least of her problems. Still, she pulled a battered Pirates hat from the side pocket of her backpack and yanked it on her head as she made her way back down the hill. She veered slightly left, away from the direction she'd come, aiming for farther down the road from where the trucker had parked.

And then… what?

She'd have to hitchhike again, and hope someone would come along on that barren two-lane highway. Someone less likely to feel her up.

Tegan used the back of her gritty arm to wipe the sweat dripping down her forehead. Damn it, she was twenty-five years old. Was she ever going to get her life together? She'd been so sure that it would be the start of a whole new life for her and Jamie when she'd packed up the car and headed out of Pittsburgh a month ago. The plan had always been for Jamie to come with her, but even with the good news about his health improving, a trip like this would have been too much.

So, she'd set off alone to travel the country, find them a place to live, and write her novel. They'd made a list of states, spending hours poring through photos and articles together. Maybe Colorado, for the mountains. Or a little town along the coast in the Pacific Northwest—Jamie had always wanted to try fishing.

But then, two weeks into her trip, her ancient station wagon had keeled over outside of Salinas and couldn't be resuscitated. Without the mattress she'd tossed in the back to sleep on, her meager savings were rapidly dwindling on campsites and motel rooms, so traveling on trains or buses was outside the budget.

For about a week, she'd hitched a ride with a grandfatherly old trucker who was carrying shipments for a grocery chain across California. He'd let her crash on the front seat of the truck while he took the sleeper cab in the back. But then he'd headed home to Santa Cruz, and she'd been on her own again.

She'd then traveled to Nevada with a woman on the run from an abusive boyfriend, but it was a relief when they arrived at a ranch outside of Vegas. They'd been looking over their shoulder for 400 miles, and Tegan hoped the woman would finally be safe with her burly ranch-hand brother who'd looked pretty comfortable with a rifle.

Next, at a coffee shop in town, she'd met a trucker carrying supplies to the oil rigs in southern Texas. She'd been eager to make it down near Austin, and he'd promised he'd be passing right through there. The trucker had a photo of a smiling red-headed woman and two ginger children in his wallet, and he'd chatted about playing for the church softball team while they ate their pancakes. Tegan didn't even think twice about climbing into the cab with him.

Somewhere past the Arizona border, she'd drifted off to sleep. When she woke, the trucker had parked on the side of the road, and his hand was under her shirt. She'd given him a hard shove and he'd lunged for her across the gear shift. In a panic, she'd grabbed the first weapon she could find, which had happened to be the pen sticking out of the pages of her journal.

Damn it, as if this whole situation didn't already completely suck, that had been her favorite pen.

She heaved a huge sigh that did nothing to clear the dust from her lungs, and kept walking. A few minutes passed, and then a couple more, and a nagging sense of unease began to settle over her. Shouldn't she have found the road by now? She hadn't run for *that* long—had she?

What if she was walking the wrong way? What if there was no road this way at all? Everything looked the same out here; it was possible she'd gotten turned around and hadn't even realized it. She gazed up into the endless, boundless blue sky, broken only by the scorching sun directly overhead and, for the first time, it occurred to her that this might not be as bad as she thought.

It might be so much worse.

She could be lost out here, and nobody would know to look for her. Only one person in the world would even notice she was missing, and it could be days before that happened.

Tegan picked up the pace, practically running now, stumbling and scraping her ankle against a rock as she scanned the horizon for signs of civilization. Just as despair began to overtake her, she heard an unmistakable *wooooosh* from somewhere ahead. She crested the next hill and almost sobbed with relief. The road stretched before her, gleaming in the unrelenting sun as a car appeared over the horizon.

Tegan flinched and took a step back. Luckily, she was so dirty she pretty much blended in with her surroundings. But as soon as the car zipped by, dust wafting behind it like smoke from a campfire, she realized her mistake. Scurrying behind a rock like a lizard every time a car passed wasn't going to free her from the scorching desert before the grabby trucker came looking for her. For all she knew, he was still parked over the next hill. That car might have been her only chance. If she were smart, she'd run after it and try to flag it down.

She saw the car begin to slow—but not for her. Across the canyon, so far in the distance that her gaze almost skated right past it, squatted a small chrome and glass building.

A diner.

A little diner with a flickering neon sign and a giant plastic cactus planted in front. There were five or six cars parked in the lot, and no sign of the tractor trailer she'd fled.

It was the most beautiful sight she'd ever seen.

She slid down the embankment and when her feet hit the road, she took off, not even stopping to glance over her shoulder. She could get herself cleaned up, order some coffee, and maybe none of this would feel so desperate. Maybe there'd be a nice family who'd offer her a ride.

She focused her gaze on that giant green cactus. God, she hoped it wasn't a mirage.

CHAPTER TWO

Jack

Jack Townsend was willing to consider the possibility that he hadn't been in his right mind when he'd planned this cross-country trip. Temporary insanity was the only explanation for why he'd let his sister convince him that enduring an endless week trapped in an enclosed space with nothing but his own thoughts was a good idea.

Well, it was too late now. He'd left California in the rearview mirror, and he wasn't about to turn around and go back. There was nothing there for him, anyway.

An accident on the highway had diverted him to this side road, and having his carefully plotted trip go off the rails wasn't helping his mood. He was behind schedule, which always made him a little anxious, and he might not make it to the hotel he'd booked in Albuquerque by dark.

Jack pressed his foot on the gas, and the V8 engine of his Mercedes G-Class easily kicked the speed up another five miles per hour. But then, out of the blue, a rusty orange pick-up truck appeared in his mirrors, hovering only feet from his bumper. The driver revved the engine and swung left, gunning it past him and then swerving back into the right lane. In another moment, the pick-up's broken tail lights disappeared over the crest of the next hill.

Jack was going exactly the speed limit, which meant that guy had to be going at least ninety. Idiot was going to get himself killed. Jack eased off the gas. No reason to join him. He'd just have to make up the time with an extra-quick stop for lunch.

And speaking of lunch—was that a diner ahead?

He slowed even further, pressing the brake as a neon-pink *Eat at Joe's* sign came into view. A couple of rusty vehicles populated the parking lot, and a ridiculous green plastic cactus sat by the entrance, holding a wholly unwelcoming sign that flickered on and off with the word, *Welcome*.

Jack almost pressed the gas again, but at the last minute he reconsidered. His GPS said it would be another thirty miles on these dinky back roads, and it was possible that this was the only option for lunch between here and Route 40.

He sighed and snapped on his turn signal. *Might as well get this over with.*

CHAPTER THREE

Tegan

"How do you know if an addict is lying?"
"How?"
"His mouth is moving."
That was what the girl with the pigtails said when we had to go around the circle at the Al-Anon meeting and share whatever we felt like sharing. She said it like a joke, and I almost expected her to say "Ba-dum-ching!" at the end. But she didn't; she just turned to me, because then it was my turn to share. I sat there frozen, with all those kids staring at me, trying to think of something to say. Finally, I whispered my name, and we moved on to the boy sitting next to me.

After we went around the circle, we had to put on blindfolds and lead each other across the room so we'd learn how to trust people.

On TV, it's always the drunk guy who has to go to the meetings, after he's crashed his car and his wife has left him and all there is to be grateful for is the bitter, burnt coffee in the church basement coffee pot. So, how did I end up there?

Jamie had seen the flyer hanging on the church bulletin board one day on his walk home from school. A group for elementary school kids like me, for kids whose parents drank too much. "It will be good for you."

"Why do I have to go and you don't?" I whined.

Jamie ran a hand through his hair. He was only fourteen but, for a second, I swore he was older than Daddy his eyes looked so worn out and tired. "Because... I think you could use a little help accepting things."

He didn't say it, but I knew what he was thinking. Jamie wasn't the one who kept making excuses, kept trying to get Daddy to sober up and act like a normal dad, like the ones whose kids went to my school. The dads who showed up for concerts and school plays without making a scene. The dads who remembered to pay the electric bill and not just the tab at Kelly's Korner Bar.

"Jamie, I promise I'll accept things if you don't make me go to that meeting."

"I don't think it works like that, T."

"It does! I swear!" I stood up straight to show him how grown up and accepting of things I could be. "Besides, I don't even care if Daddy comes to parents' night at school." I gave Jamie a pointed look. "That's what I have you for."

I don't know how, but in that moment, Jamie's eyes grew even more tired.

*

"What do you mean you don't take credit cards?"

Tegan's head snapped up from her laptop.

Damn it. Her hands were still shaking and her pulse still hammering from her run-in earlier. She'd spent the last twenty minutes trying to put her head down and work on her novel, and now she'd lost her focus thanks to some dude who didn't know how to use his indoor voice.

She glared at him from her booth in the corner, but he was busy waving his platinum American Express card at the extremely unimpressed waitress.

"Everyone takes credit cards." His voice carried all the way to the back of the diner, through the din of chatting customers and the clink of Corelle coffee cups on stained Formica tables.

The waitress shook her head and pulled her hands toward her chest as if he was holding out a rat she didn't want to touch. "Cash only."

He blew out an audible breath and Tegan rolled her eyes. What did he think, that the waitress was somehow going to stick a credit card in that ancient cash register? Did he not see the candy-colored buttons or the analog numbers that spun like a slot machine? Tegan's gaze slid from the broken jukebox advertising songs by Elvis Presley, Chuck Berry, and a group called The Dixie Cups, to the seats that had been repaired so many times they were made more of duct tape than vinyl.

What was a guy like that doing in a place like this anyway? In his pressed khaki pants and navy polo shirt, he had the air of a stodgy old senator, except he couldn't have been more than thirty. He ran his hand through his dark blond hair and every lock fell right back into place.

"Okay, well, look." He shifted in his canvas Top-Siders. "I don't have cash on me, but I probably have a check in the car."

The waitress sighed as she adjusted the apron covering her spearmint uniform. She tapped on a sign—CASH ONLY— scrawled in bright red Sharpie marker.

A couple of road workers at the counter swiveled in their seats to focus on the conversation at the cash register. Credit Card guy looked down his nose at them and then turned back to the waitress. "Well, where is the nearest ATM?"

The waitress shrugged.

One of the road workers spoke up. "There's an ATM over in Diablo." He nudged his friend, a grin forming on his lips. "But we can't have you dining and dashing on Ruby. You'll have to leave your car keys for collateral."

Credit Card guy took a step back. "How far is Diablo?"

The road worker took a gulp of coffee and plunked the mug on the counter. "'Bout five miles or so."

"*Five miles?*" Credit Card guy coughed as if the desert dust was already choking him. "You want me to walk ten miles round trip to pay for a six-dollar sandwich?"

Tegan shook her head. Those boat shoes weren't going to look so shiny after they'd hiked ten miles to Diablo and back. Her favorite pair of sneakers, now permanently smeared with cinnamon-colored dirt, were Exhibit A.

The other road worker crossed his arms over his neon orange vest. "Maybe you shouldn't have ordered that sandwich without being able to pay for it."

Credit Card guy dropped his arms by his sides. "I'm able to pay for it, if you would just…" He paused, sighing up at the ceiling as if he might find his lost patience somewhere in the red aluminum tiles.

"Fine." Ruby arched a painted-on eyebrow. "Leave your driver's license, then at least we'll have an address where the police can hunt you down if you don't come back."

Credit Card guy shook his head slowly. "It's illegal to drive without a driver's license."

Tegan bit back an incredulous snort. Was this guy serious? The chances he'd get pulled over in the five miles between the diner and Diablo were next to none. An hour ago, she would've given her future first-born to see a cop car on the horizon, but it had literally been nothing but tumbleweed blowing by.

As he negotiated with Ruby about what would be an acceptable object to leave behind—Ruby wasn't budging on the car keys or driver's license—Tegan sat up straight in the booth. A tractor trailer had pulled into the parking lot outside the window and come to a stop. Her heart dropped to her stomach when a burly trucker swung the door open, favoring his right side as he slowly climbed down to the pavement.

Bright red blood bloomed on the leg of his pants.

Heart pounding, Tegan looked wildly around the room for a place to hide as the trucker made his way to the diner door. Could she make it to the kitchen and out back in time? Tegan frantically packed up her backpack, throwing in her laptop and stuffing her sweatshirt on top as the door swung open and the trucker stepped inside. To her relief, his gaze swung past her to the hallway leading to the bathrooms. As he turned and slowly limped in that direction, Tegan dived under the table so he couldn't see her face if he happened to glance in her direction.

As soon as the bathroom door swung shut behind him, Tegan sat back up and dug in her pockets for some cash to pay her bill. But then what? She'd be out in the desert again, five miles from Diablo, apparently. She'd hoped to find a family willing to give her a ride, but the only people in the diner were the road workers and a group of older ladies who'd glared at the dirt on her clothes when she walked in.

And then there was Credit Card guy.

Tegan eyed him arguing with the waitress, and an idea slowly formed. There was no way that guy was from around here. He had to be traveling somewhere and, at the moment, it really didn't matter where. He was so strait-laced, he probably never even took a bottle of shampoo from a hotel room. And maybe that was a good thing if she didn't want to end up shoving a pen into another guy's thigh.

At that moment, the road workers slid off their stools and approached Credit Card guy from behind. "Hey, Ruby, you want us to teach this guy not to talk to you like that?" one of them asked. He nudged the other, and they bit back chuckles.

Credit Card guy spun around to face them and both their smiles disappeared, replaced by narrowed eyes.

Credit Card guy hadn't caught their teasing grins, and he went on alert, sucking in a breath and standing up to his full height.

He was tall—at least a couple of inches over six feet—but leaner than the broad, burly road workers. If they were actually serious, he'd be no match for two of them. He assumed a stance probably meant to project confidence, with his feet set slightly apart, elbows bent, and hands curled into fists. But his eyes darted back and forth between them and then flickered past them to the door, giving away his fear.

Tegan made her decision. Approaching the counter, she held out a handful of bills to Ruby. "Will this cover his meal, too?"

Ruby flipped through the money. "Sure will, honey. Let me just get you some change."

Tegan shook her head. "Keep it." She made a break for the exit, pushing the door open with a jingle and stepping outside into the dry desert air. Slinging her backpack over her shoulder, she scanned the parking lot, her gaze skimming across two pick-up trucks, an old Dodge sedan, and a motorcycle.

Nope, nope, and nope.

And then she found it. A sleek, black Mercedes SUV parked up against the building under the blinking diner sign. In the land of Ford trucks towing livestock trailers, that car stood out like… well… a drunk in a church choir.

She glanced at the door to the diner and then took a casual walk around the car, trying to get a feel for the owner. California license plate. She pressed her nose to the window, cupping her hand around her face to block out the glare. A pile of suitcases and moving boxes sat in orderly stacks in the back, like a large, anal-retentive game of Tetris. The diner door jingled, and Tegan backed away from the car and leaned against the wall.

"Hey." Credit Card guy stepped into her line of vision. "Do you have Venmo or Paypal so I can send you some money?" His voice was flat and cold, as if this whole thing were an inconvenience that was somehow her fault.

Tegan blinked, momentarily taken aback. She'd expected him to say thank you, not bark at her in that brusque tone. "No, sorry."

He blinked. "Okay, well, what about a check?"

"No, thanks. I'm not from around here." She shrugged. "I won't have anywhere to deposit a check."

Now it was his turn to look surprised. A rich guy like him probably didn't turn down money, or he never would have gotten rich in the first place. "Well, you can deposit it later, just take it and hold on to it." He held up his pointer finger. "Wait a minute." He unlocked the car and slid into the front seat, leaning over to dig in the glove compartment.

Tegan peered into the SUV. "I'm not very good at holding on to things."

He ignored her, rummaging around until he found a leather checkbook and a fat silver pen. She walked around to the passenger side and pulled the door open. He froze with the pen poised over a check. Their eyes met and, for a second, she felt a strange pull in her chest.

She looked away, past him into the dark leather interior of the car. "I can't use a check," she said, more firmly.

"Okay, well, give me your home address and I'll mail it later."

Was she not being clear that she didn't want his check, or was it that he wasn't really listening? "I don't have an address. I don't want your check."

His face flashed with annoyance, and she had a feeling that people usually did whatever he wanted without argument. "Well, how am I supposed to pay you back?"

The front door of the diner jingled, and her body tensed. Ruby, the waitress, stepped outside and lit up a cigarette, and Tegan blew out the breath she was holding. She really needed to get out of there.

"Actually, I could use a ride."

Credit Card guy started to say something and then stopped before he managed to sputter, "I don't think that's a good idea."

"Why not? You want to pay me back and I need a ride. It's perfect."

But—" He shook his head. "You don't even know where I'm going."

She bent over, propping a hand on the passenger seat so she could see him better. "Where *are* you going?"

He hesitated and, in that moment, an unexpected sadness flashed in his eyes. Before Tegan could spend too much time wondering about that, it was gone. A moment later, the hard, irritated look was back. "New York."

"City?"

"Yes."

A tiny cavern of longing cracked open somewhere behind her ribcage. He was going east. It was pretty much impossible to get to New York City without at least edging through Pennsylvania. At that moment, she would've given anything to see Jamie.

Tegan shook her head, shaking off the yearning. She was doing this for her and Jamie. He'd be devastated if she crawled back to Pittsburgh now. But she couldn't stay in Nowhere, Arizona, either, and she didn't have a lot of other options. So, she'd ride along for a few days, see where they ended up. Maybe he'd take a northern route through Colorado, or south through Tennessee and Kentucky. Both were perfect places to explore small-town America.

"Great," she said. "That's exactly the direction I'm going."

"Whoa! Wait a minute!" He held out his hand to stop her from sliding into the seat. "You can't ride with me all the way to New York City."

She didn't intend to go to New York City, but she didn't need to tell him that. "Why not? You said you wanted to pay me back, right?" She gave him a wide-eyed stare.

"Yes, but… how much did you give that waitress for my lunch? Nine, ten dollars?" He raised an eyebrow. "A ride from Arizona to New York is hardly the equivalent of ten dollars."

"Yeah, okay." She drummed her fingers on the door. "But it wasn't just ten dollars. I saved your ass back there. Is a ride from Arizona to New York the equivalent of your *ass*?"

For a second, his mouth quirked into an almost-smile, showing off his square jaw and bringing a tiny glint to his deep blue eyes. Maybe… maybe he wasn't so bad after all. Maybe riding with him would be more pleasant than she thought. But then his eyes met hers and the smile was gone. His gaze raked her up and down, and she could almost feel her skin burn under his scrutiny. She'd done her best to clean up in the diner bathroom, but without a first aid kit and a proper shower, there was only so much she could do about the scratches on her legs, or her wild, frizzing hair. She'd changed into a clean tank top at least, but her grubby backpack had already left smears of red dirt across it.

He shook his head, expelling a breath as heavy as cement.

A slow flush crept up Tegan's neck to her cheeks. Yeah, well, she didn't relish the idea of a couple of days in a car together any more than he did. If it were up to her, she'd go her own way instead of relying on rides from strangers. She was sick of relying on other people. But what options did she have? She'd worked double shifts to scrape together the money for this trip. Left Jamie behind and taken this enormous leap of faith, all because this was her shot to finally change their lives.

With her out of the way, Jamie could stay with friends for a while. Derek and Rebecca didn't have room in their tiny apartment for both of them. If she went home now, where would she and Jamie end up? Living in a rundown apartment infested with asbestos and mold, and cobbling together her two-dollar tips to pay the rent? With all the grime and pollution and neighbors yelling in the apartment next door, it was hard for her to write in the city. It wasn't good for Jamie's health, either.

Tegan squared her shoulders. She was *not* crawling back to her old life to tell Jamie she'd failed. Maybe she'd hit a little snag on this trip, but she had to look at the big picture. Her book was coming along now that she finally had time to focus on it. Out here in the sunshine and wide-open spaces, her creativity thrived like never before. And if she rode with this guy for a while, there would be plenty of opportunities to see more of the country.

Tegan's gaze swept across the SUV, from the shiny leather seats and pristine floor mats to the scowl on the face of the driver. She'd be taking a risk getting in a car with another man she didn't know. But the fact that he was glaring at her from his eighty-thousand-dollar vehicle with his face pinched like a squirrel was strangely comforting. If he found her repugnant, it was unlikely that he'd try to grope her, right?

As she stood there contemplating what to do, the door jingled again, and the grabby trucker limped out, squinting in the sunlight. Before Credit Card guy could stop her, Tegan tossed her backpack on the floor of his car and climbed in.

CHAPTER FOUR

Jack

Jack stared at the stranger in his passenger seat and watched his peaceful, solitary road trip go up in smoke. Okay, it wasn't like he'd been having the time of his life before she came along. But just because he was sick of his own company didn't mean he wanted anyone *else's* company. Especially if that person was a hippie with wild blue eyes, a ratty backpack, and scrapes on her knees. Somehow, she'd managed to climb into his car before he could stop her, and he couldn't exactly shove her back out onto the road.

This wasn't happening. He didn't pick up *hitchhikers*.

Jack watched as she settled into the seat and rooted around in her backpack. Who was she, anyway, and how did she end up in that diner in the middle of nowhere without a ride?

By the confident way she spoke, he would have guessed that she was close to his age—almost thirty—but those freckles scattered across her sunburned face gave her a more youthful appearance. Her long, unruly blond hair spilled out from underneath a baseball hat that was so worn she should have tossed it in the Goodwill bin years ago. Coppery-brown grime coated every inch of her, from her tank top and denim shorts down to her grubby sneakers. Grime that was rubbing off all over his car.

"Look," he said. "I don't even know you. I don't see how this is going to work out, traveling together."

How could he explain to her that he couldn't possibly spend day after day in a car with her—in a car with *anybody*? This was already the longest conversation he'd had with someone who wasn't in his family in close to a year. Even at work, he usually holed up in his office and let his partner handle most of the client interactions. He wasn't up for this, and maybe he never would be again.

"You won't even know I'm here." She nudged her backpack out of the way with one of her beat-up sneakers, and the sleeping bag secured to the top with a piece of twine bumped his cell phone mount. His iPhone fell to the floor with a clatter. "Oops. Sorry about that."

Jack sighed, fishing his phone out from under the gas pedal and re-attaching it to the dash. He rubbed his temples, shaking his head.

"Honestly, I promise I won't be any trouble." Her gaze darted past him out the car window and then back to meet his. "Please?"

Something about the urgency in her tone and the pleading look in her eyes had him hesitating. They were miles from civilization, and after his experience with the guys in the diner, he couldn't very well leave her there. Plus, she looked like she'd recently had a run-in with someone, or something.

His thoughts drifted to Charlotte, the way they always did lately. What if it were Charlotte stranded out there, in need of his help? He'd give anything to make sure she was safe. He hadn't been there for Charlotte, and he'd spend the rest of his life regretting it. But maybe this woman had been thrown into his path for a reason. Maybe he could help her, and atone for all the ways he'd failed Charlotte.

He planned to stop for the night in Albuquerque, and there'd be all kinds of transportation in the city. He could drop her off at the bus station—she wouldn't be stranded.

The woman flopped back against the seat, and a cloud of dust rose from her. His gaze skated from her scraped-up legs to a splatter of dried blood slashed across her elbow. "Can I ask you something?"

"Sure." She shrugged.

"What happened to you? Why are you so dirty and covered in blood?"

She rubbed her palms on her shorts, as if that was going to help, and then ran her hands down her scratched-up legs. "I'm not covered in blood."

He gestured at her elbow. She twisted her arm to get a better look, and her face scrunched up in horror. "Oh. Ew. That must be from the truck driver." She reached for her bag and dug around in one of the pockets.

Jack pulled a wad of tissues from the center console, wet them with his water bottle, and handed them to her. "Excuse me? From the truck driver?"

"Yeah…" She took the tissues and swiped at the blood on her arm. "I must not have noticed that it smeared on me when I—" She abruptly stopped talking.

Jack had a bad feeling about this. "When you *what*?" he demanded.

She cringed, wrinkling her freckled nose. "Um. Well… when I stabbed him in the leg." She mumbled it under her breath, so low he could barely hear.

His mouth dropped open. "You stabbed someone in the leg? *Today?*" Jesus. Who had he just let into his car? Maybe it wasn't too late to shove her out.

"Yeah, like an hour ago."

"*Why?*"

Her cheeks flushed bright pink. "I fell asleep and he tried to grope me, okay? He wasn't exactly a gentleman when I wasn't interested, so I had to… you know." She raised her arm and made a stabbing motion.

Jack swore under his breath. If she were his sister, or Charlotte, he'd want to hunt down the asshole who'd assaulted her and rip his head off. But then his anger turned toward the woman in the seat next to him. She'd had an experience like that, and then she hopped into a car with the next guy who came along? She had no way of knowing what kind of person he was. What the hell was the matter with her?

"So, you just happened to have a knife in your bag?" Did she still have that knife in her bag? How did he get himself into this?

"No, I used my pen."

Jack's gaze snapped to the silver pen still sitting next to his checkbook on the dash. He grabbed it and stuffed it into the side pocket on his door.

She actually had the nerve to roll her eyes, as if he was over-reacting. "I'm not going to stab *you*. Unless you plan to grope me."

"No, thank you." Jack's shoulders slumped. Damn it. How did the most irresponsible woman on the planet suddenly become his problem? If he didn't give her a ride to all the way to New York, would she take a bus in Albuquerque? Or would she hop into the next car that came along? Who knew what kind of creeps were out there?

"Look, you can ride with me as long as you're quiet, all right? I'm not here to make friends," he muttered.

She straightened in her seat. "I'll be as quiet as a mouse."

He seriously doubted that.

She crossed her legs and her backpack shifted and bumped his control panel.

"Why don't you put that thing in the back? I'd hate for you to get it dirty on the floor there." He gave it a shove. "Especially with that nice duct tape all over it."

She rolled her eyes, but picked up the backpack and swung it between their seats. It landed with a loud thump on one of the boxes stacked in the backseat. Jack winced. Hopefully, it wasn't the one holding his Baccarat etched glass bar set.

She swung back around and clicked her seatbelt together as he started the car and eased it onto the road.

They made it an entire quarter of a mile before she started talking.

"So, do you have a name?" she asked.

"Jack," he muttered, in a tight voice. He stared straight ahead, but could sense her watching him.

The silence stretched between them and, finally, she let out a small laugh. "I'm Tegan. Thanks *so much* for asking."

Okay, so he was being rude. But he didn't want to spend the next 2,500 miles chit-chatting. He had too much he should be thinking about before he had to face the rest of his life.

But she just kept talking.

"So…" She drew out the word into two syllables. "Are you moving or something? That's a lot of boxes back there."

He grunted something non-committal, but she took it as encouragement to keep blathering.

"To New York City? From where?"

He sighed. "San Francisco."

Ten dollars. If he'd only had ten dollars in cash, he wouldn't be stuck with this woman. He should have fled from the diner and driven off without stopping. Or peeled out when she suggested this ridiculous plan of traveling together. It wasn't like he would've seen her again.

But he wasn't that kind of guy, as much as right now he wished he was. Townsends paid their debts, gave to charity, and compensated their employees generously. She'd paid for his meal, and he owed her.

Plus, now that he knew a truck driver had assaulted her, he couldn't wish her out there hitchhiking with random strangers. He had a duty to make sure she made it safely to wherever she was going.

"Oh, I love San Francisco!" She was still talking. Tegan. What kind of name was Tegan?

"Me, too," Jack muttered.

"Then why are you leaving?"

He'd walked right into that one, hadn't he? "I'm transferring to my firm's branch in New York."

"What kind of firm?"

"I'm an attorney. Corporate law."

"Oh, that sounds… interesting." She said it like he'd just told her he spent every day counting a giant bucket of beans. "Why'd you go into law?"

Why did he? It used to be that he enjoyed the challenge. Reading a contract and spotting the loopholes. Researching past cases to compose a compelling argument. Negotiating the best deal for a client. But all that was a long time ago. Back when he still had everything in the world and his whole future ahead of him.

Now? He didn't enjoy anything about anything. So, he gave her the first answer he could think of.

"The law firm has been in my family for generations. It's always been my legacy. It's exciting to be a part of that."

"Uh-huh."

His gaze flickered over to her. If she raised her eyebrows any higher, they'd hit the roof of the car. "What?"

She shrugged. "Nothing."

"No, really. What's that look about?" Why was he even engaging with her? He should just shut this conversation down, but something about her tone annoyed him.

"Nothing. It's just—well, why did *you* go into law?" she asked.

"I just told you."

"No. You told me why your family expected you to be a lawyer. You didn't say anything about what you like about it."

Was she kidding? Now this woman he'd picked up in the desert was going to interrogate him about his life choices? "I'm sorry, what do *you* do?" he snapped back.

"I'm a writer."

Of course she was. He was willing to bet his Tag watch that she was traveling the country thinking she was going to write the next *On the Road* knock-off. Like people cared about her nomad lifestyle or her musings on the meaning of life or whatever it was.

"A writer?" He snorted.

"Yeah." Her voice had a defensive edge, which perversely encouraged him to keep talking.

"Are you a journalist? Blogger? Short stories? Technical manuals, maybe?" He could hear the sarcasm dripping from his voice, but couldn't help himself. There was a pause where the only sound was the car tires spinning on the dusty road. He glanced over. She was looking at him sideways.

"Well, which is it?"

Another pause.

"I'm working on a novel." She spoke slowly, drawing out each word.

"Let me guess. Is it about traveling across the country? Finding the meaning of life in truck stops and run-down diners?"

Another glance in her direction. She stared back with narrowed eyes.

He knew it. And for some reason, it disappointed him that he was right. A little part of him was hoping she'd say she was a science writer for the *New York Times*, or working on a biography of Abraham Lincoln. Or… anything that wasn't such a damn cliché. It was irrational, but it made him even more annoyed that he was stuck with her all the way to New York. That she was infringing on his trip to write some half-baked novel. "Everyone thinks they can write a book these days," he muttered.

Tegan jerked forward in her seat, her face darkening. "For your information, I'm not just some wannabe. I've had stories published in literary journals and magazines." She crossed her arms over her chest. "An editor at a major publishing house reached out and suggested I turn one of my short stories into a book."

Jack considered asking where the story was published—*Cosmo*? But he didn't actually want to know the answer. Unless it was the *New Yorker*, he was unlikely to be impressed.

They didn't speak for a while, which turned out to be a little unnerving, despite the fact that he'd been wishing for silence not five minutes earlier. It was impossible to relax when she was sighing and shuffling around next to him; when he was breathing her dusty, second-hand air.

She let out a little cough. He hadn't spotted a water bottle attached to her backpack, which was surprising, considering they were in the middle of the desert. When he'd packed for the trip three days earlier, he'd made sure to stock the car with water, snacks, and a first aid kit, just in case he broke down.

He stretched his arm around her seat to grab a bottle of water from the case on the floor. As his hand swung past her shoulder, she ducked away from him. He picked up the water and held it out to her.

"Oh," he heard her mutter under her breath. She took the bottle, but didn't open it.

"You can relax. I have no interest in making a move on you."

"I know. Of course." She peeled at a corner of the paper wrapped around the bottle. "You can't be too careful."

"That's ironic coming from a woman who just hopped into a car with a strange man. How do you know I'm not a serial killer?" And then he gave his head a tiny shake. *Why did I say that?* Bringing up serial killers to a woman who'd been groped by her last ride was pretty insensitive. But he'd only been in the car with Tegan for about five minutes, and her habit of blurting out whatever came to mind already seemed to be rubbing off on him.

"*Are* you a serial killer?" She crossed her arms over her chest in a silent challenge.

Her bold tone made him smirk. "Maybe."

"No, you're not."

He reached back to grab another bottle, and this time she didn't flinch. "How do you know?"

"Serial killers are usually charming."

He twisted the top off the bottle and took a gulp of water to swallow down his inexplicable urge to laugh.

CHAPTER FIVE

Tegan

Jamie held the phone to his ear, pacing back and forth in the narrow apartment kitchen. Mom had only been gone for a few weeks. She'd taken off with that guy she'd met at work, so at first I thought it might be her calling to say she was coming home. But then I realized Jamie was talking about me, and he'd deepened his voice the same way he did when I was playing with my Barbies and begged him to be Ken.

Finally, he hung up, turning to look at me with his eyes narrowed and his gaze sweeping from my holey socks up to my face. "When was the last time you had a bath?"

I blinked in surprise. "I don't know. Why were you talking funny like that?"

Jamie walked over to the fridge. He swung it opened and looked inside with that same intensity he'd directed at me a moment ago. "That was your teacher." He pulled out a bag of white bread with just the ends left, and an empty jar of peanut butter.

"Mrs. Schaefer? Why?"

"She was calling to talk to Dad. I couldn't tell her he was down at the bar again, especially after she told me she's worried you've been wearing the same clothes to school for days, and your hair looks like a rat's nest."

My hand flew up to my head, which immediately tangled in my unruly waves. Something burned hot in the pit of my stomach. It wasn't my fault. I was only seven, and Mom used to help with stuff like baths and hair.

Reluctantly, but still.

Jamie tossed the empty peanut butter jar in the trash. "Go look in Daddy's drawer—the one where he keeps the cash. I'm going to run down to the store to get something to make for dinner while you take a bath." He turned away from me to scrub the kitchen table with a sponge.

After my bath, Jamie and I sat at the kitchen table eating cheese sandwiches and cut-up apples.

"Listen, T," Jamie said, brushing the crumbs from his hands. "Mom's gone for good."

I stared at him, waiting for the part where he said he didn't really mean it; for him to explain that Mom just needed a break for a while, but then she'd come home. Just like he usually did.

"You don't know that for sure," I finally prompted.

He didn't answer, but the look that came over his face told me Jamie did know. That Jamie was slowly coming to understand all kinds of things that most twelve-year-old boys didn't have to think about. He arranged his apple slices in a circle on his plate and finally looked up at me. "Tegan, if they think Daddy's not taking care of us…" He put his head in his hands. His voice was muffled when he spoke again. "They'll take you away from me."

From that moment, I did everything Jamie told me to do. I took a bath every single night and held back my tears when Jamie yanked the comb through my wet hair. I did my homework and ate all the vegetables Jamie prepared, even the broccoli, which I hated. I did every single thing

Jamie told me to do because nothing was ever going to take me away from him.

*

Was Jack watching her?

Even though she was huddled against the car door, staring at the laptop propped on her leg and typing furiously, Tegan's mind wasn't really on the story in front of her. It was hard to concentrate when Jack's presence seemed to take up so much space in the car.

When she'd traveled with the grandfatherly truck driver, the gentle rocking of the truck cab and the low vibration of his baritone voice humming along to George Strait's *Greatest Hits* had been like a warm blanket wrapped around her. She'd sat in the passenger seat, oblivious to the world, and four chapters had practically written themselves.

But there was nothing warm or soothing about Jack, and the world of her book couldn't hold her attention when he was around. Every time his hand shifted on the steering wheel or he arched his back to stretch his shoulders, it was like a flag waving. When he cleared his throat or coughed, he might as well have been yelling. And his disdain was like a third passenger in the car, one that kept elbowing and poking her.

His eyes flickered back and forth between the road and her. He was probably thinking about what an idiot she was. She hadn't meant to tell him about the guy who'd groped her, and then there she was, blurting it out. She wished she hadn't said anything. She didn't need him looking down his nose at her.

So, she'd had a couple of bad experiences. If everything was easy, she'd never have anything to write about. Besides, she was back on track now, and things were looking up. Convincing Jack to give her this ride had worked out exactly as planned. Now, if she could just get some work done on her book…

Tegan focused on the screen in front of her, and finally inspiration struck. She managed to write exactly one paragraph, and then Jack coughed, and her head shot up.

Damn it.

She closed her laptop with a snap and glanced at Jack from the corner of her eye. He stared straight ahead, both hands on the wheel, driving a sensible sixty miles per hour. She tried to look at him objectively, as if she weren't a questionably welcome companion on his road trip.

His profile was attractive—straight nose, blue eyes, honey-colored hair that was close-cropped on the sides and just a little bit longer and combed back on top. Well, it would be attractive if he'd relax that tightly wound expression for one second. He had a bit of stubble on his jaw as if he hadn't shaved since yesterday. It was incongruous with the rest of his clean-cut style, but he was on a road trip. Maybe not shaving for a day was his way of really letting loose. His clothes were neatly pressed—impressive considering he'd been sitting in the car for hours—and on his wrist he wore a silver and black leather watch with all sorts of fancy little dials on it.

Jack glanced in her direction and caught her staring. "What?"

"Nothing." She turned toward the passenger window and focused on the fields rolling by. They drove a few more miles, and Tegan began to squirm. All this silence was making her twitchy.

"Want to turn on the radio?" she finally asked, when she couldn't take it anymore.

Still facing the road, Jack's eyes flickered in her direction. Without a word, he punched on the radio and hit the scan button. He zipped right past the Rolling Stones singing 'Wild Horses', and The Dixie Chicks' 'Goodbye Earl'.

She opened her mouth to object, and then snapped it shut.

The bland, folksy tones of a public radio announcer filled the car, and Jack hit the button to pause the scanner. Tegan sighed and settled back.

The announcer was interviewing a reporter who'd been at the Capitol building for a Senate vote about tax legislation earlier that day. When the reporter pointed out that the sponsors of the bill believed that the tax savings for the rich would help to improve the economy for the working class, Tegan snorted.

Jack glanced in her direction, a brow arched. "You don't agree with their assessment?"

"Bills like that never help regular people." She bent her knee and shoved one foot under her opposite leg so she could turn her body toward him.

Jack stared at her foot resting on his leather seat. "Some of the top economists in the country would disagree with you. I don't imagine that you read any of the reviews of the bill by the Center for Policy Analysis or the Brookings Institution?"

She really should stop arguing with him.

"Maybe we should agree to disagree about politics?" She smoothed her face into a congenial smile. "How about some music?"

Before he could argue, she hit the scan button and searched until she came to a song by Chris Stapleton. She settled back and hummed along.

"Country music, seriously?" Jack scoffed.

She was trying, she really was. But there was no way she could just let that go. "Don't tell me you're one of those people who hates all country music because you heard 'Friends in Low Places' at a wedding and decided the entire genre is beneath you."

"No. I hate country music because of the structural simplicity of the music, the corny, uninspired lyrics, the blind patriotism, and the sexist stereotypes."

Her eyes flew back to his profile. He stared straight ahead at the road, expressionless. Okay, that was a surprise, and maybe she was just a little bit impressed. It sounded like he actually knew what he was talking about. And a tiny part of her appreciated that he cared about sexism. Most men wouldn't even think there was anything wrong with calling grown women "girls", or all the focus on women's bodies in a lot of country music. But it didn't mean she wasn't going to argue right back.

"There are musicians in all genres with uninspired, sexist lyrics who use the same three guitar chords. Sucky music isn't exclusive to country."

"Sucky music?" He rolled his eyes. "Is that the technical term?"

"Yes! And a blanket statement like that discounts all the country artists who influenced some of the greatest musicians from other genres. I mean, Bruce Springsteen was influenced by Hank Williams. What rock musician *wasn't* influenced by Johnny Cash? Plus, some of the greatest female musicians ever came from country." She held up her hand, ready to count off the names, but the radio interrupted her as the song changed to one where the singer—unfortunately—began rhapsodizing about chewing tobacco and spitting.

Tegan cringed as Jack leaned over to turn up the chorus. "I'm sorry," he said, with a smirk. "What were you saying about the greatness of country music?"

Tegan blew out a frustrated breath and reached over to smack the radio off with the palm of her hand. "I guess talking about music is off the table, too."

How had she managed to trap herself in a car with a guy who she had absolutely nothing in common with? Less than nothing in common. She could usually talk to *anyone.* Maybe it was the writer in her, but she'd always loved getting to know people, finding out their life stories. And having spent most of her childhood moving around the city, always on the lookout for cheap rent or a free meal, she'd encountered more strangers than friends in life. She'd learned how to ask questions because people loved to talk about themselves; to make people comfortable until suddenly they were spilling their stories.

But none of that seemed to work with Jack. Aside from the fact that he barked at her when she asked him anything about himself, there was something about him that made her want to argue. Maybe it was the way that he looked at her like she was the dirt on the bottom of her scuffed shoes.

She scanned the car, looking for something else to talk about, but there wasn't much to work with. She didn't know anything about expensive cars, and he didn't seem very eager to talk about the moving boxes in the backseat. Finally, she settled on: "How about sports?"

Jack's gaze skimmed the top of her head and then slowly shifted back to the road. "You're wearing a Pirates hat. This conversation was over before it started."

She slumped back in her seat and turned back to the landscape zipping by. "I give up."

"Good," Jack muttered.

CHAPTER SIX

Jack

The hippie was squirming again. She'd spent fifteen minutes adjusting her seat with the automatic buttons, moving it back and forth, up, down, back and forth again. And Jack had been *this close* to smacking her hand away from fiddling with the vents that controlled the air flow. She sat with her dirty shoes all over his clean leather seats and spilled pretzel crumbs on the floor. On top of all that, she had to pee every hour and a half.

As if she could read his mind, she turned to him and flashed a contrite smile. "Any chance you'll be needing gas soon?"

He sighed. "I saw a sign for a gas station in five miles. Can you hold it for five miles?"

"Probably." She squirmed again.

A few minutes later, Jack rolled the car up to a red and white painted building rising up out of the flat, barren landscape. Neon signs for Tecate beer and Valvoline motor oil blinked in the window, and an antique Coca-Cola chest cooler sat by the front door, complete with a coin slot and bottle opener screwed to the side. A single gas pump squatted in the middle of the dusty parking lot.

As soon as the car stopped, Tegan hopped out and ran for the bathroom door on the side of the building. Jack got out and circled the car to the gas pump. He searched for a slot for his credit card, but there wasn't one. The convenience store had ancient, peeling Visa and MasterCard stickers stuck to the glass in the front door, though. He'd be looking for those signs at every shop and restaurant now, for as long as he lived. At least he'd grabbed some cash at the last stop, just in case.

While his gas pumped, he pulled out his cell phone and discovered he might actually have enough service to call his sister, Olivia. It was seven o'clock in New York, and he figured she'd just be getting home from work.

She picked up on the first ring. "Jack! Hi!"

At the sound of her voice, the tension seeped from his shoulders. "Liv, hey, how are you?"

"Perfect timing, I just got home and I want to hear all about your trip so far."

Jack gazed through the windows of the SUV to the bathroom door on the side of the building. There was no movement there, so he turned around and leaned back against the car. The numbers on the pump slowly flipped as the gas flowed. "I've only got a minute, but the trip is good."

There was no way he was going to tell Liv about picking up Tegan. She would only worry, and there wasn't any reason for that. This little blip with Tegan would be short-lived. They'd spend the next few days together, and then he'd drop her off wherever she was going and that would be the end of it.

"I'm glad to hear that," Liv murmured—and even from 2,500 miles away, he could tell she didn't completely believe him. Nothing about his life for the past year had been *good.* "Where are you?"

"Arizona. But we—" *No.* "I'll hit the New Mexico border soon." Jesus, he almost gave it away that he was driving Tegan. *Focus.* "It's really beautiful, I wish you could see some of this landscape."

"Oh, me too. Text some pictures, okay? Mom and Dad would love to see them too. You know they're… anxious… to hear how it's going."

Yes, there was no way he could tell Liv about his passenger. If she told his parents, his mother would be beside herself. He knew she already had plenty of opinions on the state of his mental health and what sort of diagnoses to label him with. Not that she said any of that out loud to him. No, his mother tiptoed around him, but he'd overheard her talking to Liv the last time they were visiting in San Francisco.

The gas pump clicked and shut off, signaling that his tank was full. He stood up straight. "Hey, Liv. Hold on a second, I'm pumping gas and need two hands here." He set the phone on top of the gas pump and pulled the dispenser out of the tank.

At that moment, Tegan skipped around the side of the car. "Hey, that bathroom wasn't nearly as bad as the one at the last gas station. Are you going to go before we head out?"

Jack flung the gas dispenser back on the pump, swearing under his breath. *Damn it, did she have to* yell? He lunged for his phone and hit the mute button. "I'm on the phone here," he snapped.

"Oh. Sorry." She didn't sound the least bit sorry. "I'll go grab some snacks. You want anything?"

He thought about the salt and pretzel dust ground into his floor mat. "No crumbs."

"No crumbs?" She wrinkled her forehead. "What does that mean?"

"Nothing. Never mind." He waved her toward the store. "I'll be there in a minute."

She backed away slowly, mouthing, "Ohhhh-kaaaay," as if *he* were the strange one. He watched her disappear around the car before he picked up his phone and unmuted it. Maybe Olivia hadn't heard anything.

He took a deep breath. "Sorry, what were you saying, Liv?"

"Who was *that*? Are you traveling with someone? A woman?"

So much for Liv not hearing anything.

"What gives you that idea?" *Play dumb, great strategy.* Liv had been at the top of her class at Harvard Law. She would never fall for that.

"Jack! I heard some woman talking to you. It sounded like you're traveling with someone. What's going on?"

"It's just this—hippie woman." He realized as soon as he heard Liv take an audible breath that he shouldn't have called her that.

"What do you mean, *hippie woman?*"

"I mean, she's—she's a writer. She's—" He needed to stop talking. Anything he said at that moment was only going to dig him deeper.

"And she's riding with you?" Her usually calm voice had an uncharacteristic tinge of shock. "Are you and she—*you know?*"

He almost laughed. There was no way he and Tegan would ever be—*you know.* "No," he said, calmly. "I didn't pick up some woman on this trip. I mean, yes, okay, technically, I picked her up, she needed a ride. But I didn't—*pick her up.* It's not like that." *Stop talking.*

"How long has she been traveling with you?"

"Just a few hours. It's only temporary."

"I'm worried. How do you know she's not going to rob you? What if she pulls out a weapon when you're driving? Or when you're stopped somewhere in the middle of nowhere?"

He pictured Tegan making that stabbing motion when she talked about the trucker who'd assaulted her. Liv *definitely* didn't need to know about that.

"Honestly, she's harmless," he lied. "Actually, I think you'd like her."

"*I'd like her?*"

The funny thing was, Liv probably *would* like her. She'd always had a thing for waifs and strays. When they were kids, Liv had befriended every homeless person on their walk from their Upper East Side penthouse to their private school three blocks away.

Their parents had been beside themselves that their well-bred eight-year-old daughter, who'd descended from five generations of New York aristocracy, knew the names and stories of "*every hobo in the city.*"

His baby sister was a lawyer now, and had taken charge of the pro-bono work at the family's law firm. He had no doubt she would have given Tegan a ride and had her whole life story by the time they hit Flagstaff.

But picking up a hippie woman on the side of the road was completely out of character for him. Especially the version of himself he'd been for the past year. He didn't know what he was doing with her, so he couldn't exactly blame Liv for her shock.

"How did you end up driving her?" He could picture Liv settling back into her cream-colored linen couch with the expanse of Central Park visible through the wall of windows in her living room. She'd probably laugh her head off at his description of the thugs at the diner and Ruby the waitress who didn't take credit cards. Suddenly, he missed his sister with a physical ache, and his mother and father too. What a relief to be going home to New York, and his family, instead of his empty apartment in San Francisco.

"I'll tell you all about it when I get home."

"I can't wait. It's nice to hear you laugh, Jackie," she said, reverting to her childhood nickname for him. "See, I knew this trip would be good for you."

"Don't tell Mom and Dad about her, okay? They'll just worry." They'd been through a lot, and he didn't need to add to that.

"Yeah. You're probably right. But make sure you text me when you get to your hotel tonight so I know you're okay."

"I promise."

He hung up the phone and headed inside to pay for his gas and track down his rider. He found her leaning against the counter, chatting with the store clerk. The clerk, a beefy, middle-aged guy with long dark hair and a graying beard, clutched a hand to the eagle flying across his faded black T-shirt as he laughed at something Tegan said.

Jack walked up to the counter and held out his credit card for the clerk. "For the tank of gas." While the clerk processed his payment, he turned to Tegan. "Did you find what you need?"

She shook the white plastic bag in her hand and he heard the rustle of food wrappers. "I got us some road trip snacks."

Glancing around the convenience store, Jack could only imagine what was in that bag. Whatever snacks she'd bought, he was sure he'd find them ground into his seats and floor mats in about five minutes.

Jack thanked the store clerk and headed for the door. He took two steps and stopped when he realized that Tegan hadn't followed.

"It was nice to meet you, Frank," she said to the store clerk. "I hope the next time I see you, it's not in the news for murdering your mother-in-law." She gave him a wink and he roared with laughter.

"I hear there's peace and quiet in prison, at least," Frank said. "Send me that book, if you ever get it published. And make sure when you describe me, I look just like Harrison Ford."

"I was thinking George Clooney."

Frank chuckled again. Tegan gave him a wave and followed Jack toward the door. They headed back out into the desert heat.

"I see you're making friends," Jack said, as they trudged across the parking lot. Liv really would like her. They both seemed to have a knack for charming strangers. Then he remembered their many arguments in the car.

Well, some strangers.

She skipped along next to him. "Some people enjoy my company. Hey—" Skidding to a stop, she dug around in her plastic bag. "I got you a present." With a grin, she pulled out a trucker hat with a black bill and mesh back. Across the white padded front were the words, *I'd agree with you, but then we'd both be wrong.*

"Think of it as a peace offering," she said.

The strangeness of the moment made him pause. Jack stood there in the dusty parking lot with the barren landscape stretching as far as he could see. It was so unlike where he'd been or where he was going that, for all he knew, he might have stepped onto another planet entirely.

Wild Tegan looked up at him with her blue eyes shining and a huge grin stretched across her face, holding out the most ridiculous gift anyone had ever given him.

How in the world did I end up here?

A smile pulled at his lips and he twisted his mouth in an attempt to hold it back. With a resigned shake of his head, he took the hat and popped it on his head. "Thanks."

"It really suits you." She pressed her hand to her mouth, and her shoulders shook as she held back a giggle.

"I'll wear it the next time I'm in court. It'll go over great with the judge."

Laughter burst from her throat, the sound of it foreign and familiar at the same time. There hadn't been any laughter in his life lately. It was nice to hear it, nice to remember that there were things worth laughing about. With that sound, one of the hundreds of pounds of weight that had been sitting on his chest for the past year lifted, leaving him feeling just a tiny bit lighter.

"Come on, let's go." He headed to his car with Tegan still laughing next to him.

CHAPTER SEVEN

Tegan

When the letter came that said we had to be out of the apartment in thirty days, Daddy dropped enough F-bombs to blow up a small country.

"Listen, Tegan," Jamie said, yanking me into the back bedroom away from where Daddy was pacing and ranting in the living room. "Don't ever repeat anything you just heard in school, okay?"

I nodded solemnly.

"They'll kick us out of this apartment over my cold, dead body," Daddy informed us—and the neighbors, who could hear him yelling through the walls.

And that was pretty much how it happened. Daddy wasn't dead, but he was passed out cold when the men came to put all of our stuff out on the sidewalk. Daddy didn't even wake up, and the men wanted to call 911, but Jamie said no, just put him in the car, he'll wake up in a few hours. Luckily, the car was a station wagon, because that's where we slept for a couple of months—me and Jamie in the front seats tipped all the way back, and Daddy stretched out in back.

It wasn't that Daddy didn't have a job to pay the rent. He did. He worked for the machine shop over in Homewood where he used a little press to put the threads *onto screws. But robots were taking over the world, and there wasn't always enough work for everyone at the shop, so they took turns being laid off. Daddy did okay when he had to be at work every day; it was when he was laid off that he sat around in his underwear watching Law and Order reruns. And then he'd go down to Kelly's Korner and drink away the rent money.*

*

"Hey."

At the sound of Jack's voice, Tegan looked up from her laptop.

He nudged the remains of the super-sized bag of Twizzlers she'd shoved into one of his cup holders. "The snacks you bought were... interesting... but I need to get some real food soon."

She pulled a Twizzler out of the bag and wagged it at him. "By interesting, you mean *delicious*, right?"

He grabbed the licorice from her hand and took a bite, making her smile. He'd whined about how unhealthy her snack choices were, but then he'd helped her polish off an entire package of Chips Ahoy, and he'd eaten most of the Twizzlers on his own.

"I'll keep my eye out for a diner." Tegan squinted at the road ahead and, for the first time, noticed evening was approaching. The landscape that had been a monochrome beige for 200 miles now glowed in shades of amber, gold and rust. Heading east, the sunset was at their backs, but the scrubby grasses stretching to the horizon reflected the light as if someone had set a thousand tiny fires in the fields around them.

"Beautiful," Tegan murmured, shoving her sunglasses to the top of her head. Up ahead, she spotted an exit off the highway connecting to a smaller country road. "Pull over! Jack, pull off there." She gestured wildly at the exit.

Jack wrenched the steering wheel to the right and slammed on the brakes as they hit the exit going way too fast. Regaining control, he coasted onto the smaller road and pulled over to the side. "What? Do you have to pee *again*?"

"No." She opened her car door and swung one leg out. "Come on. Come with me."

He stared at her, his eyebrows raised, and didn't even unbuckle his seatbelt.

God, this guy and his skeptical face. "Come on. We're already parked. What's the point of being in all this amazing scenery if you're just going to stay in the car?"

He sat there for another moment, and then made a big show of sighing deeply and unbuckling his seatbelt with exaggerated movements. Without waiting to see if he followed, she turned and headed into the field, wading into scrub grass up to her ankles. After she'd walked about fifty feet, she stopped and turned toward the sun sinking behind the black outcropping of rocks silhouetted on the horizon. Above it, the sky exploded into color.

Something ignited in her chest that matched the view. A glow that told her she'd done the right thing by taking this trip. So what if she'd had a few setbacks and scary moments? She was following her dreams, and she wasn't going to let a grabby trucker or anyone else stop her.

A twig snapped and brush rustled as Jack's slow, careful footsteps approached. He came up beside her and the heat from his body matched the rays of the sun.

"Wow." He stared off at the view.

She glanced up at him. "I know."

He flashed what might have been the first real smile he'd given her all day. His blue eyes crinkled around the edges and a dimple appeared in one cheek. That smile completely transformed his face, unclenching his jaw and smoothing out the hard, tense angles. "I should take a picture," he said. "But I don't think a picture can do it justice."

His gaze slid back to the horizon, where the last millimeter of sun dropped out of sight, leaving streaks of color across the sky. "This is what I'll remember when I'm slogging through slush trying to cross the street without getting splashed by a cab on my way to the office."

It was the first unguarded statement he'd shared all day. Tegan smiled, picturing the city streets in January. "When the snow looks like that pink-speckled snow from *The Cat in the Hat*, except it's black."

He let out a chuckle. "And you step off a curb, right into a giant puddle up to your ankles."

"And even when you finally dry out, you spend the rest of the day swiping at jagged salt stains all over the bottom of your pants."

Jack turned those laughing, crinkling eyes to her. "I can tell you've spent time in east coast winters. Where are you from?"

She felt her smile fade and her shoulders tense. Would he laugh at her if she told him the purpose of this trip? And if she opened her mouth to talk about Jamie, the words would get stuck in her throat. She grasped for a subject change. "It's hard to believe you've ever been forced to slog through the snow, braving the elements with the common people. Why don't you have your driver drop you at the front door of the family law firm? You do have a driver, don't you?"

Jack's face turned back to granite. He shook his head and, without a word, spun on his heel and headed back toward the road. Tegan stood there, watching his retreating back, hating the hollow feeling in her stomach. The shadows from the rock outcropping grew longer and the glow faded from the sky. She couldn't stay there in the field forever, so she shuffled back to the car. When she got in, it felt like someone had sucked all the air out.

Back on the highway, the tires spun on the road, and the engine whirred. Jack put on a podcast of two guys discussing the stock market and turned up the volume. Tegan thought about apologizing, but what was the point? They were stuck with each other for the next few days and then they'd never see each other again. It wasn't like they were going to end up as pals at the end of it. Besides, she had a book to focus on.

Slowly, the tiny fires dotting the landscape flickered out and the colors dimmed to gray, then navy, then black. They drove for what was probably only about thirty more minutes, but with the tension in the car, it felt like days.

Finally, Jack hit his turn signal and pulled off the highway toward a blue and white roadside sign.

Matorales, NM.
Population 2,631

He stopped at the first restaurant they came to—a diner that looked pretty much like every other diner where she'd eaten over the past few weeks. It had a large turquoise sign announcing the name of the restaurant, and a smaller light-up letter-board detailing the specials. Except a number of letters had either fallen off, or more likely local kids had stolen them, because the specials that day seemed to be:

DOG
MEAT
BURGERS

"Yum."

Jack wasn't amused by the sign, or he was in the mood for a dog-meat burger, because he shut off the engine and got out, muttering something about being starving. Tegan followed him into the restaurant and they settled in a booth in the back. The waitress came by to drop two menus on the table, and Jack looked up.

"Excuse me, do you take credit cards?"

The waitress nodded. "Yep."

"Good," he muttered, under his breath. "There's no more room in my car."

Tegan rolled her eyes.

After the waitress left with their orders, Jack yawned and stretched his arms back behind his head.

"Long day?" Tegan asked, grasping for a way to get back a little of that brief connection they'd had earlier.

"Long year," he mumbled, rubbing his eyes.

Tegan waited, wondering if maybe he'd finally open up and tell her a bit more. Was that one of those offhand things people said, or had he really had a difficult year? Was there more to his story about driving across the country to move to New York for work?

The silence stretched, making it clear that was all she was getting. "So, what do you think?" she asked. "This seems like a good town to stop. My guess is that I'm not going to convince you to camp, but I saw a motel down the road."

Jack sat up and picked up something from the seat next to him. He placed it on the table and, for the first time, Tegan noticed he'd brought a briefcase into the diner with them.

"Seriously? You're going to write a legal brief right *now*?"

He snapped the briefcase open and pulled out a neatly folded map. Okay, a map was even weirder than the briefcase. Who carried *maps* anymore? Jack unfolded it, carefully smoothing the creases until they lay flat. It was a map of the United States, marked up in at least five different colors of ink, with road lines highlighted, and circles, stars, and little notes covering the spaces around various cities and towns across the country.

Jack tapped his finger on Albuquerque. "Thanks to your fifteen bathroom stops, we're a little behind schedule."

"It was three stops! And that one time, you just pulled over and I ran behind a tree, so that hardly counts. Besides, you're the one who kept giving me bottles of water."

Jack kept talking like he hadn't heard her. "I'd planned to be in Albuquerque by now. There's a decent-looking Marriott that got four and a half stars on Tripadvisor."

"What? You don't stay at the Four Seasons?"

"It was already booked for a conference."

Tegan had been joking about the Four Seasons, but when she peered at the map—yep. Right there next to his finger, he'd crossed out the words "Four Seasons," and written "Marriott" in neat, straight script, with four stars and a "½" drawn next to it.

Her eyes tracked along Route 40, highlighted until Oklahoma City. "Let me guess. The next stop after Albuquerque will be Oklahoma City."

Jack tapped the map. "Well, there's a restaurant in Amarillo that had a great write-up in *Food and Wine* last month, so I want to try to make it there for lunch on the way."

He lifted his finger and, sure enough, there was the name of a restaurant, with the words "Poached pear salad" underneath, and more stars indicating its excellent rating.

"You mapped out your entire trip down to the restaurants where you plan to eat?" She was pretty sure she'd never seen anything quite so elaborate or so… anal retentive… in her life. Especially for a road trip. The whole point of a road trip was that it was spontaneous, that you took a different fork in the road just to see where it might lead. She rubbed her hand across her mouth to hide the smile, but she couldn't completely fight back the hitch in her chest from the giggle that was dying to escape.

Jack didn't seem to notice because he continued to study the map. "Well, not every restaurant. There were some long stretches where I couldn't find much on the travel websites, so I figured I'd wing it and try out a few local diners." He looked up and raised his eyebrows. "But that obviously proved to be a mistake."

"Oh, poor you, having a little bit of an adventure." Despite herself, a laugh escaped. "Now, instead of putting your golf buddies to sleep with your raptures over the poached pear salad, you can tell them you were almost in a brawl in a diner in Arizona until some woman with duct tape on her backpack swooped in and saved your ass."

The waitress came by and plunked two glasses of water on their table. Jack looked up at her. "Thank you," he said, with a polite smile. As soon as she left, he sighed and grabbed his napkin, carefully rubbing the map where a tiny bit of condensation had flown off the glasses and splattered near Tallahassee.

As Tegan studied the map, she had to admit there was something sort of appealing about being able to see the whole country displayed like this, with the possibility of all those exciting new places laid out right there in front of you. Maybe these old-fashioned quirks of Jack's weren't *all* bad.

But as she looked closer, she realized he'd planned to bypass all the most exciting places. Jack had been following Route 40 since about fifty miles outside of Bakersfield, California, which meant he'd skipped the Grand Canyon and Lake Mead entirely. Who took a road trip through Arizona and missed the Grand Canyon? And now he was heading for Oklahoma and Missouri. It made no sense.

She poked her finger at the map, in the general vicinity of Matorales. Then she slid it one state north. "What are you doing heading for Oklahoma City when you could be going north through the Rockies? You'll never see anything like it." She'd never been there, but she and Jamie had stared at hundreds of photos of beautiful mountain ranges online. There had to be a hundred picturesque little towns tucked away in the Rockies where they could be happy.

Jack swiped at the map with the side of his hand, as if her finger had left crumbs lying on the page. "I chose a southern route because there can be a lot of snow in late winter in the northern part of the country. I'm sure there's a lot to see in Colorado, but I don't relish the idea of driving through the Rockies in a blizzard."

Tegan pulled out her phone and typed in her weather app. She held it out so Jack could see. "It's says fifties and sixties and sunny all week in Estes Park, Colorado."

Jack shrugged and went back to his map. "So, my guess is that it should take us another hour and forty-five to get to Albuquerque tonight…" His words trailed off as another yawn overtook him.

"You're practically nodding off. There's a cute little motel down the street." Tegan slid her finger along Route 25 to Denver, Colorado. "Tomorrow we can take Route 25 north from Albuquerque. You can't miss out on the Rockies."

The waitress returned with their food, and Jack jerked the map off the table before she could set the plates down on top of it. "Thanks," he said to the waitress, before carefully folding the map and tucking it back into his briefcase. He closed it with a snap and moved it back to the seat next to him. "Oh, damn," he muttered, watching the waitress's retreating back. "I wanted to order some coffee. We can make it to Albuquerque tonight. I just need some coffee."

Jack rubbed his hand across his face and the purple smudges under his eyes seemed to darken. The guy was exhausted.

"You just need a good night's sleep," Tegan countered. "In the motel. Down. The. Street."

"Look, it doesn't matter if we go to Albuquerque or down the street. I'm not going to get a good night's sleep."

He didn't enunciate each word quite so precisely when he was tired. After spending half the day listening to him speak like he was at an Upper East Side dinner party, there was something sort of endearing about the way he slurred "gonna" and "goo'night." But jeez. Was he a workaholic, is that why he didn't sleep? Maybe he should leave that briefcase in the car and get some rest for a change.

Tegan picked up her fork but paused over her plate as Jack shot her a squinty-eyed look.

"Is that really all you're having? Just a slice of peach pie?" Jack asked, the scorn evident in his tone.

"You never know what can happen in life. Eat dessert first." Tegan said, with a shrug.

She expected him to roll his eyes. A guy who mapped out his entire road trip probably wasn't an *eat dessert first* kind of person. But instead, something dark clouded across his features and he turned to stare out the window.

They ate mostly in silence, occasionally asking to pass the salt, or commenting on the fact that the food was better than expected. Tegan didn't bring up their travel plans again. She'd suggest Colorado again in the morning. It wasn't that she had anything against Oklahoma or Missouri. But the whole point of a road trip was to experience the amazing scenery, the romance of the wild, untamed wilderness. And you couldn't beat the Rocky Mountains for that. The only thing in Missouri worth getting out of the car for in late winter was the world's largest roll of toilet paper. And she had a feeling that convincing this guy to stop for that was going to be a hard sell.

When the waitress brought the check, Jack reached into his pocket and handed her his credit card before Tegan realized what had happened. She tried to flag the waitress down, but she was already headed to the cash register across restaurant and wasn't looking in their direction.

Tegan turned to Jack. "You can't pay for that." She fished around in her pocket for some cash.

"It's fine, I've got it."

She pulled out a ten-dollar bill and slid it across the table. "No way. I pay my own way. Otherwise, you'll say we're even and try to leave me here." At this point, she was certain he wasn't a serial killer or the kind of guy who'd try to get in her pants. Being able to relax and not worry about her next ride—or her next driver—was comforting.

"Keep your money." He pushed the bill back. "I'm not going to leave you."

So why was he paying? He obviously had a lot of money. Did he like to flash his credit card around to show her that it was no big deal to pay for everything? No way was she going to give him the satisfaction.

"Really. Just take it." She pushed the money back.

"I'm not paying so I don't have to drive you, okay?" He picked up the bill and tossed it back on the table in front of her. "I'm paying to say thank you. You helped me out back there. At the other diner."

Tegan blinked. Of all things, she hadn't been expecting that. "Oh. Well. Thanks for the pie."

"Thanks for saving my ass."

She fought back the urge to laugh at his pissed-off expression. Even when he was trying to be nice, he looked so damn grumpy about it.

The waitress brought the receipt for him to sign and he scribbled his signature and slammed the little vinyl folder shut before Tegan could catch a glimpse of the tip he left. She wondered if he tipped well or if he was one of those rich guys who liked to show off his money with fancy clothes and expensive cars, but who wasn't always so nice to the people hired to serve him.

They stepped out of the over-air-conditioned restaurant, and the night air felt like a warm breath on Tegan's chilled skin. Jack yawned again, and she shot him a pointed look. He glanced at the watch circling his wrist.

"Fine. It's nine thirty," he said. "I don't really feel like driving for another two hours tonight. We can go off schedule for one day, and make it up tomorrow. Which way was that hotel you spotted?"

She didn't break it to him that it wasn't exactly what you'd call a hotel until they'd parked under the neon sign announcing that the Vista Verde Motel had vacancies and the rooms were only $29 a night. *Vista verde* was a bit of a stretch, given that they were in the middle of the desert and there was literally no view of anything green except for the building itself. The architecture of the one-story structure was in the adobe style of the region, but instead of the typical sand-colored walls, the entire motel was painted a shocking grass-green that, beneath the streetlights, seemed to glow like an underwater sea creature. A sign that said, *Office—Come on Inn*, waited for them in the largest window.

"You're kidding, right?" Jack said, looking from the emerald glare of the Vista Verde to Tegan and then back again.

"You're not in Kansas anymore, Toto."

He blew out a breath. "I'm sure there's something a little bit more… Uh. Maybe a Holiday Inn or even a Best Western or something."

"In Matorales, population two thousand? I doubt it. Besides, they have vacancies."

Jack eyed the building again, which seemed to pulse like a strobe light at a rave. Or maybe the overhead sign just needed a new lightbulb. "I can't imagine why," he muttered.

"Oh, come on. It's one night." Tegan opened her door and hopped out before he could turn the car around and go looking for a Holiday Inn. "Think of the stories you'll have."

Jack shook his head, but to her relief, he got out and followed her to the office. The truth was, there was no way she could afford even the Holiday Inn or Best Western. She hadn't really considered where they would spend the night when she got into the car with him, but it didn't surprise her that he was a five-star hotel kind of guy. One night at the Four Seasons would probably cost what she spent in a week on this trip. Even the $29 for a night at the Vista Verde was at the top of her budget. If they continued to travel together, maybe she could convince him to camp. It was only $12 a night to stay at the KOA campground.

But then she eyed the shiny platinum American Express card that he pulled out as he entered the motel office, and the expensive clothes that he'd somehow managed to keep clean and unwrinkled all day. No way this guy was going camping.

A short, dark-haired man greeted them and confirmed that the motel did, in fact, have vacancies. He assigned them to rooms at the far end of the building, and told them that there would be donuts and coffee available in the morning. Less than five minutes later, they stood in front of the doors to their rooms.

Jack set his monogrammed leather overnight bag down to fiddle with the key in the door, and Tegan noticed the letters JBT stamped on the side. His initials, maybe? J for Jack. They hadn't bothered to learn each other's last names. What were B and T? Probably something stuffy and rich-sounding. *Bartholomew. Bancroft.* Maybe something with a hyphen, or "thorpe" at the end. *Tipton-Tannerthorpe.* She smirked. If he was a character in one of her stories, he'd be Bartholomew Tipton-Tannerthorpe for sure.

His lock popped open, and then he paused as if he were waiting for her to go inside first. She turned her attention to her own door. When it swung inward, he picked up his bag. "See you in the morning," he said.

Tegan hesitated. Was he just saying that? Part of her had been assuming he'd ditch her by taking off while she slept, and that he'd be long gone by morning. She'd grabbed all her stuff out of his car, just in case.

"Yeah, see you." She stepped into the room, but then peeked out again, watching him disappear through his own doorway. Was this the last time she'd ever see him?

The thought bothered her a lot more than she'd expected it to.

CHAPTER EIGHT

Jack

When Jack stepped out of his room at 7:10 the next morning, he found Tegan awake and sitting in front of the office on a bench shaped like a cactus. She had a Styrofoam cup of coffee in her hand, and a plate with a chocolate donut on her lap. Her bag was already packed and on the ground by her feet.

She didn't have that ridiculous baseball cap on her head today and her hair fell down her back in loose waves. Under the fluorescent lights of the diner last night, her hair had looked blond, but now with the desert sun beating down, it appeared more strawberry. That explained the mass of freckles across her nose, and the pale, almost translucent skin on her legs. Not that he was looking at her legs. It was just hard to miss them in those cut-off jean shorts. She wore a long-sleeved, flowy shirt and a pair of dangly turquoise earrings which, it struck him when she looked up and grinned, matched her eyes.

Something clenched in his stomach that made him stop short. A tiny pull of attraction. An awareness of her as a woman and not just a person temporarily taking up space in his car and his life.

It was the first time in a year he'd felt anything like this. The first time he felt *anything* other than the crippling agony that hit him first thing, when he woke, and then the blessed numbness that followed.

He shook his head to clear it. There was no denying that Tegan was pretty in her free-spirited, bohemian kind of way. But this feeling that was clutching at his insides wasn't about her. He hadn't spent this much time with another person in so long that it was messing with his head. There was no way he was attracted to Tegan. She was loud, and pushy, and those dirty shoes alone were enough to kill any tiny bit of allure she might have had.

Her grin faded as she looked at him sideways and bit her lip.

He was staring and he really needed to get it together. Rubbing a hand across his eyes, he scrubbed away the tension. He forced a smile onto his face and started walking again.

Tegan held out the paper plate as he approached. "That guy in room five tried to take all the chocolate donuts, but I put up a fight for this one and saved it for you."

He loved chocolate donuts. It wouldn't have been his first choice for breakfast since it wasn't very healthy, especially with all the diner food he'd been eating lately. But he wasn't sorry to have an excuse to eat it. "Thanks."

"The coffee's not totally horrible, either."

"I'll grab some and we can go." He pulled the door to the office open. "Do you want anything to eat?"

She flashed him a crooked grin. "I already had two donuts."

It didn't really surprise him. Hippies who hitchhiked across the country and ate pie for dinner didn't worry about things like sugar or cholesterol.

He got his coffee, they loaded their bags in the car, and by 7:15, they were on the road again. He coasted through Matorales, past the diner where they'd eaten the night before, a gas station with one pump, and three different stores with the words "Trading Company" in the name. No Holiday Inn or Best Western. But the Vista Verde had turned out to be surprisingly comfortable after all. His room had been small and sparse, but clean, with a simple double bed covered in a southwest-style wool blanket, a small table, and a bathroom with a stand-up shower.

The only flaw, other than the unfortunate choice of paint colors, was the paper-thin walls. He could hear Tegan shuffling around in the room next to him, and the squeak of the bed shifting as she settled into it.

Although, maybe it wasn't so bad. It had been sort of comforting to lean back in his own bed against their shared wall and to know that he wasn't alone in this tiny town in the middle of the desert. Even if his travel companion was a hitchhiker who annoyed the hell out of him. After a few minutes of silence, he'd heard the bed squeak again, and then the muffled sound of her voice carried through the wall. It took him a minute to realize that she was on the phone and not talking to herself.

"Hey, is Jamie there?" he thought he'd heard her say. There was a moment of silence, and then, a disappointed-sounding: "Oh. He's asleep already?" It was too faint to hear what she said next. After another silence, where the person on the other end of the phone must have been talking, he heard, "How—how's he feeling?" More silence and then a subdued, "Oh."

Something about that one syllable, said in such a forlorn voice, had Jack's shoulders tensing. He didn't want to know who this Jamie person was; didn't want to care that she sounded worried over him.

"No, don't wake him," Jack heard next. The bed squeaked and then she'd said in a slightly louder, more cheerful voice, "Yeah, tell him the station wagon is running great. No problems at all. And it's wonderful to have some alone time, I'm getting so much writing done..."

He'd turned to look at the wall then, as if somewhere in the swirls of plaster he'd find an explanation for why she was obviously candy-coating her trip for this Jamie person. But all he heard was her murmur, "Goodbye." Something clicked, probably the lamp being shut off, the bed shifted a few more times, and then there was silence.

His mind had whirled with questions. He'd spent the entire day in the car with her, and while she'd been happy to share all her questions and judgments of what she assumed about his life, she hadn't revealed a single thing about herself, other than to say she was a writer.

Of course, he hadn't asked. He wasn't on this trip to make friends. The less he knew about Tegan, the better. He'd hadn't been eager to tell his family the whole truth about his day either, and he hadn't even been groped by a trucker.

Pushing Tegan's conversation out of his head, he'd pulled out his briefcase and worked for a couple of hours on a merger agreement before he'd nodded off. It was nice to be so tired he could barely stay awake, instead of pacing the room until his sleeping pill kicked in like usual. He'd fallen into bed, hoping maybe he'd finally get that elusive good night's sleep. But a nightmare woke him before dawn and he sat up, groping around for a lamp that wasn't on the side table.

It took him a minute to remember he wasn't in his bed in Pacific Heights. He'd sold the apartment, and all that was left of that life was in boxes in his car.

Jack had sat there in bed, shaking and nauseous as remnants of the nightmare flashed through his head. Images so painfully vivid, he didn't know where the dream left off and reality began. The sirens. The surge of people pressing toward him as he fought his way through the crowd, screaming her name. The blood.

He'd lunged out of bed to flip on the overhead light, and then sank in a chair at the small table in the corner, sucking in deep breaths. After a few minutes, his heart settled down to a normal rhythm, but he wasn't going to get any more sleep that night. He'd tried to work on the merger again, but after reading the same paragraph three times, he'd pulled out his map and spread it across the table, re-evaluating the route he'd planned.

Now, as if she could read his mind, Tegan leaned back against the passenger seat and propped her shoe on the dashboard. "So, where are we headed?"

Jack stopped at a red light and stared at her foot until she finally got the message and slid it down to the floor with a thump, leaving a smudge of tan dirt behind. She made an exaggerated cringe face and swiped at the dirt with the palm of her hand.

"Forget it. It's fine." He had some Armor All wipes in the emergency kit—he'd wipe it down when they stopped. Or maybe he'd just add it to the list, along with the crumbs from yesterday, and get the car detailed when he got to New York. She was bound to cause more chaos before this trip was over.

The light turned green and they continued through town, eventually coming to an intersection with a sign pointing right toward Route 40 east. "Look, don't get smug and start thinking that you can dictate the itinerary for this trip." He flipped the turn signal and made a left onto a two-lane road heading north. "I spent a little time last night mapping out some routes. It turns out that the weather will be better in Colorado. There have been some tornado warnings in Oklahoma. It's a little early in the season so I didn't account for them when I originally planned the trip."

Her mouth dropped open. "We're going to the Rocky Mountains?"

"Yes." He braced himself.

A wide grin spread across her face. "So, you're saying I was right."

Of course she was rubbing it in. It was tempting to do a U-turn and head back to Route 40 toward Oklahoma City, just to spite her. But they were already heading in the opposite direction.

He searched for a nice, neutral topic to change the subject from his abrupt shift in direction—literally and figuratively. Because, although the National Weather Service had issued a few weather warnings to the south of his planned route, it wasn't really about the tornadoes.

When he'd planned the trip, he'd been going through the motions. He'd chosen the easiest route and picked out a couple of hotels and restaurants that seemed comfortable and clean. All he'd wanted to do was get away for a while, not caring about the experience.

But, standing in the desert the day before, watching the sky turn into streaks of magenta and gold, something stirred in his chest. The vaguest desire to keep going; to keep putting one foot in front of the other and maybe be awake and alive for the next sunset. It seemed wrong to bypass the color and drama of the Rocky Mountains in favor of Oklahoma in late March. His life had been as flat as those plains for so long. He missed mountains and sunsets.

But he wasn't going to give Tegan any credit for that. He appreciated that she'd coaxed him out of the car to see the sunset, even if she'd turned around and insulted him a moment later. But he wasn't going to turn it into some life-altering experience, or fall to his knees to thank her.

"So how come you're such a terrible sleeper?" Tegan asked, changing the subject for him.

His hand jerked on the steering wheel. "What?"

Did she hear him last night? He didn't think he'd been talking in his sleep, but he might have been. It wouldn't have been the first time. And, as he'd discovered, those walls were thin. If he'd said anything, she'd probably heard it. His composure slipped a notch and a slow flush crept up his neck.

"Well, you said yesterday you weren't going to get a good night's sleep, then you were up half the night rerouting our trip, apparently." She cocked an eyebrow. "And you just chugged that coffee like a frat boy doing a keg stand." She picked up his empty cup and shook it for emphasis.

He looked at the cup and wished it was still full. It was pretty unlikely he was going to find a Starbucks out here.

"Plus," she continued, "last night you implied that maybe you're not having a great year."

Did he? He really did need to get some sleep. He didn't even remember that. What had he been thinking, bringing it up with her, of all people? He must be more exhausted than he realized. "I've got a lot going on. Work and the move and everything."

"So why *are* you moving?" She leaned back and lifted her foot, as if she was about to prop it on the dashboard again. At the last second, she seemed to reconsider and swung it back down to the floor. "I know it's for work, or whatever. But can they just make you move? I mean, it's your family's firm, right? Don't you get a say?"

"Who says I didn't get a say?"

"Well, you said you love San Francisco."

What was with this woman and her memory of everything he said yesterday? He did love San Francisco. He'd moved there right out of law school and he'd never been happier in his life for the first five years he lived there. But year six had nearly killed him, and he wouldn't be sorry if he never set foot in that city again.

"My family is in New York."

"So, you're close with your family?"

"Yes." That was a question he could answer honestly, and without flinching. He wouldn't have survived this past year without his family. In the early days after it happened, they were the only reason he got out of bed, took a shower, didn't starve to death. Later, they helped him make the decision to leave San Francisco and work out of the New York office. He knew it was the right move. New York wasn't full of memories that stalked him every time he walked down the street. But he'd been too paralyzed to do anything until they'd shown up and took over with their usual efficiency.

His mom and Liv had flown in and stayed for two weeks to help him pack, put the apartment on the market, and arrange for the movers. Mostly, he'd gone through the motions, filling the boxes they piled around the apartment and signing whatever paperwork they put in front of him. The only points of contention were about all the belongings he hadn't been ready to give away, and about this trip. He'd stood his ground about the belongings—most of them were in boxes in the backseat of his car.

The trip had been Liv's idea. She'd argued that he hadn't left his apartment in close to a year, which was completely false. He went to work every day and stopped at the gym to swim laps on his way home. But okay, he did have his groceries and dry cleaning delivered, and he never went out to dinner or drinks with friends anymore. Liv insisted that it would be good for him to get out of his head, do something different, and physically put a little distance between him and everything that happened in San Francisco. Her plan had been to come along, too—he'd finally agreed to go, but only if he went alone. No way was he going to spend 3,000 miles with his sister trying to get him to talk about his feelings.

Jack sighed and remembered the current occupant of his car. So much for going alone. Tegan was looking at him with her forehead scrunched up, and he had a feeling that she'd asked him another question and had been waiting a long time for an answer. "Sorry, what?"

"I asked if you have siblings."

"Yes, one sister." He drove past the junction to a smaller road snaking off to the right and hit his brakes, slowing the car down abruptly. "Damn it, did I just miss my turn?" This was exactly why he had his trip all mapped out on major highways. His mind tended to wander lately, and driving on all these back roads required attention to where he was going.

Tegan turned and squinted at the road behind them. "I can't really see the sign. Where's your map?"

"My briefcase in back." He continued to drive slowly, scanning the horizon for another sign. "Can you check your GPS? I think we want to take Route 491 north."

Tegan unclicked her seatbelt and turned around, kneeling on her seat as she reached for her backpack on the seat behind her. As she made a grab for it, her hip connected with his shoulder and her foot kicked his coffee cup, knocking it to the floor. He picked it up, shaking his head. Good thing it was empty.

Jack gave her foot a light shove. "Forget it. Sit down." He pulled his phone out of the mount on the console. "Here, just use mine." He typed in his passcode and handed her the phone open to Google maps.

"Just check if we missed the turn. Route 491."

Tegan sat back down and spent a minute studying the map. She shook her head. "Looks like it's a few miles up ahead." She shut the phone off with the button on the side, and then reached over to put it back in the cell phone mount. It didn't click in on the first try, so she it shuffled around, trying to reattach it.

Jack sighed. "Here. Give it to me."

"No, no, I got it." She finally clicked it in place. "Oh! Who's that?"

Jack's head jerked up. "What? Who?"

Tegan waved her hand at his phone on the console. She must've hit the side button again when she attached the phone, because his lock screen had lit up, and the photo that he'd saved there a lifetime ago flashed on the screen. He took one look at the couple grinning at the camera, happy and so clearly in love, and a knife twisted in his gut.

Damn it. *Damn it.*

He should have replaced that photo months ago, but he could never bring himself to do it. Just like the voicemails he couldn't seem to delete, or all the stuff in boxes that he was hauling across the country, getting rid of that photo would somehow make it really, truly permanent. He wasn't ready for that. Maybe he never would be.

He should have been more careful. The last thing he wanted was to discuss any of this with some stranger he picked up on the side of the road.

But she wasn't going to let it go. "You have a girlfriend?"

Before he could stop himself, he snapped, "Fiancée," as his lungs squeezed and his pulse picked up speed.

Her eyes widened. "Someone agreed to marry *you*?" She grinned when she said it, and he was beyond caring about whether she was kidding or not. He just wanted her to stop talking. *Please stop talking.*

"What's her name?"

He sucked in a breath. "Charlotte." Jack grabbed the phone, stuffed it in the center console, and slammed it shut. Then he leaned his arm on it, because Tegan was absolutely the kind of person who would open the console back up and grab the phone back. She wouldn't give a damn that she was violating his privacy, or that he was dangerously close to throwing up.

"Does Charlotte work in the family firm too?"

"No." His hands shook on the steering wheel.

"Well, what does she do?"

"Please stop talking."

Tegan shook her head. "Oh, come on, Jack. We've got days in this car together. Why not tell me about her?"

Jack cracked the window, but the hot, dry air that blew in did nothing to cool his burning face. "Look, I'm not going to discuss my fiancée, my work, or anything else that's not about the weather, directions, or the food at the goddamn diner. My life is none of your business. If you can't accept that, I'll pull over right now and you can get out of the car." His voice rose with every word until he was practically yelling.

Tegan slid back toward the passenger door and held up her hands as if he was waving a gun at her. That image left him so light-headed that he swung the car to the side of the road and slammed on the brake.

Tegan stared at him, eyes wide. "Okay. Okay. I'm going." She grabbed her bag from the backseat, knocking him in the shoulder as she swung it into her lap. Then she reached for her door handle.

With blood roaring in his ears, Jack wrenched his own door open and spun in his seat until his feet hit the dusty road outside. He leaned forward, resting his elbows on his knees, taking deep, gasping breaths. In reality, it was probably only a minute or two, but it felt like hours passed as he sat there, half in and half out of the car, sucking air into his lungs.

It's been almost a year, he thought with a vicious self-loathing. Shouldn't he have moved past this? Shouldn't he be able to control it by now?

Eventually, Jack took one more shaky breath and managed to wrestle his heartbeat back under control. The desert dust kicked up as he straightened, dragging his feet back into the car. He looked around, registering his surroundings as mortification slowly replaced panic. Was Tegan staring at him like he'd completely lost his mind?

But no, her seat was empty and her door hung open slightly, wobbling in the gust of wind that blew up from the hills to the east. He looked around wildly, finally spotting her on the road a hundred feet ahead with her backpack slung over one shoulder. At that moment, a dark green sedan zipped past him the direction Tegan was walking. As it drew nearer, she reached out her arm and stuck out her hand, thumb pointing toward the sky.

And then it hit him. *She's hitchhiking. She thinks I pulled over to leave her here.* He would never have dumped her on the side of the road. But of course, she had no way of knowing that. If he was shocked by the intensity of his reaction, what *she* must thought…

The green sedan slowed and another kind of panic overtook him. "Tegan, wait!" Jack called, jumping out of the SUV and taking off down the road. She couldn't get into that car. He'd promised himself he'd get her safely to her destination, and he wasn't sure he'd survive the guilt of watching her drive off with some stranger, the agony of knowing that if anything happened to her, it would be his fault.

Just like Charlotte.

"Wait!" he called, louder this time.

She turned to look at him, dropping her hand by her side. To Jack's relief, the green sedan picked up speed, zooming off over the next hill. He ran the last few feet and stumbled to a stop in front of her.

Tegan crossed her arms over her chest. "You just scared away my ride."

"*I'm* your ride," he panted.

She looked at him like he'd completely lost his mind. Which, maybe he had. "That's not what you said a minute ago."

"I didn't mean for you to get out. I—just—" He just *what*? *Had a panic attack over a photo of my fiancée?* Jack shook his head. "Forget it. I'm sorry about that back there."

She continued to stare at him warily.

"Really. I'm—you don't have to go." He reached over to take her backpack. "Please don't go." After a brief hesitation, she slowly lowered her arm, allowing him to slide it off her shoulder. They turned and walked back to the car in silence. Inside, she pulled the door shut, keeping her eyes on him, as if he might change his mind at any minute and shove her out into the dirt. He couldn't really blame her, with the way he was acting.

He should give her an explanation, that's what a normal person would do. He opened his mouth, but the words wouldn't come.

How could he tell her that Charlotte was gone, and it was all his fault?

He searched his mind for something that would be close enough to the truth to explain his outburst, but would discourage her from asking too many questions. Maybe something vague about how it was too painful to talk about. He didn't have to tell her how he should have been there for Charlotte, stood up for her. That if he had, they might still be together.

But Tegan had already flopped back in her seat with her laptop in her hands and wasn't looking at him. She flipped the cover open and huddled against the passenger door, typing away. She didn't look up or say another word until they stopped to use the bathroom and go to the ATM two hours later.

He should have been glad but, for some reason, her silence made him feel even worse.

CHAPTER NINE

Tegan

"Tegan, hurry up," Jamie said, grabbing my arm and pulling me across the gravel and broken glass. This was the part we hated the most on our walk home from school—the last half a block through the alley until we got to the rickety staircase leading to our apartment.

This was the part where we passed by the house that always had a group of people with dazed expressions and dilated eyes hanging around out back. The house where the men sold little bags of white powder from the back porch. I could feel those men sizing me up, could see how Jamie flinched at the things they said as we hurried by.

Jamie told me to never walk out there alone. "You're thirteen now, not a kid anymore." I didn't completely understand what that had to do with anything, but those looks creeped me out, and I knew enough to always listen to Jamie.

We put our heads down and kept moving. I must have heard the dog barking, but my eyes were fixed on those men on the porch, so I didn't really register it. Not until the pit bull burst out from behind the garage and clamped down on my arm. Pain shot through me, so intense I thought I'd pass out. I screamed, my voice echoing through the alley, and someone from that house yelled, "Holy shit!"

I was going to die. That dog was going to tear me to pieces, I was sure of it.

And then someone came flying out of nowhere, knocking me sideways, taking the dog down with us. In the next breath, something crashed down on the dog's head and, whimpering, the dog released me and took off down the alley.

I lay there, holding my bleeding arm and screaming at the top of my lungs. Two guys from the back porch came running, along with a woman who'd been inside the house.

The woman hauled me up and wrapped a towel around my arm. She pressed it against my wound, and squeezed it tight. My blood seeped through the thin fabric. "You'll be okay, hun," she told me. "Just hold this here."

The back porch guys towered over Jamie, who was crouching on the ground, breathing hard, my blood smeared across his chest. "Shit, kid, you just took down a pit bull with your bare hands," one of them said. The other reached out a hand to help him up.

After that, those guys never stared at me with their creepy gazes, and they never said another word when we walked by. The just gave Jamie a nod of acknowledgement and went back to whatever they were doing.

Jamie hitched his chin in response, and kept walking.

*

Tegan snapped her laptop shut and gazed out the window, suddenly overwhelmed by the events of the past few days. She wished she could've talked to Jamie last night, just to hear his voice reassure her that she was doing this for them. But he'd been sleeping again. Hopefully, all that sleep would make him stronger, and he'd be back to his old self again soon.

And now Jack's earlier outburst was consuming her thoughts, and she couldn't seem to move past it. Instead of focusing on the story in front of her, she was crafting snarky comments and indignant speeches in her head.

She knew she'd crossed the line yesterday when she hassled him about his family firm. She'd done it intentionally, because she hated how he was looking at her like she was completely beneath him. But this morning when she left her motel room and realized that his car was still there, that he hadn't left her behind, she'd been determined to start over. They had at least a couple more days together, and it would be nice if they could get along, maybe even become friends.

Keeping her head bowed, her gaze drifted around the SUV, from the expensive leather seats to the dashboard that was lit up with enough screens and buttons to control a 747. Then she peeked at Jack out of the corner of her eye. Today he was wearing another polo shirt, this time with a preppy pair of shorts. When she'd first seen those shorts, she'd almost choked on her coffee. Was he wearing *pink*? No, when he got closer, she saw that they were actually more of an orangey-coral, but it was close enough. To top it off, there were little blue lobsters embroidered all over them. If he was trying to make sure they stood out as much as possible in small-town America, those shorts were definitely the way to go.

Okay, so maybe friendship would be a bit of a reach, given how they had exactly nothing in common. Except maybe an appreciation for sunsets. But they could at least be friendly. When she saw the photo on his phone, she'd figured that it was a good chance to get to know him a little. Most people were eager to talk about their significant others. She never expected him to yell at her, or threaten to throw her out on the side of the road.

She glanced up again as the motion of the car changed and the gentle rocking slowed. For the first time in hours, Jack acknowledged her presence in the car. "Are you hungry?"

She hesitated. Was food on the list of topics she was allowed to speak of? She thought so. "Yes."

Actually, she was starving. The last thing she'd eaten was that donut four hours ago, and her blood sugar had crashed fifty miles back. But he'd been so annoyed by her one request for a bathroom break, she didn't want to push him by asking about lunch.

"How's Mexican?"

"Fine."

Jack pulled the car into the parking lot of an adobe-style building with a giant chili pepper and the words, "Taco Loco" painted on the side in bright colors. She followed him inside and blinked to adjust to the dim orange-tinged lighting. They stopped at an oval-shaped bar in the middle of the room with about fifty different types of tequila lined up on a shelf that dropped down from the ceiling. The hostess greeted them and then led them past a plastic skeleton wearing a sombrero to a table under a giant *Dia de Muertos* mural of skulls embellished with colorful flowers.

Tegan slid into her seat and snatched her menu off the table, reading it like it was a bestselling novel and pretending that Jack wasn't seated across from her. But once the server had taken their orders, she had to give up the menu and there was nothing to do but look at him.

"So…" She fidgeted in her chair and lined up the bottles of hot sauce in order from tallest to shortest. "Today's as hot as yesterday, huh?" *God.* Was that all she could come up with?

Jack cleared his throat. "When we hit the mountains in a couple of hours, it should start to cool off."

"That'll be nice."

Okay, well. That took care of talking about the weather.

Maybe she should apologize for butting her nose in his business and asking about his fiancée. Did apologizing for talking about his fiancée count as talking about her? Probably best not to take the chance. Her eyes flitted to Jack—he was staring at the mural above them like it was hanging in the Louvre—and then back down to the barrier of condiments she'd built between them.

Tegan wasn't much of a drinker, but the tequila over the bar was looking awfully appealing. Was noon too early to order shots? She pushed the bottles back to their place on the side of the table with a sigh, and then excused herself to go to the bathroom. When she returned, their lunch had arrived. She didn't have the energy to try to chat about their burritos, even though technically food was an approved topic of conversation, so she focused on the voices of the waitress and bartender sitting a few feet away at the bar.

Tegan felt bad about eavesdropping as they folded napkins and dried shot glasses, but was also grateful to have something to distract her from the silence between her and Jack. The server had a son in elementary school, which was a little surprising. Tegan had assumed the woman was just a few years out of high school, and definitely no older than her own twenty-five years. But people had kids at a young age in these small towns. Tegan couldn't imagine having a kid at all, let alone one who was old enough to play little league. The server told the bartender that she didn't know if they'd be able to afford the team this year. Her son needed a new glove, and he was growing like a weed and wouldn't fit into last year's uniform anymore. The bartender offered to dig around in his basement for his old glove, and suggested maybe they could put a collection bucket by the cash register to fundraise for the team.

Tegan felt a little tug in her heart. She'd never lived in one place long enough to be a part of a community. It was nice to think of people rallying to help a little kid's baseball team. She glanced at Jack, who met her eyes and looked like he might actually smile, but then he went back to glaring at his burrito.

After an eternity, they finished their lunch and went to pay at the cash register. Jack pulled out a wad of twenties—he must've been *really* nervous about getting caught without cash again—and handed two to the bartender. Tegan waved a few bills at him—no way was she letting him pay—and this time he took the money.

Tegan handed him another five. "Here, for the tip."

"I'll get the tip. You run to the bathroom again so we don't have to stop in ten minutes."

She shot him a glare, but since she did have to go again, she turned and headed across the bar. When she got to the hallway to the bathroom, she paused and peeked around a potted plant as Jack walked back to their table. She'd worked as a server on and off since she was sixteen years old and had strong opinions about tipping well. Leaving less than 20 percent was the worst.

When Jack got to the table, he glanced over his shoulder, back to the bar where the bartender and server were waiting on other customers. Then he pulled the wad of twenties from his pocket, peeled off a chunk, and tossed it on the table. Spinning on his heel, he strode back to the front of the restaurant. Tegan squinted at the sun that shone in through the front door as he swung it open and disappeared outside.

Did he just leave half that pile of cash for the server?

She thought about running over to look, but the server was already making her way to the table with a tray to clear their dishes. Tegan watched as she picked up the cash and then whirled around as if she was checking to see if someone was playing a prank on her. When nothing out of the ordinary happened, she turned back toward the table and stood there, staring at the cash in one hand, and clutching the front of her Taco Loco T-shirt with the other. Tegan ducked down the hall and went through the motions of using the bathroom and washing her hands, but she felt fuzzy and out of sorts.

When she got to the car, Jack was leaning against it, scrolling through his phone. He looked up when she approached. "We should make it to Estes Park in about four or five more hours, depending on how many stops you require."

A few hours earlier, she would have snapped right back at that, but she wasn't going to take the bait now. "How much tip did you leave the server?"

"I don't know." He shrugged. "Twenty percent."

She crossed her arms and took a step closer. She had to tilt her head back to look up at him. "It didn't look like twenty percent. It looked like at least two hundred bucks."

"I thought you were in the bathroom." He raised his eyebrows. "Were you checking up on me?"

"I—" She snapped her mouth shut. There was really no way to explain what she'd been doing. "I just like to tip well."

"And you thought I wouldn't?"

"No, I didn't mean—" She stopped, strangely relieved. All of her doubts over what kind of guy he was evaporated as she watched the hurt flash in his eyes. She hadn't realized until that moment how much she'd wanted to be wrong about him.

He sighed and his shoulders drooped an inch. "Look, that thing with the credit card back at the diner yesterday was an honest mistake. Maybe I was thrown for a minute, but those people automatically assumed the worst of me. I never would've walked out on my bill. If the waitress wouldn't accept a check, I would have driven to the ATM in Diablo and then gone back."

A truck flew by on the highway, the noise preventing her from having to answer. Which was a good thing, because she didn't know what to say.

Jack rubbed his temples as if the sound was giving him a headache. Or maybe it was this conversation causing him physical pain. "If I were the jerk that you seem to think I am, you wouldn't be here right now. I would have taken off."

"I don't think you're a—" Except she *had* thought that. She'd been so sure that he was unfairly judging her, while she'd been doing the same to him. Shame washed over her.

Jack shook his head and turned to get into the car. Tegan reached out and grabbed his arm. "Jack, wait."

He turned back to her.

"I'm sorry." She took a step toward him, still holding on. "I'm sorry about the tip thing. And I'm really sorry that I pushed you about your fiancée. It's none of my business."

Jack stared at her hand on his arm, and then his eyes flickered up to her face. Their eyes met and she was suddenly aware of how close they were standing. Her breath caught, and something in her heart did an unexpected flip.

He shook his head. "I'm the one who should apologize. I over-reacted back there, when you asked me about—" He swallowed. "When you asked me about Charlotte. I'm just a really private person and I'm not used to talking to strangers about—stuff that's important to me. I'm sorry I yelled at you like that."

A pick-up truck pulled into the lot and coasted into the space next to them. Jack slowly pulled his arm out of her grasp and squinted over her shoulder at the highway. Tegan took a step back and stuffed her hands into her pockets. What was she doing? Or, more importantly, what was her *heart* doing, getting fluttery over Jack, of all people? He was wearing pink shorts! And he was engaged. He'd said it: they were strangers, and they knew nothing about each other.

Maybe she'd been on the road alone for too long. And then there was that phone call last night, and now she was lonely and missing Jamie. Or maybe it was that trucker yesterday, and Jack coming along to help her. But she didn't need some guy to swoop in and save her like a damsel in distress, and she really didn't need to get all swoony about it.

Tegan whirled around and escaped into her side of the car.

CHAPTER TEN

Jack

Jack got in the car, but he didn't start it right away. Instead, he scrolled through his iPhone under the pretense of looking for a playlist, but really needing a minute to talk himself down. This trip was supposed to help him get his head straight, but the last twenty-four hours had kicked up his emotions like the car tires kicked up the dust, sending them swirling around and making it hard to breathe.

He could still feel Tegan's hand gripping his arm, still feel the warmth of her body as she leaned in and—unexpectedly—apologized. He almost wished she hadn't. It was easier when he saw her as an annoyance, as someone whose presence he had to endure until he could be rid of her. He didn't want to notice that her eyes were the exact hue of the ocean off the coast of Zanzibar—his favorite color since his parents had taken the family on a trip there when he was twelve. He didn't want to be in the path of that infectious smile, the one that made him want to smile back for the first time since—

Since Charlotte.

He didn't want to be feeling a pull toward a woman who wasn't Charlotte. It felt disloyal, like he was cheating on her. He knew that was a ridiculous thought—nothing was ever, *ever* going to happen with Tegan—but he couldn't help it. So, he could go ahead and add guilt to the mix.

Jack stuck his iPhone in the phone mount and turned on a playlist of some of his favorite music. The first chords of a song by Mumford & Sons came through the speakers and Tegan turned to him and grinned. He was glad she wasn't going to argue with him over the music again, but damn it, he wished she'd stop it with that smile.

He started the car and pulled out on the road. Instead of taking out her laptop like he expected, Tegan looked out the window and hummed along to the music. They traveled a few miles and the song changed, but she still didn't go back to her book. He wished she would. He hadn't realized how the computer had put a barrier between them until it was gone, and they were suddenly two people on the same trip together.

"How's your book coming?" he finally asked, hoping to nudge her back to it.

Her head whipped in his direction, as if she was surprised that he'd spoken to her. "It's okay. Thanks for asking."

"So, what's it about?"

She looked at him for a moment without answering, and then she turned back toward the front window and shrugged. "You know, just like you said. Traveling, the meaning of life, all that stuff."

He had a feeling there was more to it than that. The silence stretched between them and he focused on the road, trying to let his mind wander. But a minute later, he was thinking about it again. What was this story that she'd been working on in his passenger seat? Was he a character in her book now?

"So, Jacquelyn Kerouac," he asked, keeping his tone light. "If you're traveling across the country writing the Millennial version of *On the Road*, does this make me your trusty sidekick? Who was Kerouac's real-life travel companion? Neal Cassady, right?"

Tegan blew out a laugh. "Neal Cassady lived fast and died young. You strike me as more of a 'live like a tortoise and die a grumpy old man' kind of guy." She cocked an eyebrow in what he took as a silent challenge. "Going fifty in a seventy-five-mile zone isn't exactly living fast, is it?"

Jack considered hitting the brakes and slowing down to forty. But that would delay this trip even more, and he'd already added on a few extra days in his route through Colorado. Instead, he mirrored her challenging expression and shoved his foot on the gas. There was something satisfying about the little squeak she let out as she was thrust back into her seat, and the way the odometer quickly rose to 60 and then 70... 80... 90 mph.

He pushed his foot down another centimeter, and their speed hit 100. The landscape zipped past, longhorns and sagebrush blending into an olive and burnt umber blur, like a Wild West version of a painting by Monet. Next to him, he could sense Tegan tensing up and grabbing onto her seat, but he kept his eyes on the road as it disappeared over the horizon. Giving the gas pedal one final push, he gunned it over the top of the hill. The three seconds that the car sailed through the air felt more like thirty, and then his stomach did a nosedive as they reconnected with the asphalt. A cloud of dust billowed behind them as the back tires touched down and they sped toward the next hill.

Jack eased off the gas and slowed the car to a reasonable 65 mph, his heart still pounding. Next to him, Tegan let out a little sigh that at first he thought was from terror, but then he glanced in her direction. She had the wild-eyed, exhilarated look of someone who had just stepped off a rollercoaster. Probably matching the expression on his own face.

"I wasn't expecting that," she whispered, a small laugh hitching her voice at the end.

Her statement mirrored his own thoughts. It wasn't like him to speed, or act recklessly, or allow himself to be influenced by a free-spirited hitchhiker. But the strangest part of all wasn't that he'd done all those things. The strangest part was that he wanted to do them again.

Before Jack could stop it, a chuckle escaped from his throat, and then another one. And then he was laughing. How was it possible to feel completely crazy and suddenly saner than he had in months, all at the same time? Something that he'd been sure was dead forever flickered back to life, like a tiny ember turning back into a flame with a breath.

Tegan turned and, out of the corner of his eye, Jack could see her flash a crooked grin. "It's nice to meet you, Jack. I'm Tegan."

He looked at her sideways. "What?"

She shrugged. "I get the feeling that I just met the real you."

Something slammed him in the chest. How did she manage to articulate exactly what he'd just been thinking? And what was it about this woman that he'd known for less than two days, that she managed to revive something in him that nobody and nothing else had in almost a year?

He leaned back against the headrest and took a slow breath. *Don't read so much into it.*

It wasn't about Tegan, it was that he'd finally put San Francisco in the rearview mirror. And the beautiful landscapes on the drive didn't hurt. Plus, he was going home to New York, and there was comfort in that. There were plenty of reasons why he felt more like himself than he had in a year, and none of them had to do with this hitchhiker sitting next to him. She just happened to be tagging along, and she'd be gone in less than a week.

He reached over to turn up the music, feeling the beat reverberate in his chest. He cranked it up one more notch and found himself tempted to sing along.

As they crossed into Colorado, the landscape changed from flat, barren desert to pine-covered hills and then eventually to gray rock with snowy white-tipped peaks. Jack had to admit that Tegan may have been right about coming this way. At one point, he couldn't help himself, and he pulled the car over. They hopped out and leaned against the guardrail, admiring the valleys in the distance and the mountain range rising up against the dramatic backdrop of blue sky.

The temperature dropped at least thirty degrees as they rose in elevation, and they were shivering when they stopped for gas. Jack dug warmer clothes from his bag and changed in the convenience store bathroom.

His new travel plans took them north to Estes Park, Colorado, where they'd spend the night before heading east. By the time darkness descended, they'd been on the road for eight hours, and still had about two more to go. Tegan was starting to squirm again but bathroom stops were few and far between in the tiny mountain towns they'd passed through.

Finally, as Jack steered the car around a bend they saw what they'd been looking for: up the mountain sat a large wooden structure draped with banners announcing that it was wing night and that Coors Light was only a dollar a can.

Tegan nudged him in the arm. "Jack, can you pull in over there?"

He coasted into the lot and warily eyed the row of Harley Davidsons and beat-up pick-up trucks parked in front of the building. "Are you sure you want to stop here?"

Tegan grinned. "Does it make you nervous?"

Nervous wasn't the word, exactly. It was more that he still remembered the day before, and the people in the diner's reaction to him when he didn't have any cash. He didn't have any illusions that he was going to fit in at a place like this in his dark khaki chinos and navy wool Henley sweater.

As if she knew what he was thinking, Tegan's gaze swept down to his shoes and then back up to his face. He had the most ridiculous urge to blush under her scrutiny.

"You're fine. You look very nice in that, actually. Believe me, this is *way* better than the lobster shorts."

He couldn't decide if he felt flattered or offended.

"But if you want, I'll just run in and use the bathroom, and then come right back out."

At that moment, two heavy-set men in stained jeans, black leather jackets, and bandanas on their heads came out the door and headed for their motorcycles.

"No, I'm coming."

They entered the bar—a large open space with wood-paneled walls covered in antique road signs and neon beer advertisements—and Jack half expected the music to shut off with a loud scratch and for everyone to turn and stare at them. But except for the bartender—a bearded, long-haired guy who could have been the brother of Frank at the gas station the day before—nobody even looked up. Actually, other than a few guys at one end of the bar, the place was almost empty. Jack began to relax.

He followed Tegan to the bathrooms down a hallway in the back. When he finished, he waited for her at the other end of the bar from the group of older men whose leather vests and Harley T-shirts declared them to be the owners of the motorcycles parked outside.

The bartender swung by and put a cocktail napkin and a bowl of peanuts in front of him. "What can I get you?"

Jack was about to refuse, but then he stopped. *Oh, what the hell?* He ordered a draft beer from the surprisingly decent selection. When it arrived, he took a long swallow and then one more, watching through an archway as two younger-looking guys in dusty Carhartt uniforms and work boots placed bets on a game of pool.

The alcohol hit his bloodstream and relaxed his muscles as he stretched his back and cocked his head from side to side. The lack of sleep combined with the long hours sitting in a car were starting to catch up to him. His whole body ached and his eyes felt like sandpaper. He should try to find a gym or a hotel with a pool tomorrow. Swimming some laps would help with the sore muscles at least.

Tegan had been making noises about going for a hike in Rocky Mountain National Park tomorrow. It would add more time to his already lengthening trip, but it might be nice to get out of the car and move around a little. And if it would exhaust him enough to finally get some sleep, it would be worth the extra day on the road.

His travel companion returned from the bathroom with her backpack over her shoulder. She'd changed into a pair of jeans and thrown a sweater and scarf over her flowy shirt. Her eyebrows rose at the sight of his half-empty glass of beer. "Are we hanging out?"

Jack shrugged. "It seemed rude not to order something. You want one?"

"Sure." She slid onto the stool next to him.

He gestured to the bartender for another beer as a yawn escaped.

"You sure you're up for driving two more hours to Estes Park tonight? You look exhausted again."

"Well, the plan was to get there tonight."

She smirked. "And you don't deviate from your plan."

"Obviously, I do. I can guarantee that nothing in my itinerary had me drinking a beer in a biker bar with a hitchhiker I picked up on the side of the road." With that, the bartender plunked a pint in front of Tegan, and Jack handed him a twenty.

"Do I need to remind you again that these are great stories for you to tell your golf buddies?"

"That would be nice, except I don't golf. But my sister, Liv, is going to love it when I tell her about Ruby the waitress and the thugs back at that cafe."

She swiveled on the stool so she was facing him. "You said you're close with your family?"

He felt a smile pull at his lips. "I'm pretty lucky. I have a great family."

"Yeah? Tell me about them." She swiped at the condensation on her glass. "I mean, if it's okay for me to ask."

Jack felt another pang of guilt about his outburst earlier. He cleared his throat, determined to do better. "My mom is a psychologist. A PhD. She's had a private practice for about twenty years, and she spends a little too much time psychoanalyzing me, but her heart is in the right place. My dad's an attorney—" He gestured at Tegan. "You know, the family firm."

She flashed a smile in return.

"He's a great guy. He tends to go along a little too much with whatever my mom wants, but he couldn't be more supportive of me and Liv."

"And your sister? Her name is Liv?"

"Olivia. She's five years younger than me. Just finished her law degree at Harvard last year."

"So, she works in the family firm too?"

"She's always been a bit of a bleeding heart, ever since we were kids. She only agreed to join the firm if she could expand the pro-bono work we do. Otherwise, she probably would have gone to a legal aid clinic. My dad wanted her to work there so badly, he would have agreed to anything." He chuckled at the memory of his little sister negotiating her terms. Their dad represented some of the largest corporations in the country but still, he was no match for Liv.

"You must be proud of her."

"Liv is one of my best friends. I'm excited to work in the same office with her in New York."

She pressed her lips together, and something like sadness flashed across her face. She took a gulp of her beer, and when she plunked it back on the bar, the expression was gone, but his curiosity remained. Other than the fact that she was writing a book, her life was a mystery. "Do you have siblings?"

"I—um. Yeah. I have a brother. He's—" There was that look again. "He's kind of my best friend too."

"Tell me about him."

Her eyes darted to his and then quickly skated out across the bar, away from him. She pressed her lips together, staring at the blinking Pabst Blue Ribbon sign, and the sorrow on her face made him want to know more.

"Is Jamie your brother?" he asked gently, leaning in.

Her head jerked up and her face drained of color. "How do you know about Jamie?"

Jack immediately realized his mistake. He knew the name because he'd heard her talking through the motel room wall the night before, and not because she'd mentioned him. "Well, uh. The walls were thin in the hotel last night. I—I heard you talking about someone named Jamie."

"So, you sat there *listening* to me?" She crossed her arms and bent forward as if she was fighting back nausea.

He cocked his head, wondering why, all of a sudden, her face was so pale, making her freckles stand out even more than usual. "I wasn't sitting there with my ear pressed to the wall or anything. It was hard not to hear you." He'd been sitting in his own bed right against the shared wall, and she'd been talking loud enough for her voice to carry. So maybe he didn't try *not* to hear. Maybe he'd wanted to understand a little more about this woman he'd picked up on the side of the road; this woman he was starting to feel drawn to, despite his best efforts.

That anguish on her face had to do with more than him overhearing a conversation. He put his hand on her arm, wanting to offer comfort, even though he had no idea what he was offering comfort for.

She snatched her arm away and glared at him like he was some kind of creepy stalker. "I can't believe you."

The bartender glanced in their direction, and Jack lowered his voice, as if that would somehow compensate for her outburst. "What did you want me to do?"

"I don't know. Get up and do something else. *Not* listen in on my phone calls. What did you hear?"

Jack sighed. So much for their apologies earlier. What had it been—two hours? Three? Before they had started fighting again?

"I was in bed. I was trying to sleep. All I heard was you mention someone named Jamie, and then—" He stopped and snapped his mouth shut. There was the other part of the conversation. The part where she'd lied to get off the phone.

"What?" Her eyes narrowed.

Oh, hell, she was already mad. "I heard you tell the person you were talking to that you were all alone, traveling in a station wagon. Which wasn't true, since you were riding with me."

It was amazing, really, how her face went from pale white to bright red in a matter of seconds. Her freckles blended in with her skin when it flushed, which was too bad. He was starting to like those freckles. That thought surprised him, along with the realization that it bothered him to see her so upset. Maybe Jamie wasn't her brother after all. Was he a boyfriend? Someone she was in love with?

He leaned forward. "Tegan, you can talk to me."

"Right," she scoffed. "Like I'd talk to you about anything. Jamie is none of your business."

His muscles tensed at the derision in her voice. "You're right, he's none of my business." The bartender came by with his change, and Jack handed him a few dollars for a tip and then turned back to Tegan. "But I find it interesting that you think it's fine to pry into my life. You've got all these opinions about my work, where I'm living, you looked in my phone at photos of my fiancée—"

Her gasp cut him off and had the bartender glancing at them again. "I didn't look in your phone! You handed it to me, and the photo popped up on your lock screen!"

Jack leaned in and lowered his voice, ignoring her outburst. "—But you haven't shared a single thing about yourself."

She flushed even redder, if that was possible. "I apologized about the thing with your fiancée. And I did *not* pry into your life. I was making conversation. Normal people do that—people who aren't angry and bitter all the time." Her voice was rising again. "Why do you think I haven't shared anything about myself? Because you're the most judgmental person I've ever met and you've been rude to me since the minute I stepped into your car. Maybe if we could have even one conversation without you looking at me like I'm garbage, I'd actually tell you something about myself."

"*I've* been rude?" He struggled to keep his voice calm. "Excuse me if it threw me to have my trip—that I planned to take all by myself so I could have some time alone—" He raised his eyebrows and put extra emphasis on the word *alone*, "—suddenly invaded by a woman who is constantly fiddling with my heat control and the radio, spilling things and making a mess of my car, not to mention criticizing everything from my job to my politics. Under the circumstances, I'd say I've been a goddamn saint."

"You know what, Jack?" She hopped off her barstool. "I'm sorry if I've been such a nightmare for you to travel with. But don't worry, I won't ruin your solitary trip anymore." She turned as if she was going to walk away from him.

Some rational part of him overrode his anger. They were in a biker bar in the middle of nowhere. Where did she think she was going? He reached out and took her arm. "Tegan."

She wrenched away from him. "Leave me the hell alone, Jack."

The old guys at the other end of the room turned to look at them, and suddenly the bartender was directly across the bar from him with his hairy arms crossed over his ample beer gut. "Is there a problem here?"

Tegan glared at Jack. "No, there's no problem. He was just leaving."

"Tegan, I'm not leaving you here."

She turned toward the bartender. "Thank you for checking on me, but I'm fine. He's harmless." She waved a dismissive hand at Jack.

The bartender nodded and moved a few feet back down the bar, but he kept an eye trained on them.

If Jack was annoyed before, he was pissed off now. He would have left her there without a glance if they'd been anywhere else, but his conscience wouldn't let him. It was dark out, they were in the middle of nowhere, and he really didn't like the look of the guys at the end of the bar. She was upset and not thinking rationally. "Tegan," he hissed. "Stop it. I'm not leaving you here."

"Fuck you, Jack." She turned and started to walk away.

Jack followed her to the middle of the room. "Tegan," he said in a louder voice. "Come on."

In seconds, the bartender was back in front of them, this time on their side of the bar. "She told you to fuck off, *Jack*." The bartender stepped between them. "I think you need to leave now."

Two guys at the end of the bar stood up and moved in their direction. They stepped up next to the bartender and, for a second, Jack had the inexplicable urge to laugh. Was this really his life? Was he really moments away from a fight with a bunch of tattooed thugs for the second time that week?

"Door's that way," one of the thugs said, hitching his chin at the entrance. "You've got five seconds to exit on your own."

Jack glanced over at Tegan who stood, unmoving. "Are you coming?"

She gave an indifferent shrug like a bratty teenager.

Thirty-six hours ago, he'd never even laid eyes on her. She wasn't his problem. She certainly wasn't worth a bar brawl with a bunch of Hell's Angels. He spun on his heel and stalked out the door. A cold wind hit him in the face and seeped into his sweater, but his anger warmed him as he strode across the parking lot to his car. He got in and accelerated out of the parking lot.

CHAPTER ELEVEN

Tegan

Less than a minute after Jack walked out of the bar, Tegan knew she'd made a huge mistake. She turned and darted out the door, skidding to a halt in the parking lot. As she stood under a blinking orange Budweiser sign in the freezing wind blowing off the mountain, she felt a boulder drop right on her chest.

All that was left of Jack was the faint red glow of tail lights disappearing over the next hill.

He's gone.

Of course, he was gone. What person in his right mind would stick around being told to fuck off? He was probably thrilled to be rid of her, and she didn't blame him one bit. If she could somehow be rid of herself, she would.

Shame at how badly she'd treated him—again—washed over her. To say she'd overreacted would be an understatement. It wasn't his fault he'd heard her through the wall. After all, she'd heard him thrashing around mumbling, "Somebody help her!" over and over. The walls *were* paper-thin in that motel, and she'd woken to find he was having a nightmare.

But she hadn't been thinking rationally. He'd asked about Jamie and, all of a sudden, she'd hurt so badly, it was like she was the one who was dying.

She shook her head. *No.*

Jamie wasn't dying. Jamie was in remission. But how could she explain to Jack why she'd lied on the phone, why she was avoiding telling Jamie how her trip was really going? How could she admit that she'd spent a lifetime making Jamie worry about her, and she was finally trying to be the responsible one, the one who figured things out for a change?

Especially because Jack could see that she was obviously failing so miserably at it.

Another gust of wind blew up, dragging her back to her present condition. Somehow, in less than two days, she'd managed to put herself in another precarious situation. She wrapped her arms around herself, shivering as the cold cut through her sweater. Fat snowflakes swirled through the air, melting when they hit the heat from her body. She turned around and hurried back into the bar before she was soaked on top of everything else.

Sliding onto a stool at the end of the bar, she dropped her backpack at her feet and took stock of her present situation. She needed to get out of there and find someplace to stay for the night. It was cold in the mountains—a lot colder than it had been in Arizona and New Mexico—and Jack had her tiny, one-person tent and sleeping bag in the backseat of his car. He probably didn't even realize they were there. Neither of them had imagined he'd drive off alone when they'd stopped for a quick bathroom break.

All of a sudden, she was so tired she wanted to lie down right there on the pool table. Why had she been so terrible to Jack? She'd give anything to be in his car right now, listening to one of his boring stock market podcasts and arguing about where they were going to stop for the night. But she didn't have time to dwell on that now.

There had to be a cheap motel around somewhere. She pulled out her phone to look, but of course there was no cell service on that tiny mountain pass. Maybe the bartender would know someplace, but there was still the problem of getting there. He'd been quick to come to her rescue and seemed like the safest bet to ask for a ride, but he'd probably be working until well after midnight. Could she hang out there until he closed up the bar?

Clicking off her phone, she looked up to find someone sliding onto the stool next to her.

"Your friend leave?" It was one of the younger guys who'd been playing pool across the room a few minutes ago. Next to him, the other man he'd been playing with leaned on the bar.

"Yeah." She hesitated, eyeing them both. "But he'll—um, he'll be back in a little while." It occurred to her that she was the only woman in the place and it was probably better if they didn't know she was entirely alone.

The man next to her held out a hand. "I'm Bill, and this is my friend, Rob."

"Tegan." She gave his hand a firm squeeze to let him know she was tougher than she looked. "Are you guys from around here?"

Bill took a swig of his beer as he nodded. "Not too far. Me and Rob both work in maintenance at a couple of the hotels over in Telluride, 'bout thirty miles from here."

"So, you're regulars?" Maybe they'd know a cheap place to stay nearby. They could drop her off on their way home.

"Yeah, we stop by after work a few times a week." He took another gulp of his beer and then looked her up and down. "I've got to say, though, we've never had a girl like you come in before."

"Hell, no," Rob said.

"I guess today is my lucky day." Bill plunked his empty beer bottle on the bar and inched closer to her. "Can I buy you a drink?"

Tegan automatically leaned back. She didn't want to give him the idea that he'd be getting something in return. "Oh, um. Well, are you sure you guys want to stick around that long? I'm sure you're tired after working all day—" Maybe they'd be heading out soon. Home to their wives and children, preferably.

Bill leaned closer. She could smell sweat, and beer on his breath, and the faint whiff of cigarette smoke. "Baby, this place just got interesting. I'm not going anywhere. How about that drink?"

Her skin crawled as her instincts screamed at her to make a run for it. "No, thanks. I'm good. Just going to check out the music until my friend gets back." She hopped off her stool and headed over to the juke box where she flipped through the selection of songs by Kid Rock, Van Halen, and Lynyrd Skynyrd. Not exactly her style, but—she thought about Jack again—who was she to judge?

As she studied her choices, Bill came up beside her, and his arm bumped up against her shoulder. An awareness of him washed over her. He was probably at least eight inches taller than she was, with broad shoulders and a little extra weight around the middle. He wasn't fat exactly, more like brawny from all the manual labor combined with the beer that he was rapidly draining. She inched to the left, away from him, but a second later, he bumped against her shoulder again. She took a deliberate step away from him as the distinctive guitar chords of an old Guns N' Roses song played through the speakers.

Bill threw his arm around her with a chuckle that was too loud in her ear. "Great choice of songs, baby."

She hated being called "baby." She'd told him her name, but he'd probably forgotten, or maybe he didn't care what her name was. But it didn't matter, he could call her whatever he wanted if he'd stop touching her.

"Excuse me." She pushed her way out of his embrace and sat at a table by the door. Just in case she needed to make a quick escape. She watched Bill take a couple more gulps of his beer and knew there was no way she was getting in a car with him. Her gaze drifted to the biker guys at the bar. Despite their layers of black leather and gruff expression, they might be very nice. But she had her backpack stuffed with all of her belongings, and it was windy and snowing. Could she ride down those narrow mountain passes on the back of a Harley?

The problems with this situation piled on top of each other until they were teetering like a stack of blocks. Her eyes shifted to the bartender. Maybe she'd have to stick around until his shift was over.

But as she watched from the corner of her eye, the bartender lined up two shot glasses on the bar, poured in something amber-colored and handed one to Bill. Then he picked up the other glass and tossed it back. He said something to Bill and they glanced in her direction. They both laughed and the bartender punched Bill on the arm and gave him a hand slap. Her heart, which was already hovering somewhere around her stomach, dropped all the way to her knees.

Tegan slid off the stool and made a break for the bathroom down the narrow hall at the back of the building. She leaned against the sink, taking deep, shaky breaths. If the bartender had been drinking and encouraging Bill to make a move on her, he wasn't going to be her ally. She was trapped in the middle of nowhere with a bunch of semi-intoxicated men and no way to get out of there.

She wanted to sink to the floor and cry, but that would only make things worse. She needed to focus and make a plan. There was an exit door at the end of the hall. All she had to do was sneak out the back and make a run for it.

She'd be out on the road, in the dark. But surely another car would come along and give her a ride? And despite her bad luck on this trip, the chances that her next ride would be a rapist or serial killer *had* to be low, right? Or maybe she wouldn't have to take a chance on another stranger at all—if she could walk down the mountain far enough to find cell reception, she could call the cops and say she needed help. They'd give her a ride to a populated area, wouldn't they?

She slipped out the bathroom door, back out into the hallway and let out a surprised gasp as a pair of hands grabbed her.

Bill.

Startled, her backpack slipped from her grasp. Bill pulled her in and left a trail of wet kisses across her neck.

"*Stop it.*" She squirmed and pushed her forearms against his chest, but he didn't budge.

"I've been wanting to do this since you walked through that door." His breath was hot on her ear and the pungent scent of alcohol was overpowering.

She pressed harder against his chest, but he only tightened his grip. His lips moved toward her and as she turned her head away, he landed a kiss on the corner of her mouth. She arched her back away from him, but her head hit the wall behind her. "*Let go of me.*" This time she threw her shoulder into it, pushing with all her weight.

"Come on, baby, we're just having a little fun." The hand on her waist slid lower and his beefy fingers grabbed her ass. The other hand slid into her hair, holding her head still so he could plant a kiss on her mouth.

From somewhere far away, she heard Jamie's voice lecturing her about what to do if her prom date got too handsy.

Kick him in the balls.

Her knee flew up and thudded against the sensitive spot between Bill's legs. He let out a howl as he folded in half, clutching his crotch.

Tegan stumbled backward, away from Bill. She was free, for the moment, but then panic set in again. Her mind flitted from the Harley guys out in the bar to the bartender. Would they help her? If they were friendly with Bill, they might not. She'd have no way of knowing until it was too late.

Bill staggered in her direction. "*You fucking bitch.*" His voice echoed down the hall, and silence descended over the men out in the bar.

Tegan willed herself not to panic. She hitched her backpack over her shoulder, getting ready to make a run for it, when all of a sudden came the most beautiful sound she'd ever heard.

"Tegan."

Jack.

She whirled around. He stood in the doorway connecting the barroom to the hall, and she'd never been so happy to see anyone in her entire life. In ten steps, he was next to her, taking her backpack with one hand and wrapping his arm around her shoulder. "Come on, let's get out of here."

Another string of expletives came from Bill's direction, and as they hurried past the bar, Tegan could see Rob heading toward them. Jack led her out the door, and they bolted across the parking lot. He opened her door, tossing her backpack on the floor as she climbed inside, and then he jogged around to the driver's side. He started the car and peeled out of the parking lot before he'd even snapped his seatbelt into place.

When they were a couple of miles down the road, Jack pulled over and shifted in his seat to look at her. "Are you okay?"

Her heart hammered in her chest and she didn't trust her voice, but she managed a nod.

"Good. Because you're an idiot, do you know that?" His face was in shadows, but she could still sense the anger flashing there.

"Yes."

He continued as if he hadn't heard her. "Who knows what could have happened to you in there? You could have been raped. Or worse. Guys like that aren't messing around. You think this grand adventure you're on is worth putting yourself at that kind of risk? It's not. It's stupid."

"You're right." She paused, trying to swallow down the lump in her throat. *Oh god, please don't let me start crying.* But the tears welled up anyway. She swiped at them with the palm of her hand. It wasn't the yelling. He was right. She *was* an idiot.

The reality of what could've happened to her tonight—and the other day with the truck driver—finally hit her. She'd been so determined to go out on her own and prove that she could take care of everything, but all she'd done was prove that she was a complete mess.

She wrapped her arms around herself, trying to stop the shivering. Jack had the heat cranked up. Why couldn't she stop shivering? A tear spilled over and trickled down her cheek. She could feel his eyes on her, and then he reached over and rubbed the tear away with his thumb. The anger on his face was gone, replaced with an expression she couldn't identify.

She sniffed and wiped her eyes with her sleeve. "Why did you come back?"

He didn't say anything for a moment, and then a crooked smile stretched across his face. "You have all the Twizzlers in your bag."

She let out a surprised laugh.

His smile slowly faded. "I'd agreed to give you a ride, but you were right, I was rude and unwelcoming to you the whole time. If I didn't want you here, I should've bought you a bus ticket, not spent two days snapping at you." He winced and rubbed the back of his neck. "I drove about a half a mile down the road and did a U-turn. I figured I'd wait for you in the parking lot." He reached over and took her arm. "But then I got worried thinking about you in there."

She looked up and in the dim light of the dashboard, their eyes met. Before she could stop it, a shiver of a different kind ran through her.

He jerked back and looked away. "I'm sorry. After what happened back there, you probably don't want another guy touching you."

She rubbed her arm, cold now that the heat from his hand was gone. "You're nothing like that guy."

"When I walked in and saw he had you cornered down that hallway, I thought, 'I'm going to have to get her out of this.' And then you kicked him—and he keeled over like that…" Jack breathed out a laugh. "It was amazing."

Tegan pressed her hand to the smile on her lips. "It *was* kind of satisfying to hear him scream."

"He'll be walking bow-legged for weeks."

They were both laughing now and, with the sound, the tension seeped from the car.

"Jack, listen. I appreciate what you said about how you should have been more welcoming to me. But I'm the one who crashed your solo road trip." She paused, surprised by how much she hated the next thing she was about to say. "Denver is only a couple of hours from here. If you drop me off there, you could still have a nice trip all by yourself to New York. I know I set you back a few days and took you off course from the itinerary you planned, but…"

Jack stared straight ahead out the front window, and she couldn't read his expression. Shifting in her seat, she fought back the urge to ask what he was thinking.

Finally, he asked, "Do you want me to leave you in Denver?"

"I shouldn't have manipulated you into bringing me this far. You were right, ten dollars for your sandwich isn't even close to the equivalent of all this." She waved her hand to include the scene she'd made back at the bar, the mess she'd made of his car, and her general presence in his life.

"You didn't answer my question."

"Well—I—" What could she say? These feelings were irrational. "No." She glanced over at him. "I don't want you to leave me in Denver."

He was still staring out the front window. "The thing is, it turns out I'm actually not very good at traveling alone. I can get kind of moody and stuck in my own head."

"I never would have noticed that about you," she murmured.

He gave her a stern look that said he knew she was bullshitting him. She had a flash of what he must be like when he was in his element in a court room, and was intrigued.

"I've already mapped out this new route, and we're almost to Rocky Mountain National Park. Maybe we should keep going." His mouth stretched into a smile. "Keep each other out of trouble."

"I think that sounds like a good plan."

CHAPTER TWELVE

Jack

What had he been thinking? Jack had the perfect opportunity to get rid of his travel companion —she'd even offered to go—and instead, he found himself suggesting they head for the Rockies like buddies in a road movie.

His emotions felt like they'd spent two days tumbling in the dryer along with whatever rational thought he had left. The panic that rose up when he saw Tegan cornered in that back hallway still hadn't completely settled back down. And the admiration he'd felt when he watched her fight back was doing strange things to him, too. He glanced in her direction and something tugged in his chest at the sight of her leaning against the passenger door, her red-blond hair shining against her forehead in the dashboard lights. She'd closed her eyes, and the shadow of her lashes left two dark smudges across her freckled cheeks.

The dread he'd felt when she suggested he leave her in Denver shocked him. Sitting in the car for hundreds of miles of endless farmland and desert, alone with nothing but his thoughts and an occasional podcast to keep him company, had been more difficult than he would have ever imagined. Since she'd come along, he'd been incensed, aggravated, and exasperated, but, for the first time in almost a year, he hadn't been lonely. At the moment, that felt like a miracle.

And as for these other feelings—the rage when the guy in the bar had put his sloppy, drunk mouth on her, the urge to storm over and yank her into *his* arms, the desire to lean over and press his lips to the spot where he'd wiped away her tear, none of that meant anything. Those few small gestures—his hand on her cheek, his arm around her as they ran for the car—had been the first human contact he'd had in so long. He'd almost forgotten what it felt like to touch another person.

He didn't have to be in New York for another couple of weeks, and once he was back at work it could be years before he had another chance to get out and see the country like this. She needed a ride and it seemed that they'd managed to come to a truce. It made perfect sense for them to travel together. Much more sense than leaving her at a bus stop and spending 2,000 miles with his boredom and loneliness.

He drove for another twenty minutes or so until he spotted a sign for the Red Mountain Lodge at the top of the mountain. His plan had been to make it to Estes Park that evening, but that was before their little detour at the bar. It was late and dark, and they were both so exhausted that driving for two more hours on those narrow mountain passes could be dangerous. If they stopped now, it would be his second day in a row going off course, but for some reason it didn't bother him as much this time.

Tegan sat up with a bleary-eyed expression as he coasted into the parking lot of the hotel.

"Is this okay for tonight?" he asked as he parked the car.

Her gaze swept across the sign announcing that the rooms were $30 a night with breakfast included. "Is it okay with *you*? It's not exactly the Four Seasons."

He'd paid more than $30 just for breakfast at the Four Seasons, but road trips were for new experiences, right? Besides, he was so tired, as long as the Red Mountain Lodge had a bed for him to fall into, he didn't care if a life-sized wooden bear guarded the door, or that the place likely hadn't seen an update since the 1950s. "The Vista Verde did set a high bar. But I think this place can surpass it."

The interior of the Red Mountain Lodge matched the exterior and looked like a hunting and fishing catalog had thrown up all over it. Canoe oars, fishing poles, and signs declaring that someone would "rather be hunting" covered every inch of the knotty pine walls that didn't have a deer head or large-mouth bass hanging from it. Not surprisingly, securing two vacant rooms wasn't an issue, and soon they had keys in their hands and were following a worn plaid carpet down a hallway off the lobby.

Jack left Tegan at her door and then found his own room down the hall. Thankfully, there were no dead animals staring at him from the walls, but the kitsch from the lobby carried into the guest rooms, and he gazed around at the slatted wood, past a quilt with moose and bears ambling across it to a lamp made from a pair of deer antlers. Sinking down on the bed, he fought back the urge to laugh at his surroundings and once again, marvel at how he'd ended up there.

He knew he should go to sleep, but his exhaustion seemed to have disappeared somewhere back by the ice machine, and his mind whirled with the events of the day. Normally he'd get some work done, but he'd forgotten his briefcase in his car, and it didn't seem worth the effort to go and get it. The Red Mountain Lodge didn't have TV in the rooms—what did he expect from a hotel that cost as much as his Uber ride to work?—so he changed into a T-shirt and a pair of pajama pants and called Liv.

"Hi, Jack," she said, with a sleepy note in her voice.

"Did I wake you? It's a two-hour time difference here, but I thought you'd still be up."

Through the phone he could hear her shuffling around, probably sitting up in bed. "Two hours? I thought you'd be in Oklahoma by now. Isn't that only one hour?"

He'd forgotten that he'd given Liv a copy of his itinerary. She worried about him alone on this trip and was probably keeping track of his whereabouts. "Oh. Yeah. I didn't exactly make it to Oklahoma. I headed north instead."

"North?" All traces of sleep were gone from her voice. "Where are you?"

"Umm. I'm in Colorado. In the mountains, maybe an hour or two outside of Boulder? You should see it, Liv," he said, trying to refocus the conversation. "The views are amazing."

He should've known he couldn't deter Liv with talk of pretty scenery. "You sound like you're not sure where you are. What happened to the southern route through Oklahoma and Missouri?"

"Well, there was—there was a tornado." He pictured Tegan's wild hair, flashing blue eyes, and the mess she left in his car. A tornado wasn't that far off, really. "There was a tornado warning in Oklahoma, so I decided to head north instead."

"Are you still traveling with the—hippie writer?"

"Tegan."

"What?"

"Her name is Tegan."

She was silent for a moment. "So, you are traveling with her."

He didn't want to lie to his family, but at the same time, he was twenty-nine years old. Their involvement in his life for the past year was understandable—appreciated even—but maybe it was time they backed off a little. In two weeks, he'd be living in the same city as Liv and his parents again. Over the past year he'd started to grow weary of their constant clucking, the sideways looks, and the tiptoeing around for fear they'd topple his fragile mental health. Maybe now was the time to start establishing some boundaries again.

"Liv, you need to stop worrying. Tegan is harmless, and this is nothing more than a temporary ride for someone who needed help. Please trust me on this."

"Okay. I know. It's just that ever since Charlotte—" she hesitated, unable to say it. Nobody could ever just *say it*. It was like they thought that dancing around it would keep him from remembering what happened. As if he could ever forget, even for a minute. "Well, it's just been really hard to see you like that. I can't help it if I want to protect you a little."

His grip on the phone loosened. "I'm really grateful for everything this past year—I wouldn't have gotten through it without you. But I'm okay, really. I think this trip has been good for me."

She sighed. "Stay in touch, okay?"

Sleep came easily, but a few hours later, he yanked himself out of another nightmare. This one started the same as the others—the screaming, the sirens, the knowledge that someone he loved was hurt and his legs wouldn't move fast enough to get to them. But as he sat there in the dark hotel room, trying to calm his pounding heart and stop his hands from shaking, he realized that this time the ending was different. This time the woman in the dream wasn't Charlotte lying in an unnatural angle on the pavement, blood pooling under her body while two paramedics shook their heads and said over and over that there was nothing more they could do.

Jack exhaled a shaky breath as the vague edges of the dream took shape in his consciousness.

This time the woman was Tegan.

He jumped out of bed and ran for the shower, standing in the blast of hot water until his skin turned red and raw. When he couldn't stand it anymore, he toweled off, climbed back in bed, and tossed and turned for a few more hours. At dawn he gave up on sleep and got dressed and packed his bag. According to the owl clock on the wall, it was 7 a.m. Might as well get his briefcase and get some work done.

Detouring into the dining room to see about coffee, he stopped short when he spotted Tegan sitting at one of the wooden tables, glaring at her laptop. She'd been up before him yesterday, too. Was she an early riser, or was she nervous that he'd wake up first and take off without her?

He stood in the doorway for a moment and watched her. That hippie style must be growing on him because today she looked fresh and pretty in a tattered Beatles T-shirt with a turquoise knit scarf wrapped around her neck. Maybe it was how the scarf matched her eyes, or the way her T-shirt and jeans looked effortless and comfortable. Most of the women in his life wouldn't be caught dead in a ratty T-shirt, even for running errands or going to the gym. Liv, whom he loved dearly, never left the house without putting on make-up or her pearl earrings first, and unless she was actually exercising, she always wore heels.

He checked out Tegan's feet. She had replaced her scuffed sneakers with equally beat-up hiking boots. She was probably planning to make another pitch for going hiking in the park later today. Jack reached to the top of the doorframe to stretch his shoulders and back. Out the window, it looked like it was shaping up to be a nice day. Maybe some air and a hike *would* be good for them both.

Tegan looked up from her computer and spotted him braced in the doorway, mid-stretch. Two pink spots appeared on her cheeks.

Jack dropped his arms and gave her a wave, moving toward the self-serve buffet. He poured some coffee and contemplated the fruit salad and oatmeal. Definitely the healthy choices, especially given that his last meal had been Ritz crackers topped with some sort of spray cheese that came out of a can. "Easy Cheese," Tegan had said. "Easy heart attack," he'd responded, as she handed him a cracker. He'd stuffed it in his mouth, savoring the weirdly addictive, salty fake cheddar flavor. In response, she's sprayed more cheese on another cracker and held it out to him.

He smiled at the memory. Since he'd already gone completely off the rails on this trip, he might as well have a croissant. He piled two chocolate ones on plates and headed to Tegan's table. He sat in the seat across from her and slid one of the croissants in front of her.

"As much as I've become accustomed to that grumpy face," he said, "I can't imagine what your computer did to deserve it. You were really giving it the death stare when I walked in."

She pulled the croissant closer. "This scene isn't working out the way I want it to. The characters keep saying the wrong things."

He leaned back in his chair and took a sip of his coffee. "Maybe I can help. Sometimes another perspective is useful when you have writer's block. What's the scene about?"

"Well…" She eyed him for a moment. "The book is about the relationship between two siblings who have a rough childhood. In this scene, they have to have a really hard conversation. I know what they need to say, but it's so hard to make them say it."

He hadn't been expecting that. "I thought you said the book was about this trip. The adventure, the allure of the open road, all that stuff."

She hesitated before speaking. "I think you said that. You seemed to like this romantic notion of yourself as Neal Cassady, and I didn't want to burst your bubble."

He wondered if that was the real reason. From the moment he'd known about the book, he'd mocked her, and he didn't blame her for not opening up about it. But they'd come to a truce. Maybe more than a truce. "So, what is this conversation these siblings need to have?"

She pressed her lips together and stared at the screen in front of her as if she was contemplating what to say. After a moment, her eyes flickered to his and she shook her head. He was strangely disappointed as she closed her computer. "It's okay, I'll work it out eventually. But thanks for the offer." She took a sip of her coffee and peered at him over the rim. "How do you know about writer's block, anyway?"

"I don't know about writer's block." He shrugged. "But I'm an attorney, remember? I know about problem solving. At the firm we have a weekly meeting where we talk about the cases we're working on for our clients. It really helps to brainstorm with our colleagues. Sometimes they'll have an idea from a similar case, or they'll suggest another way of looking at the law that I never would have thought of."

Jack had been skipping out on those meetings these past few months, finding it easier to hole up in his office and plod through his work alone. But now that he thought about it, he missed the interaction. Part of the fun of being an attorney was that back and forth with his colleagues. Maybe he'd start going to those meetings again when he got to New York.

Tegan leaned forward in her chair and her dangly silver earrings jingled. "So, you really do like being a lawyer?"

"Of course, I do. Just because it's the family business doesn't mean they forced me into it. I've wanted to be a lawyer since I was a kid."

She smiled. "Your parents wouldn't have disowned you if you'd done something different?"

"Nope, but that sounds like a good story for you to write a book about. Actually, I have two cousins who didn't go into law. One of them is a doctor—"

She held up her palms, nodding. "Naturally."

"—and the other one is an anthropologist who studies indigenous cultures in the Amazon."

Tegan blinked. "Okay, I admit, I didn't see that one coming."

He smiled at her wide-eyed expression. "Both of them are still invited for Christmas dinner."

She cocked her head and her strawberry-blond hair tumbled over her shoulder. He was again reminded of the difference between Tegan and the women in his social circle. Most of them paid thousands of dollars for stylists to wrestle with their hair until it was sleek, shiny and stick-straight. Looking at those unruly waves across the table, he couldn't imagine why they bothered. Then again, those same women would probably do chemical peels and use heavy make-up to minimize the freckles scattered across Tegan's cheeks. He was glad she didn't. They were charming as she wrinkled her nose with an apologetic look. "Well, I'm sorry I misjudged you about your profession."

He leaned forward and met her eyes. "And I'm sorry I misjudged you about yours."

As they gazed at each other across the table, something thickened in the atmosphere around them. Tegan sucked in an audible breath and her shoulders tensed up as if she was holding the air in her lungs. In contrast, he couldn't seem to breathe at all.

He'd been hoping that whatever these feelings he was having for her was would settle down once they came to this truce and decided to be friends. That once they stopped fighting, he'd actually find her kind of ordinary.

He finally managed to take a shaky breath.

She was anything but ordinary.

He shoved the chocolate croissant to the side and stood up. "Take your time finishing your coffee. I'll meet you out in the lobby."

She didn't say anything, but he could feel her eyes on him as he stopped at the buffet, grabbed an apple and a banana, and headed out the door.

CHAPTER THIRTEEN

Tegan

When I was in fifth grade, I got to be science project partners with Sheila Smolinsky. I couldn't believe my luck. Sheila was the most popular girl in school. Her sneakers were always perfectly clean and white, she was the best at jump rope in the entire class, and she wore braces like the sixth graders did. My shoes were always scuffed, I was too clumsy and usually ended up tangled in the rope, and there was no way we could afford braces to fix that crooked bottom tooth I had. But I thought maybe if I worked really, really hard on our project, Sheila would decide to be my friend.

And that's what I did. I worked so hard for that whole month, doing my share, and sometimes her share too. And on the day of the science fair, after we'd been awarded an A triple-plus for my efforts, I worked up the nerve to ask Sheila if I could sit with her at lunch.

And do you know what she said to me? She said that she'd put up with me during the project, but if she had to sit next to me at lunch she'd lose her appetite.

I was so stunned that I just stood there for a full minute before I turned around and smacked her right in that smug metal mouth.

Boy, was Jamie mad. He had to come and get me after school because the principal wouldn't let me go home without talking to my guardian first, and Daddy was down at the bar again. And you should have seen him, pacing back and forth, charming that principal, telling him everything he wanted to hear about how I was going to be punished, how I'd have to tell the priest at confession, and "You can bet she'll be writing an apology letter to the girl she hit, sir."

I thought the priest part was taking it a bit far, but that principal ate it right up.

Later, Jamie really did yell at me, ranting and raving about how I had to keep my head down and quit getting into trouble or they were going to take me away from him. But then when he was done, he plunked down in the chair across from me and asked, "So how hard did you hit her?"

"Really hard."

He nodded slowly. "Good."

*

Tegan slumped back in her chair, her mind drifting to Jamie. Maybe it was because she'd called him again last night. It was actually his friends, Derek and Rebecca, who she'd called. Jamie had been sleeping again, and Tegan told them not to wake him. He needed his rest, and she didn't want to bother him.

But a little part of her knew that wasn't the whole story. She'd been avoiding talking to Jamie since her car broke down and her trip went south. If he knew what had really happened, he'd tell her to give up and come home. But then what would they do? Derek and Rebecca didn't have room for her in their tiny apartment; she'd only be in the way.

Jamie had been taking care of both of them for her entire life and she desperately wanted to step up and figure out this new life for them. She just didn't know how to tell him that stepping up was turning out to be harder than she'd expected.

Tegan grabbed the chocolate croissant Jack had given her and took a huge bite. The buttery, chocolate flavor exploded on her tongue, soothing her ragged emotions. She polished off the rest of the croissant and then started in on the other one Jack had left. By the time it was gone, her stomach was churning from all the fat and sugar, but it was better than the empty pit of guilt eating away at her.

She gathered up her dishes and dumped them in the rubber bin by the door, determined to get back on track and to focus on what was really important. The first step was to stop locking eyes with Jack across the table.

He was engaged. And not only was he engaged, he was happy. She knew exactly what he looked like when he adored someone, when he was in love, when the object of his gaze was his whole world.

She knew, because she couldn't get the photo she'd seen on his phone, of Jack and Charlotte, out of her head. The way Jack's body angled toward Charlotte, as if he wanted to pull her into his arms but he had to hold back so the photographer could get the shot, the way his eyes shone as he looked at her, the way the smile lit up his face as if he couldn't believe his luck.

And then there was Charlotte. At first glance, she could've passed for a young Kate Middleton with her long, shiny dark hair, glowing pink cheekbones, and full lips dabbed with just the slightest hint of pale peach gloss. Tegan wanted to ask why Charlotte hadn't come on his road trip, but he'd made it clear that talking about his fiancée was off the table.

She shoved a wayward curl out of her face and tugged at her T-shirt. It didn't matter anyway. This arrangement couldn't have been more temporary. They still didn't even know each other's last names. She could ask him, but wouldn't. In a few days, he'd be starting his new life in New York, presumably with his beautiful fiancée and a job he loved. And she'd…

Tegan straightened her shoulders. They were in Colorado, one of the most beautiful states in the country. There had to be a hundred little towns where she and Jamie could be happy. Jamie would get a job doing construction, and she'd find a job in a local diner, maybe. Their money would go farther in a small town, and they'd be able to afford a place to live. Nothing fancy, but maybe it would have a front porch, and space for a little garden. She'd get her book done, get it published and *that* would be her new life, finally on her own terms.

Tegan made her way to the lobby where she found Jack slumped on the brown log-frame couch with his legs crossed on the wood plank coffee table in front of him. He had his head tilted back against the cushion as he stared at the ceiling. She glanced up to see what he was looking at it. It was nothing more than knotty pine beams stretching to the roof.

As she got closer, she realized that he wasn't looking at anything, that his eyes were closed. The poor guy was exhausted. Did he have another nightmare last night? She was dying to know more about that, but she couldn't possibly ask.

She sank down in the cushions next to him. "Jack." He didn't stir, so she spoke louder. "*Jack.*" This time, he moved slightly, but still didn't lift his head or open his eyes. She reached over and gently squeezed his upper arm. It was surprisingly solid for a corporate lawyer who probably spent all day sitting at a desk. Jack's head rolled in her direction and he opened his eyes, hazy at first and then eventually focusing on her face. A smile twitched at his lips.

"I fell asleep."

She laughed. "You think?"

"Sorry. I guess I didn't sleep very well last night…" A giant yawn cut him off.

"You know, Jack, I could drive for a while. Just until we get to Estes Park."

"No," he replied, instantly.

She should've known he wouldn't go for it, but it was annoying that he was so quick to shut it down. "You could take a nap in the passenger seat."

"No."

"Oh, come on." She breathed out a frustrated sigh. "I'm a good driver. I have my license, I'll even show it to you."

"Not a good idea. These are narrow, winding roads. And you're not used to my car." He shook his head. "Sorry, but no. I'm not putting you in control of a two-ton vehicle when there are cliffs to drive over. Maybe when we get to Kansas I'll let you drive."

She glared at him, irritated that he was treating her like an airhead. Okay, so she was a little more disorganized and messier than him. But he was so obsessively clean and controlling, it was impossible not to be. "I had a car when I started this trip, and I even drove all the way to California by myself."

"What happened to that car?" He looked at her sideways. "Did you crash it?"

"No!" She slumped back against the couch cushions. "It broke down in California. It was old and there was too much work to do. It wasn't worth the money to fix it."

He sat up and regarded her for another moment. "You'll go the speed limit?"

"Of course."

Jack yawned again and rubbed his eyes. "Okay."

Tegan grinned and jumped up from her seat. Jack trusting her to drive his car felt like some sort of victory.

Five minutes later, she realized that "trust" might have been overstating it. She was unable to actually drive the car because he had to review the function of every single button and knob that she might come into contact with first.

"If you get cold, just push this button up, and then you can adjust where the air comes out here."

"Jack, I know how to use a heater."

"Oh." He looked up, his expression sheepish, and ran a hand through his hair. "Of course you do. Sorry. I'm just tired."

Something tugged in her heart at the sight of his uncharacteristically rumpled hair. She was tempted to reach over and smooth it down. Instead, she held out her hand for the keys. "I've got this. You go to sleep."

"Okay." He tilted his chair back and rolled to his side, resting his cheek on the seat. A second later, he yanked on the seatbelt strap and shuffled around. He tucked his legs up toward his chest and banged his knee on the center console, wincing in pain.

Tegan watched him for a moment. She'd slept in cars plenty of times in her life, but she wasn't a six-foot-something man. Even this cushy SUV wasn't really made for that kind of thing. She twisted in her seat and grabbed a sweatshirt out of her bag, carefully folding it into a neat square. She tapped lightly on Jack's forehead. "Here, lift up."

Jack lifted his head and she tucked the sweatshirt underneath, feeling the scratch of his unshaven cheek and the unexpectedly soft brush of his hair against her hand. His blue eyes shifted up to hers. "Thanks."

She focused out the front windshield. "Sleep well."

Jack drifted off to sleep almost before she'd eased the car out of the parking lot and onto the road.

True to her word, Tegan drove the speed limit—mostly—and the first hour passed uneventfully. She wound her way up one mountain pass and down the other side, her breath catching at the beauty of the landscape in front of her.

Every turn was more breathtaking than the last, with dark green pine trees stretching into dramatic canyons dotted with shimmering blue lakes. Rising up in the distance, patches of snow sparkled in the sun on sharp, silver mountain peaks.

It was too bad that Jack was missing this. She considered waking him up, but he needed his sleep. They'd get to Rocky Mountain

National Park by late morning, and there would be more to see then, so she might as well let him rest now. She'd noticed that he'd traded his boat shoes for a pair of leather hiking boots, and she took that as an excellent sign that he was going to give in to her pleas and agree to explore the park with her. Those boots had been a surprise, and so had the jeans and sweatshirt he was wearing. Of course, the jeans were dark and perfectly pressed, and the shirt said *Harvard Law* across the front. But, for once, he looked like a guy on a road trip and not a guy lounging on his yacht.

A little part of her wished he'd go back to wearing the lobster shorts. Because Jack in jeans and boots… especially with his hair a little bit messed up from falling asleep on the couch earlier…

Well.

She focused on the road in front of her, easing her foot onto the brake and taking a sharp 90-degree turn at a nice, reasonable speed.

See that safe driving, Jack?

The car rounded the bend, and the road curved into a slight downgrade. As she coasted down the hill, her hands began to vibrate—just the slightest bit on the steering wheel. *Weird.* Up until that point, driving the car had been so smooth, she'd started to understand why rich people liked these big, expensive vehicles.

The vibration grew stronger, and Tegan held on tighter to the steering wheel as the shaking reverberated up her arms. This couldn't be good. She slowed the car a fraction, her gaze swinging back and forth across the road as she searched for a place to pull over. There was no shoulder, and she'd just gone around another blind turn, so this would be the worst place to hit the brakes. Up ahead, another bend in the road loomed. Whatever was wrong with the car couldn't be as dangerous as stopping on a narrow mountain road where another vehicle could fly around the curve at any moment.

She took the turn and something began clanking on Jack's side of the car. How it didn't wake him was a mystery. She scanned the road and, with a sigh of relief, spotted a narrow shoulder up against the rocky cliff ahead. There would be room to pull over there. Easing the wheel to the right, she steered the car toward that strip of asphalt when she heard a loud thump and then the clank of metal. She slammed her foot on the brake as the car banked to the right, pitching into the outcropping of rocks. She flew sideways, banging her elbow on the center console, and Jack woke with a start as his body made contact with the passenger door.

The car came to a stop and everything was quiet. Jack sat up in his seat and blinked, pressing his hands to his eyes to clear the haze that sleep had left. Tegan sat as still as a statue, her hand pressed over her mouth in shock.

Oh God, his car was a crumpled mess on the side of the road. Jack seemed to finally wake up as his shoulders tensed and his head swung in her direction.

She looked at him with wide eyes. "Jack, I don't know what happened—"

Her voice trailed off as he took hold of her arm and squeezed it like a mother checking her child for broken bones. "Are you okay?"

"I am so *sorry*." The car had stopped vibrating but she could still feel it all the way down to her bones. Or maybe she was shaking from the shock. "One minute, I was going around the bend and the next minute the car was rocking and—I don't know what happened. I didn't want to stop in the road, but it was really vibrating and—I was trying to pull over and then all of a sudden—How did you not wake up—?" She was aware she was babbling but couldn't seem to stop.

"Hey." Jack took her by the shoulders and turned her to face him.

She braced herself for his anger, but all she saw was concern reflected in his blue eyes. The tension in her shoulders loosened a fraction.

Jack rubbed his hands up and down her shoulders. "Don't worry about the car right now. Are you okay?"

She nodded, still dazed. Was she okay? Her elbow hurt a little, but it was probably just a bruise. And she was shivering, but Jack's hands on her arms were warm and comforting.

She took a deep breath and managed to give him the play-by-play without stumbling over her words. He held her gaze, nodding until she finished, and then he turned to peer out his side window. "Good thinking, not stopping in the middle of the road. A car could have come along and slammed into us."

"What do you think happened?"

"I have no idea. Let's go look." He pulled his door handle, but could only swing the door a couple of inches before it hit the rock outcropping they'd crashed into. "I think I'll have to climb out your side."

Tegan got out, staying as close as possible to the side of the road in case a car came flying around the bend. Jack did an awkward roll across the middle console and followed her. They rounded the front of the car, and Tegan's mouth dropped open.

"*Jesus*," Jack muttered.

The front passenger-side tire was missing. All that was left was a metal rim where the tire used to be. Several shiny new scratches ran across the rim where the steel hit the pavement and the car careened into the rocks. Tegan swung around. About fifty feet ahead, the tire lay in the road. How had she missed it rolling across her path? Probably because her focus had been on trying not to go crashing into the rocks. So much for that.

As Jack jogged up the road to get the tire, Tegan surveyed the rest of the damage. It wasn't as bad as she'd imagined by all the clanking and vibrating, or the sickening crunch of metal against rock. She didn't know anything about cars, but it didn't look like the engine or vital parts inside the hood were damaged. Or maybe that was just wishful thinking.

Jack came up beside her and propped the tire against the rocks. "I had the tires rotated before I left San Francisco. Just to be…

safe." He slowly shook his head. "They probably didn't tighten the lug nuts properly. It explains the clanking and vibrating before we crashed."

She shuddered. What if the tire had flown off when they were going seventy-five on the highway?

At that moment, a pick-up truck swung around the bend, slowing as it approached. Jack's car didn't leave much room on the narrow shoulder, but the Dodge Ram inched up toward the back bumper until only the cargo bed stuck out partway into the road. The door swung open and a man in his mid-forties wearing jeans and a plaid flannel shirt hopped out.

He walked around the SUV to where Tegan and Jack stood. "Everyone okay here?" They nodded and the man surveyed the front of Jack's car with a whistle. "I assume the tire fell off before the crash, and not the other way around?"

Jack nodded. "That's what we're thinking."

"Damn. Loose lug nuts, I'd bet." The man adjusted his green canvas hat with *Triple Crown Horse Feed* stitched across the front, and shook his head. "You're lucky you weren't on one of the steeper parts of the road when this happened. You could have flipped right over the side."

Tegan hadn't thought of that. Even though the day was sunny and approaching sixty degrees, she shivered and pulled her cardigan tighter. She looked up to find Jack giving her an odd look.

"My name's Gil Miller." The older man held out his hand. "I live over in Copper Canyon. It's just down the mountain and around the bend, maybe fifteen, twenty minutes from here."

Jack took his hand, and they shook. "I'm Jack and this is Tegan. Thanks for stopping. You wouldn't happen to know anyone who can fix this, would you?"

"My cousin runs the service station in Copper Canyon. Let me give him a call and have him send up a tow truck." He pulled a phone out of his pocket. "I see you've got California plates. Where are you from?"

"San Francisco. Headed to New York."

Tegan didn't bother to chime in. She was busy feeling nauseated at the idea that they could've gone over the side of the mountain. She balled her shaking hands into fists and wrapped her arms around herself.

Gil scrolled through his phone. "Well, my cousin should have you back on the road in no time. The damage doesn't look too bad, considering." He wandered back in the direction of his truck with his phone pressed to his ear as Jack opened the back door of the SUV and rooted around inside.

Tegan wandered across the road and peered over the guard rail. The cliff dropped off steeply, and the valley stretched out like a carpet of evergreens far below. Her mind formed an image of the SUV in a smoldering heap at the bottom of the mountain. She spun on her heel and hurried back to the car.

Jack closed the back door, holding a down jacket in his hands. He walked over to where she stood and in a swift move, wrapped it around her shoulders. Had he seen her shaking? She couldn't seem to stop.

"You okay?" He tugged the jacket closed around her. "You're never this quiet."

She snuggled in, breathing in the crisp, citrusy scent that floated off the jacket. Or maybe it was coming from Jack. He was standing awfully close, his hands still holding the jacket closed around her.

She tilted her head to look up at him and wanted nothing more than to lean in. In that moment, she wished it was his arms wrapped around her instead of his jacket. "How are you so calm? Why aren't you upset?"

"It's hard to get worked up about a few dents and scratches when I know we're lucky that we're okay."

"But aren't you worried this will slow you down even more? I bet you expected to be almost home by now."

Jack turned his head and looked across the road, past the place where the cliff dropped off and the valley stretched to the snow-tipped mountain peak jutting into a cloudless sky. His gaze shifted to hers, and she stared back into his perfect blue-sky eyes.

Those eyes crinkled around the corners as he smiled at her. "How could I wish for New York City when this is my view?"

He meant the mountains. Of course he did. Except that he was looking at her. The wind picked up and blew a lock of hair across her face. He reached up, smoothing it to the side, and the heat from his hand trailed across her skin.

At that moment, Gil rounded the car, pocketing his phone. "Rick says he can be here with a tow truck in about twenty minutes."

Jack turned away from her, and headed over to talk to Gil. Tegan hung back, her mind whirling from the accident, and from her reaction to Jack. As she stared off into the distance, bits of conversation drifted over. Jack chatted with Gil about the damage to the car, the small towns and farms sprinkled throughout the nearby valleys, and the Colorado hockey team's latest loss to the New York Islanders. If she didn't know any better, she wouldn't have believed he was the same sullen, grumpy Jack whose sandwich she'd paid for earlier that week.

Except that wasn't completely true. She'd definitely gotten off on the wrong foot with Jack. But she'd seen another side of him now—a side that could be funny, and caring, and thoughtful. She was beginning to suspect that there was something deeper he was struggling with, something causing that dark, distant sadness in his eyes. Maybe it was the reason he was on this trip, and leaving California. For a second, she wondered if it had something to do with Charlotte, but she quickly pushed that thought out of her head.

A few minutes later, a tow truck with the words *Miller Automotive* painted across the side pulled up, and a man who could have been Gil's brother jumped out. He shook hands all around, spent a few minutes discussing the accident with Jack, and then got to work hitching up the SUV. In a surprisingly short amount of time, he had it on the bed of the tow truck and ready to take to the garage.

"You can ride with me," Gil offered. "I'm headed that way too, and you might be more comfortable. Rick here is a bit of a slob and his truck is always a mess."

Tegan smiled, finally snapping out of the daze she'd been in since the accident. She climbed into Gil's passenger seat and slid over to the middle to make room for Jack. He followed her to the truck, but stopped at the door and eyed the space in the seat next to her. His gaze drifted from her right shoulder down to her leg and Tegan knew what he was thinking. He'd fit, but it might be a tight squeeze, and there was no way he could avoid pressing up next to her.

Jack took a step back. "You know, I think I'll ride in the tow truck." He didn't meet her eyes. "I want to talk to Rick about the damage, see what he thinks it will take to fix it. I'll see you down the mountain."

Before she could respond, he closed the door and disappeared around the truck. She sighed and slid back to the right side of the seat, snapping on her seatbelt. It was better they kept their distance. Because he was engaged, and she was an idiot.

CHAPTER FOURTEEN

Jack

Jack had to admit that Tegan had done a pretty good job of keeping the car under control after Rick talked him through the damage, remarking on how much worse it could've been. Just as Gil predicted, the damage to the car was minimal, which was surprising considering that it had collided with a rock wall.

Rick wiped his hands on his grease-stained coveralls and squinted into the late-morning sun. "My guys and I can easily fix this in a day, but the problem is, it's Sunday. I won't be able to get the parts until tomorrow."

Jack nodded, resigned to the fact that they'd be spending at least one night in Copper Canyon, Colorado. What was one more thing to throw him off his plans? At this point, his map and itinerary were crumpled in the bottom of his briefcase.

When Rick disappeared into the office to get the paperwork together, Jack turned to Gil, who'd hung around to hear the diagnosis. "Thanks for all your help getting us here. It looks like we'll be sticking around tonight. Can you point us to a hotel?"

Gil stuffed his weathered hands into his pockets. "I'm sorry to say we don't have any hotels around here. Mary Murphy runs the bed and breakfast over on Pine Street, but my guess is she's booked up today. We've got Copper Canyon's bicentennial celebration tonight. Did you see the banners when we came in on Main Street?"

Jack had vaguely noticed the shiny red and white signs declaring *Copper Canyon, Colorado, Celebrating 200 Years* draped across the streetlights as they drove through town.

"There are people coming in from all over for it. Bud McCaffey who played quarterback for the Copper Canyon Mountain Lions back in the day—you ever hear of him?—he played three or four years for the Miami Dolphins before he blew out his knee. Anyway, he'll be coming in to give the dedication. And Sarah Delaney, she graduated from Copper Canyon High and then moved out to Silicon Valley to start some tech company. They say she sold it for half a billion last year. The mayor will be giving her the key to the city. Lots of other folks have family coming in for the festival, too."

"Is there anything nearby?" Jack gazed out at the mountains that loomed in the distance. Those peaks were probably visible from pretty much anywhere in Copper Canyon. "Maybe the next town over?"

Gil shook his head. "We're pretty remote out here. There are plenty of hotels over in the ski areas, or up in Estes Park, but we don't get a lot of tourists down in this valley. Copper Canyon is really an old mining town, although all the mines have closed down. Now, we're mostly farmers, or people commuting up to the tourist areas for work. The nearest hotel might be over in Salida Springs, but that's about twenty-five, thirty miles away."

Without a car to get there, it might as well have been a hundred miles.

At that moment, Tegan emerged from the garage, where she'd gone to get her bag from the backseat of the car.

Gil's gaze swept from Jack to Tegan. "I'm sorry I can't offer you my guest room, we have my in-laws in town for the festival. But you're welcome to stay in my barn if you'd like."

"Your barn?" Jack asked.

"On the drive, I was telling Tegan here that I've got a little dairy farm right outside of town. Some of the cows sleep in the barn at night. There's a bathroom downstairs—it's not fancy, but it works. You can sleep upstairs in the loft. The kids like to camp up there sometimes, and they threw some old mattresses on the floor." He nodded at Tegan. "I see you have sleeping bags."

Tegan dropped her backpack at her feet and patted the sleeping bag tied to the top. "Oh, I have one, but I don't think Jack..."

"I have a sleeping bag."

Tegan wrinkled her nose. "You do?"

"Sure." He turned to Gil. "Thanks. The barn sounds great."

Gil shrugged as if it was no trouble at all. "I've got a few errands to run in town, but I'll be ready to head out in about two hours. You can pack up whatever you need and leave your bags here in the office with Rick." He gestured toward the road. "If you walk about three blocks that direction, you'll hit Main Street. We're a small town, but we've got a few shops you might like, and a coffeehouse that might even impress you city folks."

The adrenaline from the accident was starting to wear off, and coffee sounded great to Jack. Had he really just agreed to stay in a barn tonight? After the Vista Verde and the Red Mountain Lodge, where would he be sleeping next? A jail cell?

But he found he couldn't quite get that worked up about it. Gil had been so kind to offer, and maybe it would be nice to have a story or two to tell about this trip someday. Maybe someday, he'd actually look back and laugh.

Gil got in his truck with a promise to meet them back there in two hours, and Jack headed into the garage to pack his bag.

Tegan trailed behind him, leaning against the car as he swung open the door to the back. "You really have a sleeping bag?"

"Why is that so shocking?"

"I don't know. I can't picture you sleeping on the ground, out in the woods."

He crossed his arms and looked at her. "I'm about to sleep in a barn."

Tegan laughed. "You know there will be actual animals living in there. And dirt and straw and cow manure."

"My parents keep horses in Connecticut. I'm aware of what a barn is. And I've shoveled plenty of manure." Jack shrugged. "My dad believed that if we wanted to ride the horses, we had to learn how to take care of them. So, I spent a lot of weekend mornings hauling bales of hay and shoveling shit."

Tegan's eyebrows rose, and her grin grew wider. "Well, you're just full of surprises."

Jack turned back to the trunk of his car, and surveyed the moving boxes. He hadn't bothered to label any of them, a decision he now regretted. His sleeping bag could be anywhere, and he didn't really want to dig through the contents of some of those boxes in order to find it. He sighed, pulling the nearest box toward him and peeking in the top. *Nope.* He quickly slammed the cardboard flaps shut, smoothing his hand across the packing tape to reseal it. He grabbed the next box, opened it and then shut it again.

"Here, I can help." Tegan reached for a box.

"*No.*" It came out more forcefully than he'd intended.

Tegan pulled her hands back like the box had burned her.

"It's just that there's—uh—work stuff in here. Confidential files."

She squinted at him, and he was pretty sure she didn't believe him, but then she shrugged. "Okay, I'll wait for you on the bench."

She disappeared around the corner and he quickly sifted through the boxes until he found his camping gear. He grabbed his sleeping bag, stuffed some clean clothes into his overnight bag, and headed back out into the sun.

They stopped in the office to leave their bags with Rick. When the bell on the door jingled, he looked up from his paperwork and smiled at them. "Will I be seeing you at the bicentennial celebration later this evening? There'll be all kinds of food, and bands playing. The local breweries will all be there with tables too. Should be a good time."

"Oh, I don't know—" Jack began, but Tegan cut him off. "*Yes.*" She clasped her hands together. "That sounds like just what we need after the day we've had."

Rick grinned, and even Jack had to admit that her enthusiasm was contagious. Maybe it would be good for them to go, to have a beer and listen to some music. The two of them had been alone in the car for way too long.

"How are you at line dancing?" Rick asked. "We've got a local country band that's as good as anyone coming out of Nashville."

Jack felt Tegan's elbow connect with his side. "Jack loves country music."

"Well, great," Rick said. "I'm glad our little town has something to keep you entertained while you're here. You can catch a ride in with Gil later."

Tegan nodded. "We're off to explore now. We'll see you later."

They headed in the direction that Gil had pointed them in earlier. The whole town stretched only a few blocks in each direction, and standing at one end of the business district, they could see all the way to the other end. There were no stop lights, and not enough traffic to warrant them. The few cars gliding down the road braked for pedestrians crossing the street, and nobody seemed to be in much of a hurry. Jack found himself slowing his step too, taking in the scene in front of him instead of heading straight to the coffee shop like he would've back in the city.

Main Street was wide and lined with rows of brick buildings that looked like they'd been there since the Wild West days, but had been carefully refurbished since then. Signs over the well-maintained awnings announced the coffee shop, a clothing boutique, and a general store. Jack felt his shoulders relaxing and the stress of the accident finally slip away as a light breeze blew the scent of early spring flowers from the pots lining the windows. A black and white marquee hung in front of the Manor Theater, greeting visitors and announcing the bicentennial festival, and suddenly, Jack was glad to be on the receiving end of that warm welcome.

He turned and almost ran into Tegan, who'd stumbled to a stop and stood gaping at the scene in front of them. The expression of longing that moved across her face did something to his heart that he didn't want to think about. They'd seen their share of beautiful sights on this trip, but he'd never seen her as enthralled as she was with this charming small town.

Finally, Tegan blinked and seemed to snap out of her reverie. "Let's check out that coffee shop that Gil recommended."

They ordered at the counter and found seats at a table in the window. Jack eyed Tegan's untouched drink as she watched the townspeople set up for the festival. Her gazed skated from the men on ladders hanging strings of Christmas lights across the street to a couple of older women setting up tables for crafts and baked goods. Only when a box truck pulled up, blocking their view, and two men in cowboy boots and flannel shirts hopped out to unload amps and guitar cases, did Tegan finally pick up her coffee.

Jack couldn't help but wonder what her reaction to the town was all about. "Have you ever lived in a small town like this?"

She shook her head. "No."

"You said you moved around a lot as a kid?"

She bit her lip and fiddled with her silverware. "Yeah. But we were always in apartments in the city." She ducked her head with a faint smile. "I read a lot of Fannie Flagg when I was a kid. So, I built up this romantic notion of living in small-town America. You know, where everyone knows each other, and come together to help each other out. Where the big social event is the bicentennial celebration." She gestured out the window with a rueful laugh.

"Fannie Flagg." He squinted, searching his memory. "*Fried Green Tomatoes*?"

"Have you read it?"

"No, but I remember my sister crying over the movie." He smiled. "So, is that part of what this trip is about? Looking for the perfect small town to settle down and write your book?"

"Not just to write my book." She hesitated, shrugging. "But it's a silly childhood dream that I probably should have given up a long time ago." Her laugh sounded forced.

He'd caught her excitement at attending the bicentennial festival, and that expression of naked longing on her face when she saw the town. There was no way it was just a childhood dream. He wanted to know more, but he didn't know how to ask without prying into her life. And, even more surprising, he suddenly had the urge to tell Tegan about Charlotte. Maybe it was the sadness in her eyes that told him that she would understand, because she'd been through a lot too. Or maybe it was that she was the first person to help him feel anything other than that crushing sorrow he'd been carrying around for the last year.

But then Tegan slid off her stool and began stacking their plates, signaling that the conversation was over. "I'm going to grab a coffee to go. Do you want one?"

"Sure. Thanks."

"Large? Cream, no sugar?"

He looked up, surprised, but then he shrugged it off. It was no big deal that she knew his coffee order. They'd spent a lot of time together in the past few days, and he drank a lot of coffee. But somehow, it made him feel less alone.

CHAPTER FIFTEEN

Tegan

We didn't always live in the city. The summer after Mom took off, Daddy sent us to live with Grandma in West Virginia. We never knew Grandma before that summer. When Mom was still pregnant with Jamie, she and Grandma had some kind of falling out. I once heard Mom cursing Grandma for saying she'd made "poor choices when it came to men." But once Mom took off, I guess Grandma took pity on the fact that now me and Jamie were stuck with Mom's poor choices, and she invited us to come stay.

Grandma's house wasn't fancy. Jamie said it was a trailer which meant that at any minute someone could come along and drive away with it, although that never actually happened. But she lived in the woods next to a creek, and I could run around barefoot without watching out for broken glass or needles. We spent so much time running around outside, sometimes I forgot to miss Mom or even feel sad about her. And Grandma had a dog who splashed in the creek, and a whole bunch of neighbors who came with tuna noodle casseroles and cleaning supplies to help out when she found that lump in her breast.

By fall, Grandma was too busy with her treatments to watch us kids, so we had to go back to the city with Daddy. But I never forgot what it was like that summer. Never having to lock our doors. Going out and playing without worrying about creepy guys in the alley following us. And all those nice people who showed up to help, just because Grandma needed it.

*

On the drive over, Gil told them about his farm: a working dairy business situated on fifty acres a couple of miles outside of town. Tegan had been expecting cows and tractors, and fields covered in bales of hay. But when Gil turned off the main road and steered the car over the crest of the hill, she didn't anticipate the postcard image of America stretched out before them. She couldn't have written it any better if she tried.

A weathered white farmhouse, complete with a wraparound porch and swing, sat in the middle of lush fields dotted with black and white cows. A short stroll from the house, wood-fenced animal paddocks surrounded a two-story red barn. Parked in front of the barn was a collection of farm equipment painted a familiar green hue and a rusty pick-up truck loaded with animal feed. In the background, the peaks of the Rocky Mountains rose up, keeping watch over it all.

As Gil parked in front of the house, a golden retriever came running to meet them, and three children playing cards on the front step waved enthusiastically. Tegan and Jack hopped out of the truck, and a middle-aged woman with a long, graying braid and worn, faded jeans on her sturdy frame stepped out on the porch. Gil put an arm around her and introduced her as his wife, Linda.

Tegan was immediately drawn to her kind eyes and warm smile, and a childhood longing rose up from somewhere buried deep. It lodged right in her throat, making it hard to say more than a whispered greeting. She swallowed hard. How many times had she imagined a scene like this as a little girl? An old house that was worn but comfortable, two loving parents sharing an easy affection, a dog who came running to greet her. How many stories had she scribbled in notebooks about a home, a real home, where she could stay forever?

She felt Jack nudge her, and she looked up to find him watching her with an odd look. "Gil and Linda just offered us a tour of the farm."

"That would be great." She managed a weak smile, shoving her childhood longings out of her head.

As they strolled past the paddocks where the cows gathered in the fields, Tegan found her eyes sliding to Jack when he wasn't paying attention. He asked Gil about the farm operations and got into a discussion with Linda about how the economy had affected the price of dairy. Funny that when she met him she thought that he was cold and aloof, and even worse than that, a snob. Here he was, locked in an engaging conversation with a couple of farmers in the middle of a cow pasture.

Gil and Linda ended the tour inside the barn—an open, spacious building with concrete floors, thirty-foot ceilings, and wide, wooden plank walls that let the sun shine in through the cracks. Most of the cows grazed out in the pastures, but Gil led them past the milking equipment to the far end of the barn where wooden stalls scattered with straw contained a few animals.

"I hope you don't mind having a couple of roommates tonight," Gil said. "These heifers are pregnant, so we separated them from the herd." He gestured for Tegan to follow him to one of the stalls and look over the side.

She stood on her tiptoes and peeked over, gasping at the sight of a tiny cow standing on spindly little legs and staring up at her with giant brown eyes. "Oh my gosh, there's a baby cow in there!"

Gil chucked. "We call them 'calves.' This girl was born about two days ago."

"Jack, look." Tegan waved Jack over. "Those cows are so big, I didn't expect the calves to be so little."

Jack moved over to the stall and easily peered over the top. "She's pretty cute."

The calf's mother shuffled her giant body over to where they stood and aimed her nose at them, sniffing audibly. Tegan jumped back with a little squeak.

"She won't hurt you, honey." Linda laughed. "She's just hoping you have a little treat for her." She dug around in a wooden bin and pulled out a couple of apples. "After all her hard work, she deserves it. Here, go ahead and give it to her."

Tegan eyed the apple in Linda's hand and shook her head. "Jack is used to horses. He'll do it."

Jack gave her a smirk as he took the apple and fed it to the cow. "I never expected you to be such a wimp." The cow crunched happily on the apple and rubbed her head against the stall, looking for more. Jack scratched between her furry ears.

"You two must be tired, and wanting to clean up," Gil said. "The stairs to the loft are just down this way."

Gil and Linda headed back the way they came, and Jack followed. Tegan paused for another minute to study the cow and her calf, and then she hurried after them. When she caught up to Jack, she shot him a glare. "I grew up in the city. The only animals I've ever been around are pit bulls tied up in people's back alleys, and I learned to avoid those." She slid her sleeve up her arm, showing Jack the scar where a dog had bitten her as a kid.

"Jesus." Jack's eyes widened. "I apologize for calling you a wimp."

She shrugged and tugged her sleeve back down.

"I am a little surprised, though," he said. "I wouldn't have guessed you were a city girl."

"Why not?"

"I don't know. There's something free-spirited about you. You don't seem jaded enough to have grown up dodging pit bulls."

He was probably referring to how stupid she'd been, getting into cars with strange men and storming off in the biker bar. Well, she'd certainly learned her lesson. That was the point of this trip, wasn't it? To learn to go out and make it on her own. There wasn't anyone around now to chase away dogs. She had to do it for herself.

"Yeah, well," she muttered. "I'll have to work on that."

Jack stopped walking. "Don't."

She stumbled to a halt next to him. "Don't what?"

He cocked his head and studied her for a moment. "Don't become jaded." His lips quirked into a barely there smile. "Free-spirited is one of your best qualities. There are enough of us who are sad and bitter in this world."

Before she could answer, he turned and headed back across the barn after Gil and Linda, leaving her standing there, wondering what he had to be sad and bitter about.

Tegan showered in the small, unheated bathroom off the milking area on the first floor of the barn. After dressing in a flowered dress and denim jacket, she headed outside to see if everyone was ready for the festival. Jack was out in the yard, leaning against a tractor. He looked surprisingly at home there in his jeans, hiking boots, and dark gray button-up shirt. His hair was still damp from his shower and waved slightly around his temples.

Just like that, she was buzzing with excitement about the evening ahead—the fun of a party, and dancing, and music—and hanging out with Jack. Over these past few days, she'd seen him so much more clearly. She kept catching little glimpses of him that were so contrary to the aloof, angry stranger she'd met a few days ago. His thoughtfulness when he offered to help with her writer's block, his kindness after the crash, the ease in which he interacted with Linda and Gil.

Flashes of the kind of guy she could fall for, if she let herself.

As for those moments of real darkness—the nightmares, the exhaustion, the defensiveness when the conversation turned too personal—well, it was clear that he was wrestling with something. She wanted so badly to know what was going on in his head. If only he'd trust her enough to open up—

At that moment, Tegan realized Jack was on the phone, so she settled on an oversized rocking chair on the front porch. Out of the corner of her eye, she snuck little glances at him. He was too far away for her to overhear his conversation, but he was talking more animatedly than she'd ever seen him, and every once in a while, the sound of his voice drifted across the yard. Was he telling Charlotte about the car accident, or about how they ended up at Gil and Linda's farm? Did Charlotte know that *she* was the one who'd been driving when the car crashed? Had he mentioned that she was tagging along at all?

If Jack were her fiancé, she was pretty sure she wouldn't be happy about him spending days in a car with another woman, or sleeping next to her in a barn loft. But maybe Charlotte wasn't the jealous type. Tegan flashed back to the photo on Jack's phone. If Jack ever looked at her the way he looked at Charlotte in that photo, maybe she wouldn't worry about other women either. Tegan smoothed the skirt of her dress. Especially other women with wild, unruly hair and wrinkled clothes.

The front door swung open and Gil and Linda stepped out on the porch, both freshly showered and wearing clean jeans and flannel shirts. Their three children, ranging in age from five to eleven followed, talking in excited voices about funnel cakes and who was going to win the biggest stuffed animal in a ring toss game.

Tegan and Jack piled into the back of a muddy van with the family and they headed into town for the festival.

In the few hours since they'd left, the townspeople had transformed downtown Copper Canyon. Roadblocks stopped traffic on either end of Main Street, and crowds swarmed the space in the middle, lining up at food trucks and carnival games. On a large portable stage at one end of the street, a big-haired woman who could've passed for a young Dolly Parton strummed a guitar and sang a cover of 'Jolene' for a crowd bouncing and swaying on the dance floor below.

Tegan squinted as the afternoon sun began its slow descent over the mountains, and at that moment she fell in love with Copper Canyon, Colorado.

The song ended and young Dolly switched to an electric guitar. A cheer went up as the first notes of an upbeat Garth Brooks song reverberated over the crowd, and people began lining up in front of the stage. Gil and Linda's kids took off, followed at a more reasonable pace by their parents.

"Come on, Tegan." Linda glanced back with grin. "You and that boyfriend of yours better get out here to dance with us."

Tegan stumbled to a stop at the same moment she felt Jack freeze beside her. "Oh, um—" But Linda was already wading into the crowd. Tegan peeked at Jack and he looked as flushed and embarrassed as she felt. "I—um." She shrugged. "Well, this is awkward."

Jack took a deep breath and blew it out slowly. When he turned back, he flashed her a smile. "It's fine. Come on. Something tells me you've been waiting your whole life to line dance at the Copper Canyon Bicentennial Festival."

They made their way to the dance floor and lined up with Linda and the kids. Jack was a surprisingly good dancer—ballroom dancing class in prep school, he said—especially compared to her. She kept going left instead of right and crashing into him, but he just laughed and caught her by the arm before she stumbled.

When the band took a break, they piled around a picnic table with Gil, Linda, and the family. Linda settled the kids with funnel cakes, and Jack and Gil got in line at a tent for one of the local breweries.

While they waited for the men to return with their drinks, Linda and Tegan sat on the table with their feet propped on a bench and looked around at the crowd.

"This is really wonderful," Tegan murmured.

Linda smiled. "I'm glad you're enjoying our little town. Gil says you and Jack are from San Francisco, and moving to New York? Copper Canyon is a far cry from the big city."

Tegan absently rubbed the toe of her sandal on the bench. "Yeah. Um. Jack's not really my boyfriend. I'm just traveling with him for a little while."

Linda looked at her with wide eyes. "Oh! You two just seemed so—well, I shouldn't have assumed. I'm sorry."

"It's okay. He's—he's actually engaged. I don't really know much about her."

Linda gave her a long look and Tegan had the feeling that Linda could see right through her. "Huh. I wonder why his fiancée isn't on this trip with him."

Tegan's eyes found Jack chatting with Gil and another man in line at the Rocky Mountain High Brewery tent. Why *wasn't* Charlotte on the trip with him? It seemed like the kind of thing a couple would do together, especially if they were getting ready to start a new life all the way across the country. But maybe Charlotte couldn't get the time off from work. Or maybe she already lived in New York and Jack was moving there to be with her. There could be a million reasons.

As if he sensed her gaze, Jack's head turned, and his eyes met hers. The pull of attraction was so strong it nearly yanked her off the table. From the look on his face—wide eyed and stunned—it had hit him just as hard. A beat passed, and then Gil leaned over and said something to Jack, holding out a beer for him to take.

Tegan looked away and found Linda watching her with a half-smile on her face. Linda patted her on the knee and hopped off the table. "I'm sure you two will figure it out." She rounded the table to scrub the funnel cake off her five-year-old's face before Tegan could tell her there was absolutely nothing to figure out.

After a few more hours of line-dancing, beer, and carnival games, Tegan and Jack piled into Gil and Linda's van and headed back to the farm, laughing and admiring the kids' prizes. When Gil pulled up in front of the house, they said goodnight to the family and made their way up to the loft. Tegan used the bathroom, changing into leggings and her warmest sweater. When she got back upstairs, she found Jack in sweatpants and a Columbia Law T-shirt, folding a sweatshirt to use as a pillow.

Tegan tried not to stare, but there was something so appealing about him when he was like this—comfortable and just a little bit unkempt—that she couldn't seem to help it. There were no lights in the loft, only a single bulb that glowed up the stairs from below, making the space feel smaller and more intimate.

With a murmured "Goodnight," she climbed into her sleeping bag, just a couple of feet away from Jack's. He slid into his own sleeping bag and a minute later, his breath slowed to a steady rhythm.

Tegan was envious of his ability to fall asleep so quickly, while she lay there, distracted. Remembering how her heart had kicked her in the chest when Young Dolly pulled up a stool and launched into an acoustic version of 'When You Say Nothing at All', and Jack had held out his hand, asking her to dance.

She wasn't imagining this attraction. But Jack wasn't the kind of guy to cheat. Even though she'd only known him for a few days, she was sure of it.

Why isn't Charlotte on this trip with him?

Tegan tossed and turned in her sleeping bag, unable to get comfortable.

"Tegan."

She jumped at the sound of Jack's voice. "God, you scared me. I thought you were asleep."

"How can I sleep with you flopping around over there?" He sounded more amused than irritated. "What are you thinking about?"

She hesitated. He'd made it clear that talking about Charlotte was off limits, but she had to know. They couldn't keep skating around this. "I was just thinking that… you must really miss Charlotte. You know, being away from her all this time."

He paused for long enough that Tegan wondered if he was going to answer. She squinted at him in the dim light and watched him flop from his side to his back, staring up at the overhead beams.

"Yeah," he said in a voice so low she had to strain to hear him. "Yeah, I miss Charlotte."

She rolled to her side, irrationally angry at her disappointment. What did she expect him to say? It was her own fault.

"Well, it's good that you'll be getting back home soon then."

He didn't answer, and she wondered if he'd fallen asleep again.

Tegan's eyes flew open. Someone was yelling. Her hip and elbow pressed against the floor through the thin mattress as she struggled to sit up.

Her head whipped around to the person thrashing on the mattress a few feet away.

Jack.

He was in the throes of another one of his nightmares. She blinked to adjust to the darkness, and from the moonlight streaming in through the window, she could see his face contort with anguish and his hands curl into fists.

"*No. No.*" He thrashed around on the floor.

She needed to get to him. Her sleeping bag had tangled around her legs, so she scooted her way across the space between them, dragging it with her. Laying a hand on his arm, she found his skin hot and clammy.

"Jack. *Jack.* Hey." Tegan gave him a shake.

He rolled over and yelled, "Help her!" He grasped at Tegan wildly, as if he were drowning and she was the life raft. "Somebody, *please help!*" He was almost screaming now, and she was afraid Gil and Linda might come running.

"Jack!" Her heart pounding, she shook him harder. "*Wake up!*"

With a gasp, he sat up and stared at her, his eyes wide and unblinking. *Oh, thank God.* She rubbed his arm. "Jack," she murmured in a low voice, the way she would talk to a child. "You're okay. It's okay." She repeated it over and over again.

Slowly, his eyes focused and he gave a slight shake of his head. "Tegan." He held his hand out as if he was reaching for her, but pulled it away.

"Yeah, it's me. I'm right here, okay?" She gave his arm a squeeze, and his skin was slick with sweat. "You were having a nightmare."

He blew the air from his lungs and then he flopped on his back on the mattress. "God. That was—*God.*" He brushed his hands over his temples as if he was trying to wipe the dream from his mind.

Tegan slid down and propped herself up on her arm so she could look him in the eyes. "Want to tell me about it? My brother used to say that if you tell someone your scary dream, it'll go away."

He stared up at the ceiling without speaking, his breath coming in and out in short gasps. Slowly, he rolled his head toward her. He didn't say anything, just studied her in the dark. Finally, he shook his head. "I—I'm okay."

She longed to reach out and touch him, to comfort him, to take away the pain that was tearing him up. She inched closer, sliding her hand into the space between them. Her fingers brushed his arm. Other than a small intake of breath, he didn't move. Slowly, she slid her hand across his arm and over his chest until she found the sharp, steady rhythm of his heart. She pressed her hand against his sweaty T-shirt.

"I'm sorry, Jack," she whispered. "Whatever this is that's hurting you so much, I wish—" She hesitated, afraid of what she really wished. "I wish it wasn't."

His chest rose under her hand as he took a slow, steady breath. When he released it, the tension followed, and his muscles relaxed. He moved his hand to cover hers, holding it tightly.

"I'm glad you're here."

She slid her other arm out from under her and lay down next to him. "Me too."

He closed his eyes and after a moment, the gentle rise and fall of his chest under her hand told her that he was asleep. She slid an inch closer, until her forehead was almost pressed to his shoulder. The heat from his body chased away the chill, and her eyes slowly drifted shut.

CHAPTER SIXTEEN

Jack

From somewhere out in the yard, the distinctive *cock-a-doodle-doo* of a rooster's crow drifted into Jack's consciousness. He opened his eyes and squinted at the slant of sunlight that fell across his makeshift pillow from the slats between the pine walls of the barn. He blinked to adjust to the brightness, waiting for the heavy feeling of exhaustion to wash over him, but it never came. For the first time in a long time, he felt refreshed and alert. He couldn't remember the last time he'd managed to sleep all the way until morning. Usually the nightmares dragged him from bed long before dawn, leaving him pacing like a ghost in the darkness until the gray light finally released him to stagger through the day.

Was it possible that the nightmares were subsiding, and that he might be able to sleep like a normal person again? A tiny flicker of a memory kindled in his mind. *The screams. The panic that threatened to choke him. The blood.*

No. He'd *had* a nightmare last night.

Slowly, it came back to him. Tegan leaning over him, gently shaking him awake. Her hand pressed to his pounding heart, and her voice, low and soothing, telling him that she was there and everything was okay. His usual terror and panic replaced by the comfort of her presence and the warm lure of sleep.

He felt movement at his hip and looked down at the tangle of strawberry-blond hair spilling across his shoulder, and the freckled cheek pressed against his arm. Tegan was there, she'd been there all night. And he'd finally slept—really slept—for the first time in almost a year.

She shifted in her sleep, reaching out to grasp his arm like a child pulling a teddy bear to her chest. The scent of something fresh, like cut grass and spring, drifted up from her hair, and he turned his head to breathe it in. He lay as still as a statue, hoping he wouldn't wake her, savoring her warmth against his side.

Jack knew the exact date that he'd last slept next to a woman. He knew the moment almost to the minute that she'd climbed out of bed for the final time, walked out the door, and never come back again. He could recall it intellectually, but the feelings were fuzzy. He hadn't thought about sex in almost a year. Charlotte was gone, and he hadn't cared if he ever touched another woman, kissed another woman again. If he didn't get close to someone he'd never have to go through the pain of losing them.

But in that moment, lying next to Tegan, breathing in her scent and feeling her against him, something that was frozen inside him finally thawed.

A breath drifted from the back of her throat, and he wondered what she was dreaming about. She let out another sigh, the sound like a quiet mix of satisfaction and anticipation he imagined she'd make if he leaned down and pressed his lips to hers.

His muscles tensed as the image flashed in his mind. The rooster crowed again, and she stirred.

Her eyes opened and she slowly sat up, propping herself on her elbow. "Morning, sunshine," she mumbled, with a sleepy smile.

"Good morning." He shifted on the thin mattress, unable to meet her gaze. Afraid if he did, she'd see right through him and know what he was feeling.

"Did you sleep okay? After… you know…" Her smile faded. *The nightmares.* She remembered.

"Yeah." He paused, clearing his throat. He waited for her to question him about what happened. He wondered if he should tell her. In the beginning, she'd been a stranger, an unwanted passenger in his car. But since then she'd become… a friend.

Jack flashed back to the night before and remembered Tegan laughingly stumbling into him while they line danced. Holding her in his arms while they swayed to a slow song. The way their eyes connected across the crowd and it felt like he'd been hit right in the chest with a cattle prod.

Her quiet presence soothing away the fear that had been stalking him for almost a year.

Maybe Tegan wasn't just a friend. Somehow in the last few days, the hippie woman he hadn't even wanted in his car had started to worm her way into his heart. She'd become someone he cared about. Someone he wanted to open up to. He took a deep breath.

Under the loft, a barn door creaked open and the shuffling hoofsteps of a herd of cows crunched across the straw on the floor below. Gil's voice drifted up the stairs, talking to the animals in the same encouraging and exasperated voice he'd used when talking to his children on the way to the festival the night before.

"Come on now, get on in there. Where do you think you're going, missy?"

Jack shook himself, half-relieved and half-disappointed by the interruption. He pushed aside his sleeping bag and sat up.

Tegan rolled out of her sleeping bag and dug through her backpack, keeping her head down as she piled clothes on the floor next to her. The silence pulsed between them, punctuated only by the occasional moo of a cow or murmur from Gil. Finally, she tossed her backpack aside. "You want to use the bathroom first?"

"No, you go ahead."

She nodded and stood up. Without another word, she grabbed her clothes and headed across the loft.

He watched her retreating back as she descended the stairs. Why did he feel so let down?

Jack threw on his jeans and hiking boots from the night before and went downstairs to see if Gil needed help with the cows. Gil gratefully accepted his offer. Apparently two of his farmhands had overdone it on the local beer last night and were running late.

Gil laughed and shook his head. "At least the bicentennial only comes by once every two hundred years."

He showed Jack how to secure the cows in their metal pens and hook their udders up to the industrial-sized milking machine. Out of the corner of Jack's eye, he noticed Tegan leave the bathroom and slip out the big barn doors, probably heading over to the house to visit with Linda, but he concentrated on the task at hand. Gil wasn't a big talker—he spoke to the cows more than he did to Jack—and there was something meditative about moving down the assembly line to attach the metal cups to the cows' undersides, listening for the steady suction of the machines drawing out the milk, and then moving back down the line to unhook them.

He settled into his task, enjoying the hard work and sense of accomplishment. Living in an apartment in San Francisco, he'd gotten most of his exercise at the gym. On occasion, he and Charlotte had driven into Marin County to go hiking on Mount Tam or in Muir Woods, but those opportunities had been rare when they were both working eighty hours a week. They'd had a tiny container garden out on the patio, really just a couple of pots of herbs and vegetables, but he'd stopped watering it months ago. Those sad brown basil and tomato skeletons had mocked him every time he looked out the kitchen window until he'd finally tossed them, pots and all, in the dumpster in the back alley. Now, surrounded by the scent of milk and hay and the outdoors, feeling the pleasant ache of his muscles, he began to understand the appeal of a life like this.

That thought brought a smile to his lips. If his family and friends could see him right now, could read the thoughts going through his head, they'd call a doctor. Sure, he'd shoveled his share of horse shit, but that had been at the stables of his parents' Connecticut horse club, where he'd learned to ride English style and play polo. Rolling out of bed in a hay loft and crawling under a cow wasn't what anyone had probably imagined when he'd taken off on his solo road trip across the country. Hell, it wasn't what he'd imagined. Not even close. Nothing about this trip had gone the way he'd planned, and yet…

There he was, standing ankle-deep in straw and cow manure with his hands encased in a pair of blue rubber gloves, trying not to get kicked in the head while he grabbed for a cow's udder. And he was happier than he'd been in a long time.

The little town in the middle of nowhere, the farm, the cows…

The company of one person in particular.

He and Gil milked the last of the cows, and then they headed over to check on the new calf. The pregnant cows mooed for their breakfast, and then in protest when Gil sent them out into the paddock so he could clean their stalls. Jack helped Gil shovel out the manure, lay down a fresh layer of straw, and move four dozen bags of feed to the back of the barn. By the time they finished, another hour had gone by and Jack's muscles were protesting.

He pulled off his sweaty, dirty sweatshirt and reached for one of the wooden beams overhead to stretch out his sore back. When he let go, he looked up to find Tegan in the doorway of the barn, watching him with wide turquoise eyes. The air crackled between them, and his heart thudded.

"You have straw in your hair," she finally murmured in a low voice, taking a few tentative steps toward him.

Jack ran his hand through his hair, coming up empty. She took a few more steps and then reached up and plucked a piece of straw from his head. Her mouth twisted into a smile. "You smell like cow shit."

He took the straw from her hand. "You smell like cut grass and spring flowers," he said, before he could stop himself.

She blinked, and her cheeks turned pink. "It's my shampoo."

He reached out and twisted a lock of her strawberry hair between his fingers. "I like it."

She stepped back, shoving her hair behind her ear. "I'm sure Charlotte's shampoo is nice too." Her eyes, bright and open a moment ago, were shuttered now. "I just came to tell you that Linda said to wash up. Breakfast is in half an hour. I'll go and tell Gil." She swerved around him and headed across the barn.

She thought he was engaged. Jack dragged his hand through his hair as he watched her retreating back.

Maybe it was time to tell her the truth.

He took a quick shower, threw on a pair of clean khaki trousers and a pale blue button-up shirt, and then strapped on his watch. Breakfast was in fifteen minutes, so he pulled out his cell phone. There was a text from Rick at the auto-body shop saying that the parts had arrived and the car should be ready that afternoon, and one from Liv asking how the trip was going.

He hit the button to call her, and she answered right away. "Hi, big brother!"

"Hey. You at work?"

"Yep, just got here. I'm starting a class action suit against that drug company that didn't disclose all the side effects from its anti-seizure medication, and a bunch of people had heart attacks. I can't wait until you get here so I can rope you into working on it with me."

Jack chuckled. "We'll see. I've got tons of work for my own clients to catch up on after this trip. I doubt I'll have time for your bleeding-heart projects."

"So, speaking of when you're getting here—where are you? Are you headed east yet?"

Jack tried to remember what his many-times revised itinerary had looked like before the crash. They were supposed to have been in Rocky Mountain National Park yesterday morning. According to that plan, they would've made it to the middle of Kansas by the end of today. Well, that wasn't going to happen.

"I'm not quite as far along as I planned. I had a little car accident yesterday, so I'm in some small town in Colorado."

Her gasp echoed through the phone. "Jack, are you okay?"

He told her about the accident, downplaying it as much as possible and leaving out the fact that Tegan had been driving. He also didn't bother to mention that they'd slept in a hay loft last night. Liv was pretty upset, and he spent the next five minutes reassuring her that he was fine.

She paused after that, and then finally said, "And was that woman—Tegan—there during the accident?"

He thought about lying, but he didn't have anything to hide. Besides, his sister was one of the best lawyers he knew. He wasn't going to fool her. "Yes."

He knew she wanted him to say more but she was trying to give him some space, and he appreciated that. He wished he could reassure her that traveling with Tegan was no big deal, and that they'd be going their separate ways soon. But the thought of that left a hollow feeling in his gut. He wasn't sure of anything anymore, so he told Liv that he'd text her that night and hung up.

He folded up his dirty clothes and was about to head over to the house for breakfast when his phone buzzed and a text came in from Liv.

I messed up! I'm so sorry. I called Mom to let her know I'd heard from you, and you know how she does that psychologist thing where somehow you end up telling her things. I might have told her about the accident and I let it slip that you're traveling with Tegan. I swear I didn't mean to. Please don't be mad.

Jack stared at the phone. The last thing he wanted was his parents getting involved in this. He knew Liv would never have blabbed on purpose: his mother was a professional at getting people to talk. He sat down on his mattress and waited for the phone to ring. Sure enough, five seconds later, the phone buzzed in his hand, and the word *Mom* appeared on the screen. He swiped to answer.

His mother's slightly frantic voice pierced the quiet of the loft. "I'm so glad I caught you. Livie told me that you had a car accident and that your tire fell off? Jack, that's awful. Are you okay?"

Despite his dread over this conversation, it was good to hear her voice. His mom could be overbearing, sometimes worrying too much about appearances, but that was everyone in their Upper East Side social circle. Deep down, she only wanted him to be happy, and she'd always been supportive of him. She'd certainly been there for him that past year and, because of that, the concern in her voice sent a frisson of guilt through him that he continued to worry her.

"I'm okay. Really. Not even a scratch. And the car was barely damaged. It should be as good as new by this afternoon."

"Well, thank goodness for that." She breathed out a sigh. "I'm just glad to hear that you're okay. And your—" she paused "—travel companion? Is she okay too?"

He sighed. *Subtle.* "Yes, Tegan is fine."

"So, where is Tegan from?"

He didn't know. There was a lot he didn't know about her. They'd been tiptoeing around each other, and he still hadn't asked her last name, a fact that he definitely wasn't going to tell his mother. "I think she grew up all over the place. Her family moved a lot."

"Is she from a good family?"

Jack knew that was code for "Is she rich like us?" Judging from her clothes and duct-taped backpack, he seriously doubted it. Either way, he wasn't going there with his mother. "I haven't met her family, but I'm sure they're nice."

"So, you two are friends? Or—more than friends?" The pitch of her voice raised an octave at the end, as if she was trying to be breezy and casual, but Jack's mother was never breezy and casual. He knew she had perched at the end of the couch cushion, her spine stick-straight as she squeezed the life out of her phone.

"We're not—" He stopped abruptly. It would've made his life about a hundred times easier to outright deny it, but for some reason, the words didn't come. This connection he had with Tegan was the first thing that felt real in his life in a long time.

"Jack, I'm sure she's a lovely young woman—*whoever* she is." She just couldn't resist that, could she? "And I'd love nothing more than for you to come home, get settled, and meet a nice woman. God knows you deserve a little happiness after all you've been through. But I'm concerned about you having a—a fling—with someone you picked up on the side of the road."

"It wasn't on the side of the road. Technically it was in a diner," he muttered, more to himself than his mother.

"Your whole life is in flux right now. And I worry that you're focusing on this young woman to avoid facing your feelings about Charlotte, or your future here. If you met her in New York—at a party or at work maybe—is she the sort of person you'd date?"

Jack stared at the dust swirling through the sunbeams that slanted across the loft. He never would've met someone like Tegan in New York. He didn't know much about her life, but it was pretty clear they didn't move in the same circles. She certainly wouldn't be at any parties he attended, and he couldn't imagine how they'd ever cross paths at work.

"Can you see her fitting into your life here?" his mother pressed gently.

Jack imagined taking Tegan to dinner with his law firm colleagues and their spouses. Or to a party with his parents' powerful friends. She was pretty good at talking to people, so maybe she'd get along fine. But that thought lasted for about ten seconds before he shook his head. Chatting with a clerk at a gas station in Arizona wasn't the same as socializing at a party with senators and CEOs. There was a certain delicacy and balance that you needed to strike. You couldn't just blurt out whatever came into your head without them judging you and whispering behind your back.

He flinched as a wave of disgust rolled over him. It would be awful. She'd hate every minute of it. Those kinds of social pressures had destroyed everything he had with Charlotte, and he'd never put Tegan in that position. He'd never forgive himself if he dulled the light inside of her.

"Jack? Are you there?" His mother's voice cut into his thoughts. "I think we might have a bad connection."

"No, I'm here." He sighed deeply. "Look, you don't have to worry. We're just friends. She'll probably be heading her own way soon. And I'll be home in a few days."

His mother's relief radiated through the phone. "Please be safe driving the rest of the way home. I love you."

Jack's heart tugged. He knew that, deep down, his family had his best interests at heart. Maybe his mother was right. These feeling he had for Tegan weren't rooted in reality, and whatever connection they had out here on the road would never survive at home. He didn't even know where *home* was for Tegan.

Jack clicked off the phone and headed downstairs. His car would be ready that afternoon. It was time to get back on track, to start sticking to his plan: get home, and get on with the rest of his life.

No more detours, no more distractions.

CHAPTER SEVENTEEN

Tegan

Stupid stupid

*

By late afternoon, they were back in the car on the way to Estes Park, and Tegan was back to huddling against the door with her laptop open. Not that she was getting any work done. Mostly she sat there musing about how the word *stupid* started to look really stupid after staring at it for too long, and replaying the events of that morning in her head.

That moment when she was lying next to Jack and he'd looked like he was about to open up to her about his nightmares. Later, when she pulled straw from his hair, and for a crazy second she'd thought he was going to kiss her.

So, so stupid.

They were back to uncomfortable silence in the car, unless you counted the sound of Jack's boring economics podcast, or the way he cleared his throat and looked away when he accidentally bumped her arm on the center console. By the time they rolled into Estes Park and stopped for a quiet, stilted dinner, the awkwardness was almost too much to bear.

I should be happy right now. She'd never felt more at home in a place as she had that morning with Linda, making a mountain of pancakes while the kids and dog ran in and out of the kitchen. She'd even opened up to Linda about her feelings for Jack, and Linda hadn't judged. She'd just given Tegan a hug and promised it would all work out. And somehow, back there in Linda's kitchen, it had felt like it *would* all work out.

Copper Canyon was the small town she and Jamie had always dreamed about, with the sort of kind, welcoming people they'd hoped to find as neighbors. Really, she'd found exactly what she'd been looking for. It was the whole reason she'd come on this trip in the first place. She could ask Jack to drop her off in Pittsburgh, pack up Jamie, and the two of them could be on a bus heading back here by next week.

But the thought of Jack driving off without her, of never seeing him again, left her feeling hollow and shaky, like she'd had a few too many drinks the night before. A Jack hangover. She knew the best thing to do was go cold turkey. Let him go and get on with her life and her plans. But, instead, here she was, pushing a piece of pie around on her plate and wondering what he'd been about to say before Gil and the cows interrupted them.

Stupid.

The waitress swung by to drop the bill in front of them. Tegan reached for her wallet, but it wasn't on the table, or the bench next to her. She looked at Jack. "Did I have my wallet with me when I came in?" She didn't speak loudly, but her voice sounded like a bullhorn after all that silence.

Jack's eyebrows knit together. "I don't think so. I didn't notice it."

"Can I have the car key to go and get it?"

He picked up the bill. "Don't worry about it, I've got this."

Tegan chewed on her thumb nail. "Would you mind unlocking the car? I'm a little worried about my wallet. I want to make sure it's in my bag." The last thing she needed was to lose all her money and credit cards. Of course, the way this trip had been going, it wouldn't surprise her if she'd dropped it on the ground at the last gas station.

Jack clicked the remote unlock button, and she ran out into the parking lot. When she got to the car, she opened the back door and grabbed for her backpack. She'd tossed it on top of all of his stuff in the backseat earlier and, at some point, it had slid off and gotten wedged in between two boxes. She gave it a yank and it came free, but one of the boxes tumbled bottom-up onto the floor of the car. The lid popped open, and out spilled a mess of framed photos, pens, paperclips, and other junk that looked like Jack had dumped it from the top of a desk into the box with little concern for organization. It seemed so contrary to everything she knew about Jack and his intense need for order that for a moment, she didn't even notice the details of the mess. Then she looked around the floor of the car.

Photos. Of Jack and Charlotte.

She shouldn't snoop, but she knew she was going to. Heart pounding, she picked up a frame and held it closer. Jack and Charlotte at some sort of fancy party, or maybe a wedding. Her breath caught. Jack wore a slim-fitting, charcoal-gray suit with a matching vest and navy tie, looking as effortlessly wealthy and handsome as a movie star on his way to a premiere. Her gaze shifted to Charlotte with her Duchess of Cambridge elegance, standing next to Jack in a pleated lavender chiffon gown, her long, dark hair waving over one shoulder. Could she have looked any more perfect for Jack?

Tegan's head swung back to the diner door. He'd be out any minute and she needed to clean up the mess. He would definitely freak out if he caught her in his stuff. But she couldn't seem to stop herself. She picked up another frame. A candid photo of Jack and Charlotte on a boat—or really, that thing was probably a yacht. Jack wore the preppy lobster shorts, which made much more sense in that context, and Charlotte wore a pale blue gingham dress. The photographer had captured them laughing, Jack's head tilting forward, and Charlotte's cheek pressing against his shoulder. They looked so… happy. An ache throbbed in her heart, and she tossed the frame back in the box.

She knew she should stop tormenting herself, but instead, she grabbed a newspaper clipping from the pile and flipped it over. It was from a San Francisco paper and had that same photo of Jack and Charlotte that was on his phone. It looked like a professional photographer had taken it. Was this their engagement announcement?

As soon as she read the headline all the blood rushed from her head. *Fiancé of San Francisco Marathon Mass Shooting Victim Starts Charitable Fund in Her Honor*

"Oh my God," Tegan breathed. She scanned the article, reading the text but unable to absorb what it said. It was completely wrong. It couldn't be. But as she scoured the page a second time, the words began to sink in.

> *The fiancé of a victim of the tragic San Francisco Marathon shooting donated one million dollars to start a charitable fund in her honor. Charlotte DeYoung, 30, was crossing mile eighteen of the marathon when the gunman opened fire. She died at the hospital two hours later. The Charlotte DeYoung Foundation will provide grants to support pediatric brain cancer research, a cause that was close to Ms. DeYoung's heart.*

Tegan flung the article on the car seat like it was on fire and pressed her hands to her mouth in horror. She'd watched the news stories, obsessively scrolled the articles like everyone else. About a year ago, a gunman with an AR-15 had opened fire at the San Francisco marathon, injuring dozens and killing seventeen. *Charlotte.* Charlotte had been one of the runners.

Jack's fiancée was dead.

Tegan bit back a sob. The nightmares, the sadness in his eyes, it all made sense now. What Jack must have gone through, must still be going through. It was unbearable.

And then she remembered. Jack—where was he?

Her head whipped back to the restaurant, and she saw him in the window, handing his credit card to the woman at the cash register. If he caught her digging through his stuff she didn't know what he'd do. Maybe kick her out of the car for good this time, and she wouldn't blame him. She'd found the article by accident, but he wouldn't see it that way. He'd only see his private pain spilled out all over the floor mat.

She grabbed the box and threw in the photos, pens, and other junk before shoving it back on the seat. As she picked up her bag and backed away from the car, footsteps crunched across the parking lot behind her.

"Hey, did you find it?" His voice sounded so normal. How was that possible? His fiancée had been murdered. How could anything about his life ever be normal again?

She spun around and stared at him, blinking to fight back the tears that pricked her eyes. "What?"

"Did you find it?"

He couldn't mean—no. What was he talking about? "Find what?" she mumbled, pressing a shaking hand to her forehead.

He stepped back and shot her an odd look. "Your wallet."

Her wallet? Oh, she'd gone out to the car to find her wallet. It seemed like hours ago. Days ago. She ducked her head, unable to look at him, as she fumbled in her backpack. "Yeah. Here it is." She held it up and then dropped it.

He was still looking at her sideways. "Are you okay?"

How could she know this about him and not say anything? Was she supposed to hop in the car and ride along, arguing over the radio station or which exit to take, as if she had no idea the terrible tragedy he'd suffered? In the last few days, she'd grown to care about him. If the enormous crack slowly working its way across her heart was any indication, she cared a lot.

Any minute now, she was going to lose it and start crying. She needed to get out of there. She needed—

Jamie.

CHAPTER EIGHTEEN

Jack

Jack watched in confusion as Tegan stumbled backward, away from him. Her eyes darted around the parking lot, landing everywhere but on his face.

"Are you okay?" he asked again.

"What?" She shifted from one foot to another as if she was trying to hold back from taking off running. At this point, he was used to her odd behavior, but this was strange even for Tegan.

"Are you okay?" he repeated.

"Um. I have to make a phone call." And before he could say another word, she spun on her heel and took off across the parking lot.

"Tegan, wait." But either she didn't hear, or she was ignoring him. Jack watched her retreating back as she disappeared around the building. Should he follow her? For a second there, he had thought he saw tears welling up, but maybe it was just the mountain wind making her eyes water.

He hesitated, and then turned toward the car. *No more detours or distractions.* He'd promised himself not even twelve hours earlier, after speaking to his family, that he wasn't going to get involved. She'd been fine in the diner a minute ago, and this was just Tegan being Tegan.

As Jack walked toward the car, he sighed. Tegan being Tegan was right. She'd left the back door open. He walked over and was just about to swing it shut when something made him pause.

One of his boxes—the one closest to the door—had been pulled out of line, and the corner hung over the edge of the seat. Not only that, the lid was slightly ajar. Had Tegan been snooping in his things? A few days ago, he would have automatically jumped to the conclusion that she had. But, no, he knew her better now. Tegan was always dropping and spilling things. She'd probably grabbed her bag and knocked the box out of place. As he reached in to push it back into line, something caught his eye.

And then a chill ran through him.

There, on the floor. It was impossible to miss it on the otherwise spotless mat. The newspaper article about Charlotte's death. Her face smiled up at him from the photo the reporter had taken from their engagement announcement. At least the reporter had kept his name out of it, had respected his privacy.

Jack picked the newspaper clipping up, crumpling it in his hands. Tegan must have seen it.

The knowledge knocked the wind out of him, and he leaned breathless against the car. No wonder she'd looked like she wanted to cry. Everything she needed to know about him was laid bare in that piece of paper. The whole, terrible tragedy.

And what the article didn't say, she could probably fill in for herself. Why he was closed off and cold. Why he was broken.

In that moment, he knew his feelings for Tegan couldn't be trivialized as simply *detours or distractions*. It didn't matter that she might not fit in at a dinner with his law firm colleagues, or that she wasn't the kind of woman he'd normally meet in New York. He felt disgusted with himself that he'd even compared her to that world.

He might not be able to look at that photo of Charlotte without feeling dizzy, but the ache in his heart had everything to do with Tegan.

And, just like that, it hit him with blinding clarity. He'd been such an idiot. Shouldn't he have learned this year that life was short, and chances were fleeting? He should have told Tegan. Should have grabbed the opportunity last night in the barn, or this morning, to open up and be honest about his past. Told her before she found out in this horrible, shocking way.

Would she look at him differently now? If he chased her down, told her he had feelings for her, would this color everything?

Jack gazed out across the parking lot in the direction of the spot where she'd disappeared around the diner. Where had she gone? She wouldn't take off after something like this. Tegan would've stayed, she'd have challenged him, and pushed him to open up, even when it was the last thing he wanted to do.

So, where is she?

He paced along the white line that marked his parking space and then turned back to the diner. If life was short, and chances were fleeting, there was only one thing to do.

Go after her.

CHAPTER NINETEEN

Tegan

Tegan rounded the corner of the building and skidded to a stop next to the back wall of the restaurant. By the kitchen door, she found a couple of overturned buckets and sank down on one.

Jamie answered on the second ring.

"Hey, T." He sounded so tired. Did she wake him? It was only nine o'clock on the east coast.

"Hi." She fought to keep the tears out of her voice. If he knew she was close to crying, he'd want to know what was wrong. The last thing he needed was to worry about her more than he already did. She couldn't tell him about Jack. But God, it was nice to just hear his voice.

"So, how's your trip going?" Jamie asked. "Did you find the small town of your dreams yet?"

"You mean *our* dreams," Tegan corrected.

"Right. Of course." There was that exhaustion in his voice again.

He was so tired; he'd been struggling for so long, while she was out here on this carefree adventure. It was for both of them but, all of a sudden, Tegan felt pretty damn selfish. She *had* found the town of their dreams, and she'd driven away because she wanted to be with Jack.

Jack, whose own dreams had been shattered, and who was mourning the love of his life.

Oh my god, what have I been thinking? How could she have forgotten what was important?

"You'll never believe it, but I think I might've found us a place to live," she told Jamie, adding as much cheer to her voice as she could muster. "It's in Colorado, and you're going to love it. It's so beautiful. And the people I met are wonderful. Start packing because I'll be home in less than a week."

For a moment, Jamie was silent. Taking it all in, maybe. *This was it.* This was what they'd spent their whole life looking for. But when he spoke, his voice was flatter than she expected. "Tegan, I don't think I'm going anywhere. Well—" he breathed out a little laugh, but there was no humor in it. "Not to Colorado anyway."

Tegan clutched the phone to her ear. "What do you mean? You don't want to stay in Pittsburgh, do you? I haven't even told you about Copper Canyon yet."

"No, I don't want to stay in Pittsburgh. And you have no idea how happy I am that you found someplace wonderful to live. But I don't think I'm going to make it there with you. I—" His voice wobbled through the phone. "I had a scan about two weeks ago."

"Two weeks ago? Why didn't you tell me?" But she knew why. They'd been missing each other's calls, with her out of cell-range half the time, and Jamie sleeping the other half. And then she'd been leaving chipper voicemail messages, going on about how great her trip was. The weight of the guilt pressed down on her. Jamie had undergone tests that he hadn't been able to tell her about.

He lowered his voice. "T, the cancer is back."

She froze, momentarily unable to breathe as that news sank in. But then she sat up straight. "Okay." They'd been through this before, and the doctors said it might happen. But there were new medications to try, other treatments. Jamie's cancer had gone into remission before, and it would again. "Okay," she repeated. "So, the cancer is back. We can handle this. What are the options?"

Jamie's silence stretched through the phone, louder than a scream. Finally, he murmured, "There are no options."

Her heart pitched. "What do you mean, there are no options? Of course there are. The doctor said there are new drug combinations coming out all the time. And then there was that research trial you're a great candidate for."

She heard him take a breath in and then blow it out slowly. "There are no options for *me*, Tegan. I'm done. I'm not doing it anymore. The cancer has spread, none of these options are going to cure me, and I'm tired. The side effects of the drugs are worse than…" He trailed off.

She gripped the bucket beneath her thighs. "Worse than what, Jamie? *Than dying?*"

"Yes." His voice was so firm. So final.

"*No.*"

"Tegan, I think maybe you should stay in this Copper Canyon place. You sound so excited about it, and there's nothing I want more than to know you're settled and happy—"

"No." Tegan cut him off. "No. I'm not going there without you." She shook her head slowly. "This is crazy, Jamie. I'm going to call the doctor tomorrow and tell her you've decided to enroll in that research trial." If there was even a chance it could work, she'd have to *make* him do it.

He let out a hoarse chuckle. "You sound just like you did when you were eight and kept trying to get Dad to sober up. How'd that work out for you?"

"Jamie, this is *not funny*."

"No, T. It's not." His voice was more subdued now. "I'm dying."

This couldn't be happening. After everything they'd been through, Jamie was supposed to have beaten the cancer. Things were finally turning around for them. She'd found them a place to live away from the stress and noise and city pollution, away from the bad memories, and they were going to start over.

She had a plan.

A tear rolled down her cheek and she swiped it with her hand. "Jamie. *Please.*"

"Tegan, I can't do it anymore. I just… can't."

Her whole body shook as she tried to hold back a sob. She opened her mouth to argue, but her throat felt packed with sand. On some level, she knew it was useless anyway. She was well acquainted with that note of finality in his voice. Jamie knew when it was time to let go, so much better than she did. All those times she'd convinced herself that their dad would stop drinking, that their mom would come back; Jamie had been the voice of reason. If Jamie said he was done, he was done.

She took a deep, gasping breath and finally managed to whisper, "How long do you have?"

"I don't know. A couple of months probably."

"Okay. I'll…" Tegan trailed off. She had no idea what she'd do.

"Tegan," Jamie cut in. "*Go to Copper Canyon.*"

"I—" *I can't.* Not without Jamie. "I'll call you soon." She hung up the phone and crossed her arms over her stomach, bending forward at the waist and fighting to breathe through the vise squeezing her lungs.

Jamie.

Jack.

"Tegan."

She jumped to her feet and whirled around. Jack stood next to the building with his arms hanging at his sides and his face ghostly pale in the dim fluorescent street lamp.

How much did he hear? She scrubbed her hand across her cheeks to wipe away the tears.

"Who is Jamie?" He took a step toward her and then stopped.

She stared at the dumpster at the end of the parking lot, and finally managed to whisper, "My brother."

"Did I hear you say—is Jamie—"

Oh God, he'd heard everything.

He took another step toward her and she heard the crinkle of paper brushing against his leg. Her eyes darted to the crumpled piece of newspaper clutched in his hand.

She gasped. Oh God, he knew she'd found the article. In her rush, she must not have put the box away properly. He was so orderly, it was exactly the kind of thing he'd notice. How could she have been so careless? Her gaze flew to his face, where pain slashed across his eyes. He'd packed away all that agony, and she'd dragged it out and forced him to remember.

She pressed a trembling hand to her mouth. "I—did you—" She couldn't do this. Her whole body was shaking, shivering from the cold, but she was sweating at the same time. Her head pounded as her thoughts whirled between Charlotte and Jamie, and the incredible, hopeless tragedy of it all. She closed her eyes as if that would make it all go away. She wanted nothing more than to go back to ten minutes ago, when Jack was engaged to the love of his life, and Jamie was still willing to fight.

"Jack." She needed to move, to get out of there. "Can we go? Please? I need to go." Her voice cracked at the end, and his face softened.

As soon as he nodded, she darted past him and ran for the car. The doors beeped and clicked as they unlocked. She was already strapped into her seat, leaning against the door with her eyes closed, when she heard Jack slide in next to her. She squeezed her eyes tighter.

He started the car without a word, and pulled out of the parking lot. A few minutes later, she felt the car turn and then come to a stop. She opened her eyes. They seemed to be somewhere right outside of town, in the parking lot of a hotel that was way too nice for her budget. Estes Park was full of places to stay, and Jack had certainly picked an expensive one.

She couldn't afford this. But how could she possibly argue with him now? Hopelessness rose inside her like a river after days of rain. One more drop and the whole thing would spill over and sweep away everything in its path. Who cared about the price of the room? She'd put it on her credit card and figure it out later.

She trailed after Jack as he got out of the car and crossed the parking lot to the office. He stood at the front desk, his expression unreadable as he requested two rooms and handed the clerk his platinum American Express.

Wearily, Tegan pulled out her credit card and held it out. She jumped as Jack's hand pressed down on top of hers. "*Don't.*" He finally looked at her, his face like granite. "I'm paying for this."

She opened her mouth to argue, but he cut her off. "We're not staying in some shithole motel tonight. So, don't say a word."

They made their way to their rooms in silence, a fact that Tegan was grateful for. She couldn't have gotten a word out anyway. They stopped at her room, and Jack stood there with his hands stuffed into his pockets as she pushed the door open and stepped inside.

Thirty seconds. You just need to get through the next thirty seconds, and then you can fall apart.

She turned and finally looked at him, but he gazed past her into the room. She didn't blame him if he hated her for snooping in his things. In one disastrous night, all the bridges they'd built had come crashing down. Jack was right in front of her, but he stood on the other side of a vast canyon. She had no idea how to jump over to his side. In that moment, she finally understood how much he'd come to mean to her.

She took a step back and quickly closed the door. Shoulders shaking with sobs, she dropped her backpack and then spun around and pressed her back against the door. Her legs gave out and she slid to the floor. She sat there, her head tilted back against the wood frame until she heard his footsteps tap down the hall, and the click of his door opening and closing. Then she dropped her forehead to her knees and let the dam break.

Pressing a hand to her mouth to muffle the sobs, she thought of her big brother who had been the only constant in her unstable, chaotic childhood. Jamie had been no more than a child himself, but he'd stepped in to take care of her. He'd sacrificed so much for her, putting off college because he couldn't leave her alone with their father. He'd said they couldn't afford it, but Tegan knew that he could've gotten a scholarship if he didn't have her to think about. Instead, he'd gotten a job working construction. He'd go to college later, he said. After she finished high school.

But the year she finished high school was the year he'd gotten sick for the first time.

Jamie had never ended up going to college, never met a nice girl and got married, never had a chance to follow any of his dreams.

And now he never would.

Tegan wrapped her arms around her knees and sobbed harder.

She thought of Charlotte. A woman she'd never even met, but whose smile would forever burn into her memory. Charlotte, who'd had everything, and then had it stolen by a terrible, senseless act of violence. Charlotte, who'd never get to live out her dreams. Who'd never get to marry Jack.

Tegan's heart folded in on itself. The agony Jack must be experiencing. She'd give anything to be able to take that pain away from him, but it was impossible. A person didn't get over a loss like that.

Tegan didn't know how long she sat there on the lush hotel carpeting with the door digging into her back and her body wracked with sobs. Eventually the tears stopped, and all that was left was a soul-deep pit of misery and exhaustion. She managed to drag herself to her feet and stumble across the dark room. Sinking down on the bed, some part of her registered the luxury of it—the firm mattress that gave just the right amount under her weight, fluffy white duvet made of the softest cotton—but it offered little comfort. She longed for the blissful ignorance of life back when she'd stayed in dive motels and still felt hope and excitement for the future.

Tegan flung herself across the bed and stared up at the ceiling, her only hope that sleep would come quickly and take it all away, just for a little while.

CHAPTER TWENTY

Jack

Jack paced from the door of his hotel room to the bed, and then back again.

Tegan's brother—*Jamie*—was dying.

Jack remembered the affection in her voice when she'd told him her brother was her best friend, and then the sadness that flashed in her eyes when he'd inadvertently mentioned knowing Jamie's name. That Tegan had lied on the phone that first night—asking the person on the other end of the call to tell Jamie her car was running well—made so much more sense now. She wouldn't want to worry him, not if he was sick.

Jack tried to imagine what he would do if his sister had cancer and he'd gotten the news that it was terminal, but he quickly backed away from that thought. It hurt too much to even consider it. He sank down on the edge of the bed, consumed by Tegan's anguish. Her stricken face when she'd looked up and saw him standing by the diner. Her pale skin and red-rimmed eyes on the drive to the hotel. The way her hands had shaken as she'd shoved the keycard into the door.

Her voice begging Jamie not to give up on treatments.

Had Tegan run off to call Jamie after finding the newspaper article because his story of losing Charlotte had reminded her of her own suffering? Or was Jamie the person she turned to for solace? Jack knew Tegan well enough to know she'd be devastated by Charlotte's death. And instead of comfort, she'd gotten the worst news of her life. His heart broke thinking of her all alone in the hotel room next door with the earth shifting beneath her and nobody to turn to.

He lunged off the bed and leaned against their shared wall, pressing his ear to the drywall, but all he heard was the faint rush of air blowing through the vents. What he'd give to be at the Vista Verde right now; what he'd give for those thin walls that gave away secrets.

Was she crying over there, or had numbness overtaken her? He'd never, ever forget sitting alone in his apartment that first night after Charlotte had died. The walls echoing with every tiny movement he made. The hopelessness that stole his breath like a riptide pulling him under. The fervent wish that the gunman had taken him too.

Jack stood up and strode to the door, but then paused. Should he go to her? Would she even want to see him right now? Maybe he was nothing but a stranger to her. A stranger who hadn't always been as kind as he should have been, and who'd kept things from her. Maybe having to face him, and his own tragedy, was the last thing she needed right now.

He jumped, the buzz of his phone ringing on the side table jolting him out of his thoughts. He hurried over and picked it up, checking the name of the caller. *Mom.* She was probably just checking in on him again, calling to ask the status of the car repairs and find out if he was back on the road, headed toward home.

Jack hit the side button on his phone, sending her to voicemail. He couldn't face his family right now, or their judgment and opinions about what he should be doing or whether or not Tegan was the right kind of person for him. They would never understand his connection with her, and he didn't know how to explain something that he didn't fully understand either.

Jack paced to the door and then back to the bed. What he *did* know for sure was that everything about this felt wrong. How could he possibly stay here in this room when Tegan clearly wasn't okay? How could he climb into bed tonight while she was right down the hall, hurting and alone?

Jack paced one more groove in the carpet from the bed to the door, and this time, he swung it open. He'd go down the hall, knock on her door, and offer to talk. To listen. Offer a shoulder to cry on. If Tegan didn't want to see him, she wouldn't be shy about telling him so. But he had to go. He had to at least try.

CHAPTER TWENTY-ONE

Tegan

Tegan jumped as a knock pounded on the door. It had to be Jack. There was nobody else it could be. Rolling off the bed, she swiped at her still-damp cheeks and made her way to the door. Had he come back to yell at her for snooping in his stuff, or to tell her once and for all that he was done with her? She didn't think she could feel any emptier, but the thought of him leaving chipped one more hole in her heart.

She swung the door open. Jack stood there with his shoulders slumped under his plain white T-shirt and his hands stuffed into the pockets of his khaki pants.

"Hi." She stared at his blue and yellow argyle socks. He hadn't bothered with shoes for his walk down the hall to her room.

"Tegan, I—" He stopped.

The silence stretched, long and endless, and she finally forced herself to tilt her head up and meet his eyes. He flinched, and for a moment she wondered if he couldn't stand to look at her. But then he reached out and put his hand on her cheek, gently wiping the tears away. "Tegan, I'm so sorry," he whispered.

Her heart rapped painfully against her sternum. She took a step toward him, longing for the comfort of human connection. And longing for… so much more than that. For so many things that were dangerous to think about because they were impossible. How could she so desperately wish his fiancée was still alive and, at the same time, desperately wish for him to return her feelings for him?

Jack took an audible breath, but he didn't move away. He stared at her, palm still pressed to her cheek. Her eyes flew to his—questioning, craving—and her heart nearly pounded out of her chest at the desire she saw in their blue depths.

Then she did what she'd been wanting to do for what felt like forever, even if it had only been a couple of days. She leaned in and kissed him, wrapping her arms around his neck and pulling him against her. He slid one hand behind her head, kissing her back, and the heat and solidity of his body grounded her.

She took a step backward, tugging him with her into the hotel room, but he gently pulled away. "Tegan, we shouldn't do this. This—isn't what you need right now. I don't want to take advantage of you."

This was *exactly* what she needed right now. If she had to face this awful night for one more second, face Charlotte and Jamie and the crushing tragedy of it all, she didn't think she'd make it through. "Jack," she murmured, grabbing his T-shirt with both hands. "Stop talking."

His eyes widened, but he didn't step away. Instead, he snaked an arm around her back, and slanted his mouth across hers. At that moment, all traces of gentleness and hesitation disappeared, replaced by an urgency that consumed all rational thought. She yearned to comfort, to be comforted, to share heat and pleasure instead of deep, dark emptiness. She yanked him all the way into the room at the same time as he pushed his way forward, slamming the door. They stumbled across the narrow space and fell on the bed in a jumble of arms and legs. His mouth found hers again—rough, hot—as his hands tangled into her hair.

His weight pressed on top of her. His hands slid across her skin. His mouth explored her jaw, her neck, then went lower. How could she have ever thought that Jack was staid, or boring, or buttoned up? He was warm, generous, both rough and gentle, and he took care to give as much pleasure as he received.

And, in that moment, she didn't think about Jamie. Didn't think about Charlotte. She got lost in the feel of him, and didn't think about anything at all.

CHAPTER TWENTY-TWO

Jack

As Jack lay on his back in the dark hotel room, staring at the narrow strip of moonlight slashing across the ceiling from a crack in the curtain, a feeling of contentment washed over him for the first time in as long as he could remember. The smell of spring floated over him from Tegan's hair splayed across his shoulder, and he reached up to gently feather his hand across her cheek. She flashed a tiny, hesitant smile.

He pressed a kiss to her forehead. "You okay?"

"Yeah."

He carefully pulled his arm out from under her head and turned on his side so he was facing her. It somehow felt like they'd shared everything but, in reality, there was still so much he didn't know about Tegan. "Can I ask you something?" he asked.

She bit her lip, and then nodded.

"Why are you really on this road trip?"

She took a slow, heavy breath and for a moment, he was afraid she was closing off. "It's a long story."

"I have all night."

Tegan shifted so she was looking back at him, their faces only inches apart on the shared pillow. "I had a rough childhood. My mom left when I was seven, and my dad was an alcoholic."

"Your mom left? For good?" He thought of his own mother, overbearing but endlessly devoted to her family.

Tegan nodded. "She wasn't really cut out to be a mother. Even as a little kid, I could tell that she wasn't happy. She was never that parent who gave hugs, or wanted to read books with us, or came running when we had nightmares. She did the bare minimum—food, clothes, a ride to school. We were pretty much on our own for everything else. And then she met some guy at work, and I guess she saw a chance at a better life than what she had with two kids she didn't really want, and a husband who spent ninety percent of their marriage in a drunken stupor, and she took it."

It was the one of the most heartbreaking stories Jack had ever heard, but she just shrugged. As if she could see the direction of his thoughts, she continued, "It was okay. She was someone who wasn't really present in my life, so the hole that she left when she took off wasn't as big as you'd think. And besides, I had Jamie." The wistful smile that lit up her face was almost as sad as her story, now that he knew about her brother.

"Jamie is five years older than me, and for as long as I can remember, he took the place of both my mom and my dad. He was the one who came in when I had a nightmare—"

"If you tell someone about it, it'll go away," Jack murmured, remembering her response to his own nightmare. She'd said her brother told her that.

"Yeah." Her smile dropped a notch. "He cooked meals and made me do my homework. Taught me to read, and encouraged me to write. He's my whole family. He's everything—" Her voice cracked, and he reached over and took her hand, lacing his fingers with hers.

"It sounds funny, but I grew up sheltered. My dad was an alcoholic and my mom was gone, we were dead broke and sometimes living out of our car. But Jamie never let me think that our lives were anything less than an adventure. We weren't sleeping in the car, we were in a spaceship on our way to Mars."

He smiled sadly at the image of a freckled little girl and her older brother, camped out in a rusty old car, blasting off on an adventure to outer space.

"We weren't dumpster diving for food, we were on a treasure hunt." She let out a wry laugh. "Sometimes I felt sorry for the other kids who had to live in houses with parents who bought food at the grocery store."

If Jamie had that kind of fortitude and imagination at age twelve, he must be a pretty amazing guy now.

"Even after Jamie got sick, he still took care of me, protected me. He kept his illness from me for a long time. I was finishing high school and he didn't want to distract me. And then even when he couldn't hide it anymore, he downplayed it, not letting me know how really serious it was. He has acute myeloid leukemia and needed a bone marrow transplant, but he wouldn't let me donate—even though I was a match—because it's incredibly painful and he didn't want to put me through that. It was the first time I really fought him on anything, and eventually he gave in."

Jack tried to imagine what he would have done if it he'd been responsible for Liv the way Jamie had been for Tegan. Would he have gone to the lengths that Jamie had to protect his sister? He'd like to think so, but he'd grown up with two loving parents, so it was impossible to imagine being solely responsible for anyone. "That's pretty selfless."

Tegan seemed to think about that for a moment. "I think he took our mom leaving a lot harder than I did. He was older, and he felt responsible. Like if he'd been a better kid, she would have stayed. Which is ridiculous, of course. You couldn't have asked for a better kid than Jamie. But I think on some level, he thought he was making up for her leaving by going above and beyond to look out for me. Which is selfless, but it's also sad. Sometimes I wish he'd been a little more selfish—had lived his own life, followed his own dreams a little more. Especially now."

Now that he doesn't have much time left.

She didn't say it, but it hung in the air. Jack felt the pain radiating from her and he wished there was something he could do to take it away. But he knew from experience that was impossible. "Where is Jamie now?"

"He's in Pittsburgh—that's where we grew up. Moving from apartment to apartment, and sometimes to our car when we got evicted." She paused, looking away from him. "Jamie's hospital bills were huge, and he was still pretty weak from all the treatments and couldn't work. I waited tables, but tips on two-dollar diner coffee don't add up to much. I couldn't juggle it all, we got evicted, and there was no way to pass that off as some sort of adventure. I felt like such a failure. The worst part was that Jamie blamed himself and tried to make *me* feel better. Luckily, he has some friends with a guest room where he can stay."

In the dim light, Jack watched a tear trickle from her eye, leaving a wet mark on the pillow. "We'd always dreamed of moving far away. One summer when we were kids, we lived with my grandmother in a small town in West Virginia, and it was the best summer of our lives. But then my grandma got sick and we had to go back to our dad. But we always said we'd find a place just like that, far away from Pittsburgh, and start over."

She squeezed her eyes closed, holding back more tears. Heart aching, Jack reached over and pulled her against him. She burrowed her face into his chest, and took a couple of deep breaths. Finally, she lifted her head and met his eyes.

"Once the doctors gave him the all-clear, I took off in the old station wagon. The plan was that he'd focus on getting stronger, and I'd find us a place to live. But now I wonder if he knew more than he let on. I wouldn't have gone if he was sick, and he was still protecting me." She scrubbed a tear from her cheek. "Maybe he didn't ever plan to go with me. Maybe he just wanted me to have somewhere to go when he was gone."

"So now that you know… what happens next?"

Obviously, this was the end of their adventure together. It was just a matter of figuring out the details to get her home to Jamie.

She rolled on her back and stared up at the ceiling. "Jamie wants me to go back to Copper Canyon. He wants to know that I'm settled someplace before he—" She shook her head. "But I can't go back there without him. It was *our* dream. We were supposed to do this together."

Jack nodded. "So, you'll go back home?"

"I don't know."

He sat up. "You don't know?"

She took a shaky breath. "I don't know if I can watch my big brother die. I don't know if I can sit there while he slowly… fades away."

Jack watched the sheet rise and fall with her breath. How much of that was the real reason she was on this trip? A reason that she probably couldn't even admit to herself. He suspected that she'd been in denial about the reality of Jamie's illness for a long time. Because acknowledging that the only constant in her life was abandoning her was too much to bear.

"I can't imagine how painful it will be." He paused. "Actually, yes, I can. It will be awful. I know that. But I can promise you that if you don't go, it'll be worse. You'll spend your life regretting that you weren't there." He gently turned her face to meet his eyes. "Tegan, you have the chance to be there for him. To tell him you love him one last time. And to say goodbye. Don't miss it because you're afraid it will hurt."

She blinked, and he looked away. They both knew that he wasn't just talking about Tegan and Jamie. He flopped back down on the pillow next to her, and it was her turn to prop herself on her elbow and stare him down.

"Tell me something about Charlotte."

Was she serious? They were in bed together. They'd just... She really wanted to talk about his fiancée right now? "What do you want to know?"

"How'd you meet her?"

If the story could distract Tegan from thinking about her pain for a little while, so be it. "She stole my cab."

"Really?" Tegan let out a teary laugh.

"Yes. Well—sort of. She *tried* to steal it. It was rush hour, and raining, and I had gotten lucky enough to flag it down. Getting a cab in the rain during rush hour in New York City is pretty much the equivalent of finding a unicorn. And then before I realized what was happening, Charlotte came running down the sidewalk, soaking wet, and yanked the door open before I could."

Tegan gasped in mock indignation. "Was it on purpose?"

"No. She'd just had a really shitty day, and was so desperate to get home that she didn't notice I was standing right there."

"What did you do?"

Jack ran his hand through his hair, laughing. For the first time, a memory of Charlotte made him feel a little bit lighter. "Well, I'd like to say I was a complete gentleman and gave her the cab right away."

"But..." Tegan asked, her voice tinged with amusement.

"But I'd had a shitty day too, and I admit I wasn't at my best."

Tegan clamped her hand over her mouth, shoulders shaking with laughter. "Having met you on one of your shittier days, I can't say this surprises me."

He could laugh at that too. Laugh at himself for the first time in a long time. "We ended up sharing the cab, and by the time we'd made it fifteen blocks, I knew she was the one."

It should have been weird to talk about Charlotte with Tegan... but it wasn't. It was weird that for the past year, people *didn't* talk about Charlotte. His friends, family, co-workers all tiptoed around him, pretending she never existed. They were afraid that if they brought her up, he'd think about her, remember that she was gone. But they didn't understand that he thought about Charlotte every single minute of every single day.

He felt like he was dishonoring her when he *didn't* talk about her. When he tried to act like everything was fine and sit around idly chatting about the weather or what was on Netflix or whatever other inane conversation people tried to engage him in. As if there wasn't a Grand Canyon-sized hole in his life that Charlotte used to occupy. Even worse was knowing that his grief made other people uncomfortable, and having to pile the guilt of that on top of everything else. So, he'd retreated. Hidden out in his office or in his empty apartment so he wouldn't have to talk to anyone.

Until now.

"Was Charlotte a lawyer too?"

"No, she was a doctor. A surgeon. She'd just finished her first year of her fellowship in pediatric surgery when she—" He inhaled, and his heart didn't ache quite much as he expected. "When she died."

"I've seen the photos, I know Charlotte was beautiful, and I guess she was pretty smart too. I bet you were perfect for each other." She reached out and brushed her hand across his bare shoulder. "I'm so sorry, Jack."

He knew she really meant it. That being with him like this, and still allowing him space to mourn Charlotte, didn't have to be mutually exclusive.

"We were perfect for each other, in a lot of ways. But it wasn't always perfect. It's easy to romanticize now that she's gone, but we had our problems, too." He paused, remembering. "You think my family pushed me into my career? You should've seen Charlotte's family."

Tegan's eyes grew wide. "She didn't want to be a doctor?"

He sighed. "She did. But surgery… and then pediatric surgery. It's brutal. It's years of training longer than general medicine. Super competitive, old boys' club. She hated it. She would have been happy as a family doctor, or a pediatrician with a private practice. She was great with kids and she loved them. As a pediatric surgeon, the only time she really interacted with kids was when they were knocked out by anesthesia. But her dad was a surgeon and he really pushed her. I hated how she went along."

He stared at the ceiling, remembering the endless discussions, the arguments. She said he didn't understand, that he wasn't being supportive. In the end, he'd given in, let her make up her own mind, even when he could see how miserable she was. If only he'd pushed harder. "It's not like going into family practice was anything to be ashamed of. It was her whole career—her whole life—and she was letting someone else dictate it. That's how we ended up in San Francisco. She did her surgical residency and then her fellowship there."

"You didn't want to go?"

"Don't get me wrong, I loved San Francisco. But I would have liked it to be *our* decision instead of her father's decision. And then, you know, there's a part of me that thinks that if I'd stood my ground, if I'd argued against surgery and hadn't let her father have so much influence, we would've stayed in New York and she'd still be…" He trailed off.

There it was. The truth that had haunted him every day for the past year. He was to blame. He'd allowed this to happen. Like one domino knocking into the next one, triggering row upon row of collapse, he hadn't stood up to her family when he should have. He'd allowed some messed-up sense of duty and the unreasonable standards to dictate what they did and where they lived. And because of that, Charlotte had moved to California to pursue a career she hated. Charlotte had taken up running to deal with the stress.

Charlotte had been crossing mile eighteen of the San Francisco marathon when a gunman opened fire on her.

"Oh, Jack. *No*," Tegan said, breathlessly. "You can't. Life isn't like that. You have no idea what could've happened if you'd stayed in New York."

He shook his head. "There's so much pressure in the circles where Charlotte and I grew up. But I should have been stronger. More forceful. Told her father to back off."

But he hadn't.

"Charlotte was so stressed out all the time, and it was me who encouraged her to take up running… I should have encouraged her to quit her job instead. *Insisted* on it." He pressed his hands to his temples.

"Jack." Tegan flopped on her stomach, her face inches from his. "I know you blame yourself, but *none* of this is your fault. You loved Charlotte, and you were being supportive. How could you possibly know what would happen? I never met Charlotte, but I know she wouldn't have wanted you to do this to yourself. Nobody would."

He watched the light from a car on the road outside shift across the ceiling and then fade away. Was Tegan right?

For the first time, he considered what Charlotte *would* have wanted for him. *Move past the grief and move on with your life. Be happy.* Charlotte's voice. A whisper. Or maybe it was the wind in the trees outside the window.

Rolling onto his side, he gazed at Tegan. Her hair shone in the moonlight, and her freckles played across her face. Up close, they were just thousands of tiny dots, but when you stepped back and took a wider look, they blended together to make up something beautiful.

He didn't know if he'd ever be able to move on from Charlotte and be happy. But for the first time, it felt possible that he had a fighting chance.

CHAPTER TWENTY-THREE

Tegan

Paper crinkled, a pen scratched.

Tegan slowly returned to consciousness, stretching in a bed that was too lush to be anywhere that she recognized. It came to her in flashes.

Charlotte.

Jamie.

Jack.

Tegan sat up in bed.

Jack.

She found him on the other side of the hotel room, bent over the map he'd spread across the table. A set of multi-colored pens sat in a neat row, perfectly spaced like railroad ties. He chose a green pen, made a note on the map, placed the pen back on the table and then reached for the red pen.

Jack was freaking out.

He had the map out, he was back in planning mode. He must be feeling out of control, and this was how he reined it in. She hadn't known him very long, but she knew this about him.

He finished with the red pen and then looked up, finally noticing she was awake. "Hi." Back to the pens. This time he chose orange.

She rolled out of bed, grabbing the sheet to wrap around her. Her clothes lay scattered across the room, she had no idea where her underwear had gone, and her hair was like cotton candy frizzing around her head. While Jack sat there already showered, in a pressed button-up shirt with his still-damp hair neatly combed. If he was going to sneak out of bed at dawn, why didn't he go to his own room until she had a chance to shower and get dressed? Then they could've done this awkward morning-after routine on equal footing.

She'd never had a connection with someone like they'd had last night. It had meant so much more than just sex and the desire to ease each other's pain for a little while. At least, it had for her. But while they'd bared their souls about Charlotte and Jamie, they hadn't talked about what any of this meant between the two of them. And that map was making her nerves bubble up. Did he regret what happened?

It shouldn't surprise her that he was freaking out. Maybe it was appropriate that she looked like the poster girl for the walk of shame, and he looked like he was on his way to the office. This was who they were—opposite, incongruent—and it was better to have it all out there.

Tegan found her T-shirt and jeans on the floor and made a break for the bathroom to quickly pull them on and brush her teeth. Then she took a look in the mirror. Her hair was still flying everywhere and she'd forgotten her bra on the floor, but it would have to do for now. She slipped out of the bathroom and perched on the edge of the chair across the table from him. "So… you're back to the map, huh?"

"I woke up early, so I started thinking about the route home."

Did he wake early because he'd had another nightmare? Last night it was a question she could have asked him. This morning… were his walls back up?

"Yeah? What did you figure out?" The question came out flat, emotionless. Jack was thinking about getting back home, and maybe he was looking for the shortest route to have this over and done with.

Well, what did you expect? That he'd drop his whole life in New York to go on your grand adventure?

She had zero plan, and Jack had a map the size of New Mexico. The two of them would never fit. After everything he'd been through, why would he want to get involved with a woman he barely knew, one with a sick brother and a complete lack of direction?

He tapped his finger on the map, somewhere in the general area of Colorado, and slid it along a highway line. "Well, I had planned to take this route through Kansas and Missouri. But now I think we could go a northern route. Wyoming, Nebraska, eventually through Chicago."

"Okay." At this point, she didn't really know what the difference was. It was all just farmland.

Jack paused and gave her an odd look, as if he'd expected her to argue with him, or at least have an opinion on the subject. She didn't because she wasn't sure she was going to be in the car with him. What was the point with riding along with him for a few more days? After everything they'd shared, it would only hurt more when they went their separate ways. Maybe she could ask him to drop her in Denver. There'd be plenty of buses and trains there.

Jack went back to the map, sliding his finger east. "I know you're dying to see the world's largest ball of stamps, so we'll swing by that in Nebraska. And the world's largest frying pan here in Wyoming."

Tegan's head jerked up. He wanted to take her to corny tourist attractions all of a sudden?

He smiled, and kept moving his finger across the map. "Then I thought we could spend a night in Chicago." He paused and cleared his throat. "And then from Chicago, we could head down

I-90 through Cleveland, and then from there, it's a straight shot to Pittsburgh."

Pittsburgh. Was that what this was all about? The tourist attractions and everything? He hadn't had a chance to say goodbye to Charlotte, and he didn't want her to make the same mistake. So, he thought if he turned it into some kind of adventure, she'd go home to Jamie? But then what?

He'd drop her off in Pittsburgh, and probably wouldn't even need to spend the night. "From there, you can make it to New York in under seven hours." And that would be the end of the road for them.

But he met her eyes and lowered his voice. "I was thinking I'd come with you to Pittsburgh. Maybe stay a while and help out with Jamie."

She opened and closed her mouth before she was able to get any words to come out. "You want to stay Pittsburgh with me? To help with my brother?"

He smoothed out a crease in the map. "I thought maybe you'd want me to come along. For support."

Her heart lurched in his direction. More than anything she wanted him to come along. More than anything she wanted everything he was offering. But what was his real motivation?

"I guess I don't understand, Jack." One of his pens was out of alignment. She reached over and nudged it until it was parallel to the others. "Don't you have to be back in New York? Don't you have a job?"

He leaned back in his chair. "I transferred most of my clients in California over to my partner before I left, and I took leave for six weeks. I've still got a couple of clients that I need to keep up with, but I don't start in New York until next month."

Next month. So, they'd spend a few more weeks together. Driving through the Midwest, stopping at tourist attractions. He'd be there when she went home to Jamie and maybe he'd hang out for a week. But then he'd go back to New York and she'd—she'd do what?

Say goodbye to everyone who'd ever mattered to her. What Jack was offering would only make it hurt worse when he left too. And then she'd be alone.

"Why?"

"Why what?"

"Why do you want to spend the next few weeks with me? I mean, I guess I get it on some level. You don't strike me as the type to go out and hook up with women you meet in bars or whatever. So, it's probably been a while since you—you know."

Jack's eyes narrowed. "Tegan—"

She cut him off. "But all this with the tourist attractions, and then going home with me to see Jamie. Why? None of that is how you want to spend your vacation."

He leaned in so abruptly that she jumped. "How do you know? Maybe it's exactly how I want to spend my vacation."

"And again, I go back to—why?"

Jack took a breath and blew it out slowly. "First of all, this isn't just about sex. You're right, I don't generally go out and sleep with random women, but I'm not that hard up. And you're not just some—" He waved his hand as if he was looking for the right word.

"Fuck buddy?" she supplied.

He cringed and ran his hand through his hair. "No. You're not just some *fuck buddy.*" He leaned in closer, grabbing her hand as she fiddled with his pens. "I know it's only been a short time, but I care about you, and I know what you're dealing with right now is awful. I hoped you'd want me to be there for you. And as far as the rest of it…" He sighed. "I thought you'd enjoy the silly tourist attractions, that they'd make you happy. You could use a little joy right now. Honestly, I don't know what happens after I have to go back to New York. But can't we figure it out when the time comes?"

She stared across the table at him, trying to shove down the hope in her chest, but it kept bobbing to the surface. Part of her knew that it was a fantasy to think they could make this work between them. Their lives were so divergent, they might as well have lived a million miles apart. But she didn't want to think about that right now. Right now, she wanted—needed—to have faith.

She gave him a tiny nod.

"So that's a yes?" He looked at her sideways.

"Yes."

"To which part? The ball of stamps?"

She laughed. "Definitely yes to the ball of stamps."

"And the rest of it?"

She looked up at this man who she'd only known for a short time, but who had somehow become important to her, despite both of their best efforts. His blue eyes glinted with flecks of gold and crinkled at the corners as his lips curved into a tentative smile. Maybe going out on her own didn't mean she had to do everything by herself. Jack wanted to go with her, to be there for her through whatever was next. Maybe she could face whatever heartbreak was going to come because she wouldn't have to face it alone.

"Yes. To all of it."

He gave a heavy sigh, almost as if he'd been holding his breath. Almost as if he'd been nervous that she'd say no. And with that, Tegan stood and took a few tentative steps toward Jack's side of the table. As soon as she was in arm's reach, he pulled her onto his lap. She leaned in and pressed her mouth to his, and he kissed her back, sliding his hands around her waist and holding her tightly against him.

Almost as if he didn't want to let her go.

*

They finally made it to Rocky Mountain National Park that afternoon. Finally got to go on the hike they'd been talking about for days. Tegan knew she couldn't avoid Jamie's illness forever, but maybe she could avoid it for a little bit longer. Maybe she could build her heart up with Jack, and with these beautiful landscapes, before she went home and had it completely shattered.

Once they were out on the trail, she distracted herself by watching Jack's tall frame moving on the path next to her and the dimple in his cheek that she'd finally become acquainted with, now that he wasn't afraid to smile at her.

"What are you staring at?" he asked, as he sank down on a rock where they'd stopped to take a break. He handed her a bottle of water from the Patagonia daypack he'd meticulously stocked with trail mix, a first aid kit, and other emergency supplies for their five-mile hike.

"How does a corporate lawyer end up with arms like that?" She'd been surprised when she finally saw him in the light of day without a shirt on. She thought back to the day when the road workers at the diner had threatened him. At the time, she thought he was afraid of getting hurt in a fight. Now that she knew him better, she could easily guess it was that he'd been wary of causing a scene.

Jack's shoulders shook with laughter. "Of all the things I thought you might say, that wasn't it."

Her cheeks grew hot. "Well, I mean, you sit around all day writing legal briefs. And I can't imagine that you get ripped playing golf."

"Swimming." He shrugged. "After Charlotte died, the only thing I could do other than work was go to the gym and swim laps. It was that or lie on my living room floor and stare at the ceiling." He said it calmly, as if the statement was a simple fact and not laced with pain. "Besides, we've been over this. I don't golf."

"How can you not golf? I thought it was a requirement of being rich, like worrying over your stock portfolio and eating with a bunch of different forks."

He was laughing again. "Well, I *can* golf. I did learn. But I'm from New York City, so it's kind of an ordeal to get to a golf course. Business deals are more likely to be made over billiards or racquetball at the Harvard Club than on the golf course."

"Harvard. Is that where you went to college?" College was the kind of thing people usually discussed on the first date, but she and Jack had spent so much time tiptoeing around each other, they hadn't gotten around to all that small-talk stuff. In some ways, she knew him so well, and in other ways, they were still strangers.

"Yes. I did my undergrad at Harvard. But I went to Columbia for law."

"They didn't blackball you at the club for that?"

He handed her a bag of trail mix. "Not quite." Jack chuckled. "My family almost blackballed me, though."

"Really, why? Columbia wasn't good enough?" She sifted through the trail mix in her hand, picking out the cashews and dried cranberries and leaving the raisins and peanuts in a pile on Jack's backpack.

"You know all those generations in the family law firm? They all went to Harvard."

"Uh-oh. Why didn't you go, then?"

He shook his head at her pile of discarded trail mix and scooped it up, tossing it in his mouth. After he chewed and swallowed—Jack would never talk with his mouth full—he said, "I knew I was going to work at the firm after I graduated. If everyone there went to Harvard, I thought it might be a good idea to get a different perspective. Some of those law professors at Harvard are so old, they've been there since my dad was a law student."

"But you said that your family didn't care if you became a lawyer at all. So, what was the difference to them if you went to Harvard or Columbia?"

"It's hard to explain. I know my parents love and support me. But appearances are a big deal, especially to my mom. Honestly,

I think she was worried that people would think I didn't get accepted to Harvard Law."

"*Did* you get accepted to Harvard Law?"

He knit his brows together. "Of course."

Tegan rolled her eyes. "Of course," she repeated in the same cocky tone, and he grinned.

But what would his family have done if he hadn't gone to Harvard or Columbia? She knew what he'd said about his cousin the anthropologist, but she was willing to bet that cousin still had an Ivy League degree and a respectable academic job. What if Jack had chosen a career that they couldn't brag to their friends about? Or a girlfriend who didn't meet their standards? Would his family accept him anyway? And would Jack go against them if they didn't?

Jack brushed peanut dust from his hands. "So, I'm guessing that you studied English, or creative writing? Where did you go to college?"

Tegan busied herself with closing up the bag of trail mix and putting the cap on her water bottle. She didn't have anything to be ashamed of, and she *wasn't* ashamed… exactly. She knew she was a good writer, and she'd worked hard, staying up late every evening to write after double shifts at the diner. Her list of publications might be short, but they were in well-respected magazines and journals. And she and Jamie had high hopes that the editor's interest in her latest book might lead to something. Her little bit of success was hard-won and she was proud of that. But she wondered how her 'career' might appear to Jack—and to Jack's family. She didn't even have a degree in creative writing.

Tegan sensed Jack watching her as she stuffed the trail mix and water into his backpack, but didn't look at him. She reached over to zip it shut and his hand came down on top of hers.

"Hey." He gently tugged the backpack away from her and tossed it on the rock next to him. "Tegan, listen. I don't care where you went to college."

She sighed. "The thing is, I didn't go to college. Or—well, at least, I didn't finish. I went to community college for two semesters—I did half of an associate's degree in nursing and then I dropped out because we couldn't afford it, and I needed to work full time."

She turned to look at him, and a smile tugged at the corner of his lips.

"Nursing? Really?"

"Yeah. I would have loved to study creative writing, but Jamie was sick. We didn't have the money for a four-year college and I knew I should go into something where I could get a good job. Since I never finished, I ended up waiting tables anyway."

He jumped off the rock and stood in front of her. "Why did you feel like you couldn't tell me that?"

"It's not you, Jack. It's—everyone else." She looked down at her hands.

"My family? You think they'd judge you?"

"Wouldn't they?"

"My sister Liv will adore you. And my parents might have these expectations for my career, but they'd have nothing but admiration for you if they knew how much you've overcome. They love me and want me to be happy. And *you* make me happy. So, I know they're going to adore you too."

She studied the earnest expression on his face. Over and over, she'd misjudged him. If he could take her background in stride, maybe his family could too. More than anything, she wanted to believe what he was saying.

CHAPTER TWENTY-FOUR

Jack

After the hike, Jack waited in the car while Tegan paced the parking lot talking to her brother on the phone. When she got back to the car, he wasn't expecting her bright eyes or happy smile.

"How's Jamie doing?"

"Good. He sounded really good," she said, her voice upbeat. Maybe *too* upbeat. Jack couldn't miss the tension in her shoulders or the fear peeking out beneath the hope on her face. "The doctors said he has a couple of months, but they don't know Jamie. He's the strongest person you'll ever meet, and if anyone can beat the odds, it will be Jamie. Besides, doctors never really know, do they?"

Jack hesitated, torn between wanting to reassure her, and not wanting to encourage her denial about the reality of Jamie's illness. This slow and winding trip home was Tegan's chance to process what was happening, and to prepare for the worst so it wouldn't be a shock when the time finally came.

If there was one thing Jack wouldn't wish on anyone, especially Tegan, it was the shock of losing someone unexpectedly.

When a gunman had opened fire on Charlotte and dozens of other runners at mile eighteen of the San Francisco marathon, he'd been in his car on the way to meet her at the finish line. With the road closings, traffic, and the chaos of rescue vehicles racing to the scene, it had taken him almost two hours to get to the hospital. The worst two hours of his life. He'd finally ditched his car and run the last mile and a half to UCSF Medical Center, but when he got there, she was already gone.

Jack hadn't believed it. He'd actually argued with the doctor. If Charlotte were really gone, he would have sensed it somewhere deep down. Would have felt some sort of seismic shift in the atmosphere. Instead, all he'd felt was numb.

He hadn't known at the time that the pain would come later. When he'd gone home and stumbled over Charlotte's abandoned work shoes in the hallway of their apartment. When he'd tried to fall asleep in the bed he used to share with her. When he'd realized that nothing mattered if she was gone.

He shuddered at the memory. It was duller now, less like a knife to his heart and more like a broken bone that didn't heal correctly. It would probably ache forever.

Jack didn't want the same thing to happen to Tegan. She'd been through so much in her life already. He couldn't imagine it—her mother leaving, her father drunk all the time, moving from place to place, living in a car—and now her brother dying. He was becoming protective of her, wanting to shield her from any more pain.

He reached out and took her hand. "I hope so, Tegan. I really hope so."

She flashed him a grateful smile, and some of the tension eased from her shoulders.

He never would've imagined feeling this way when he'd picked her up at the diner a week ago. The last year had been the darkest of his life, and he'd been sure it would stay that way forever. But then Tegan came along. They had a few more weeks before he had to start his job in New York and, for the first time, he didn't need to analyze what it all meant, didn't need a plan for what was going to happen next. He just wanted to be with her, and be there for her. They'd figure out the rest later.

*

Jack leaned back in the driver's seat and settled into the ride across northern Colorado. Tegan alternated between typing in her laptop, fiddling with the car radio, and feeding him junk food. When she wasn't writing, they drifted between conversations sparked by stories on the news, whatever song was playing on the radio, or the beautiful scenery that whipped past the car windows. Jack had spent so much time alone that he'd forgotten how nice it was to have someone to laugh with, or to share the awe of a beautiful view.

The sun dropped beneath the horizon as they crossed from Colorado into Wyoming and pulled into a town that Jack's research showed had a couple of hotels and restaurants. They found a nondescript diner and went inside, choosing a corner booth. Jack ordered a salad—he'd been eating way too much greasy diner food lately—and Tegan ordered a slice of lemon pie. When their food arrived, Jack eyed her plate.

"Pie, again? Really?"

She waggled her fork before plunging it into the meringue fluff. "Like I said. Life is short. Eat dessert first."

He shook his head disbelievingly as she looked up at him over her pie. "Don't tell me you're one of those people who thinks there are only certain foods for designated mealtimes."

"Dessert is for after dinner."

"Not today, it's not." She stuffed a bite in her mouth. "Today it's just… dinner."

"I bet you eat leftover pizza for breakfast, don't you?"

"Oh, come on, Jack. You went to college. I know it was Harvard—" She put the word *Harvard* in air quotes, "—but surely, you've woken up hungover and eaten leftover pizza for breakfast before."

He shook his head slowly, as if he was sorry to break it to her.

"Well, that's very sad for you. You've obviously lived a deprived life." She took another bite. "If you're nice to me, I'll share my pie with you."

"No, thanks. I've had enough junk food on this trip. Thanks to *you*."

She grinned and slowly licked lemon filling off her fork, her shoulders shaking with laughter. It shouldn't have been sexy, but it was. Her comfort in her own skin and her ability to laugh at herself were more seductive than anything. Tegan wasn't afraid to say what was on her mind, or to act silly, to laugh a little too loud, or cry when she felt like it.

The world he'd grown up in was so focused on expectations and appearances that sometimes he'd felt suffocated. It wasn't as if he'd ever had a strong desire to rebel, so growing up, it hadn't bothered him so much. But then he met Charlotte and had to sit by as she gave in to her parents' expectations for her career. And when Charlotte was killed, most people in his social circle expected him to put a smile on his face and act like he was fine.

When he'd fallen apart at Charlotte's funeral, everyone had looked away and whispered behind their hands until his mother put her arm around him and led him to a private room. Some part of him had known that her concern wasn't solely about his well-being. She'd worried that his grief was making other people uncomfortable. She was conditioned to care about appearances, and he knew that she would've preferred that he stand up straight and compose himself until he was alone.

His gaze swept across Tegan, from her wild hair and jingling turquoise earrings to her faded gray T-shirt printed with the words, *I'm better in writing.* She sat back against the booth with one foot propped on the seat next to her, completely comfortable in her own skin. Tegan wouldn't have cared if he'd laid down on the floor in the middle of church and sobbed. She probably would have flopped right next to him, and to hell with anyone who felt embarrassed or uncomfortable.

His chest filled with a blend of anticipation and hope as he watched her from across the table. Maybe his mom was right, and Tegan wouldn't fit into his life in New York. But maybe he didn't completely fit in there anymore either.

"You know, I think I'd like to taste that pie." He climbed out of his seat and slid into her side of the booth.

She stabbed a bite with her fork, but before she could hand it to him, he leaned in and pressed his mouth to hers. A surprised hum vibrated from the back of her throat, and her lips curved into a smile under his as she kissed him back. She dropped the fork on the plate with a loud clatter and from somewhere far away, he sensed diners in the surrounding booths turn to look at them. People were staring, and public displays of affection usually made him uncomfortable. But Tegan tasted like lemons and sugar, and she was messing with his head.

After dinner, Jack consulted his notes and located the hotel he'd mapped out earlier that day. It was a nice-looking place that had a high rating on Tripadvisor. The five-star hotel they'd stayed in the night before had been more to his standards, but in small-town Wyoming, this was the best they were going to find. At any rate, it was certainly a step up from the Vista Verde or the Red Mountain Lodge.

In a few days, he'd take Tegan to Chicago. His parents had a downtown condo they'd bought a few years ago for when his dad was in town for business, but they rarely used it. Jack had already contacted the building manager to let him know they'd be coming. The manager confirmed housekeeping would stop by on the morning of their arrival to dust and vacuum. But for now, this place looked decent enough.

"Jack, we can't stay here." Tegan shook her head as he pulled into a parking spot at the hotel.

"Excuse me?"

"We need to find someplace else."

His gaze skated over the brick and stone façade. "What's wrong with it?"

She stared down at her hands, and her blue eyes that had been laughing and open back at the diner looked shuttered now. "I can't afford this."

His heart gave a painful kick. He reached over and took her hand. "It's okay. I'm paying."

Her head wagged back and forth, over and over.

Jack pulled the keys from the ignition. "It's not a big deal. I've got it."

Finally, she met his eyes. "It's a big deal to me. I don't want you paying for everything."

She knew he had money; she'd even made jokes about him being rich. But maybe she didn't understand that a few nights in a couple of decent hotels really were nothing to him. Pointing out just how little of a dent this hotel would make in his budget would be crass. But he didn't want her stressing over the cost when she had enough to worry about. Finally, he settled on: "I promise I can afford this."

"Jack, I'm guessing you could probably afford to walk in there and buy the whole damn hotel. I don't care. It's not about that."

Okay, he really didn't understand. "So, this is about your pride? You can't let me pay for anything?"

"It's about making an equal contribution. I've spent my entire life with my older brother taking care of me. I told you this." She blew out a breath and rubbed her temples. "I'm here, on my own, to finally take care of myself. Not to find another guy to pick up the slack."

His head thrummed with frustration. "I'm not sheltering you by paying for a couple of hotel rooms. Why should we be uncomfortable if we don't have to be?"

"Why do you need to be in a fancy hotel to be comfortable?" she shot back. "I was happy sleeping next to you in a hay loft. I could curl up in the back of this car as long as you were there with me."

He couldn't argue that he'd been more content on this trip— sleeping in barns and rundown motel rooms—than he'd been in a long time. When he was with Tegan, he didn't miss the fancy hotel rooms or gourmet meals or any of the other luxuries of his regular life. In fact, part of him dreaded going back to it. Dreaded giving up the simplicity of what they had out on the road for the social pressures and expectations that were sure to inundate him the second his Mercedes passed through the Lincoln Tunnel.

He flashed her a crooked grin. "If we sleep in the car, can we turn it into a rocket ship and take it to Mars?"

"*Yes.*" Her face lit up and at that moment, he would've given every penny in his bank account just to keep her smiling. "Jack, that's *exactly* what I'm talking about. I don't want you to pay for stuff, or to take care of me, or ease my way. I just want—" She hesitated, grabbing his hand and locking her fingers with his. "I just want you."

He kissed her then, leaning over the center console to pull her closer. And when she kissed him back, another weight lifted from his chest, leaving him lighter. For all he knew, he *could've* been on Mars. Because in that moment, he felt about as far as possible from that cold, dark apartment in San Francisco where he'd spent the past year of his life just trying to survive... and sometimes wishing he *hadn't* survived.

"Jack," Tegan murmured against his mouth when they finally stopped to take a breath. "We passed a perfectly good motel down the road. How fast do you think you can get us there?"

*

The moment they were inside their motel and had the door closed behind them, Tegan dropped her backpack on the floor and was back in his arms. He tugged her shirt over her head, and when they broke apart so he could pull off his own, she eased backward on the bed.

He paused then, his gaze tracing her from the scattering of freckles across her bare shoulders to the wild hair fanning out across the pillows. And finally, his eyes found hers, and his breath caught.

I might be on Mars. But if Tegan is with me… I could stay here forever.

CHAPTER TWENTY-FIVE

Tegan

"Well," Jack said, gazing at the World's Largest Ball of Stamps with his chin in his hand. "I think they've done an outstanding job with the color palette but, I must say, the size leaves something to be desired."

Tegan pressed a hand over her mouth to hide her grin as Jack continued to analyze the beach-ball-sized object in front of them as if it were a work of art on display at the Metropolitan Museum, instead of butted-up next to a gas station and a shop selling Western shirts in a Nebraska truck stop.

"I admit I expected something a bit grander in scale. The World's Largest Ball of Twine had at least ten times the diameter."

"Surely, sir, you know you can't compare the two," Tegan said in her best imitation of a nasally upper-class accent. "It would be like comparing Michelangelo and Picasso."

Jack arched his brow and nodded his head like a serious art critic before they both broke up laughing.

True to his word, Jack had veered off the highway—going a sensible speed, of course—at every corny tourist attraction they passed, placing bets on how many eggs they could cook in the World's Largest Frying Pan and gamely posing for selfies in front of the Clown Motel. He drew the line at staying there, however, and Tegan had a lot of fun arguing with him about it. But despite her teasing, it meant a lot to her that he'd planned all these ridiculous activities to take her mind off Jamie along the way.

They gave up on the ball of stamps, and Tegan grabbed Jack's hand, tugging him toward an archway into the store next door. A neon sign hung on the wall blinking *The Saddle Shop: Western shirts to make you look snappy.* Inside, oak shelves displayed rows of cowboy boots and clothing racks showed off colorful Western shirts.

"You should get a shirt," Tegan said.

Jack blinked. "You want me to buy clothes here? I don't think these are quite my style."

"It's not about style. When in Rome, and all that. Or in this case—" She flashed him a grin. "Where are we now? Nebraska?"

He shot her that skeptical expression she was growing sort of fond of, and rounded the clothes rack to look through some of the more restrained designs. She shook her head as he grabbed a couple of plain chambray shirts and headed for a changing room in the back that had swinging saloon doors straight out of a Wild West film.

Tegan turned back to the clothes rack and began flipping through the shirts until she found the perfect one. Moving around the store, she gathered several other items in her arms until she had everything she needed. Then she made her way toward the changing room.

"I found you some more things to try on," Tegan called to Jack. She eyed the black Western shirt with white piping sewed in a V across the chest and embroidered red roses tumbling over each shoulder, holding her breath as she slid it under the door. She followed the shirt with a box of pointy-toed black cowboy boots with a pale gray wing-pattern etched into the side, and a belt with a giant silver buckle.

She'd only meant to give him the clothes as a joke, another riff on their game of embracing the silly tourist activities. But somewhere beneath the surface, maybe there was a little more to it than that. The buttoned-up New York lawyer she'd met at the beginning of this journey would have scoffed at these ridiculous clothes. And maybe a little part of her worried that he was still under there somewhere. That this was all just a diversion until he got back to his real life. One where there was no room for her.

"Are you serious?" The jingle of the belt buckle and flip of the shoe box lid carried through the door, followed by silence. Tegan shifted her weight. Finally, with laughter in his voice, Jack called out, "Where's my hat?"

And with that, Tegan's shoulders relaxed. Less than a minute later, she tossed a black wool cowboy hat with a silver-studded band over the door.

"Okay," Jack said, after another moment of shuffling. "Are you ready?"

"God, yes," she said.

"I'm coming out, and you better take it all in, because I don't think this is ever happening again."

Tegan sank down on a bench against the opposite wall, facing the changing room. "I'm ready."

Jack swung the dressing room doors open and stepped out like a cowboy on his way to a shoot-out in the street. Tegan slapped her hand over her mouth as a giggle escaped. Jack stuffed his hands in his pockets and took a couple of steps toward her, widening his steps into a bow-legged stance, as if he'd just hopped off his horse.

"Howdy, little lady," he said, in a terrible Western accent, tipping his hat.

"Oh my God—" Her whole body shook with laughter now.

Jack ambled around the room, getting into the spirit of things. "Whaddya say we head on down to the saloon to wet our whistles?"

That buttoned-up New York lawyer she'd met at the beginning of this journey was nowhere to be seen. Tegan laughed so hard she fell off the bench and slumped on the floor. Jack sat down and pulled her back onto the bench with an affectionate grin stretched across his face. "You're the only person on Earth who could get me to do that. If my family and friends in New York could see me right now…" He trailed off with a shake of his head.

And with that, the little nagging uncertainty was back. "Yeah? What would they think?"

Jack stared past her at the dressing room doors for a moment, and then his gaze snapped back to hers. "I don't care what they'd think." He flashed her a grin and headed back in the dressing room to change his clothes.

While Tegan waited out in the shop, she grabbed a pair of weathered dark brown leather boots and pulled them on. Standing to admire how they looked with her jeans, turquoise scarf, and chunky cardigan, she was transported back to the Copper Canyon Bicentennial Festival. Back to Linda and Gil's dairy farm, and the kind older couple who'd welcomed two strangers into their home. And back to the dream of a small town she'd been chasing since she was a kid.

Jack appeared in the mirror behind her. As if he could read her thoughts, he remarked, "If you really plan to settle down in a small town, you look like you'll fit right in."

Tegan met his eyes in the reflection, her smile faltering. Jack lived just about as far from a small town as you could get. His family and his job were both in New York City and, at least until a couple of days ago, he'd been eager to get back there. Sure, he'd fit in at the bicentennial festival in Copper Canyon better than she'd expected. But that was one stop on his journey, not a whole change in lifestyle. And even if he wanted her to move to New York to try to make this work—a big *if*—could she ever be happy living there? She'd spent her whole life trying to escape the city.

"You should get those boots," Jack said, interrupting her thoughts.

Tegan shook her head, moving away from the mirror. The price was far more than she could ever afford. She pulled the boots off and set them back on the shelf.

Outside, Tegan's phone buzzed with Jamie's name. In a second, all the laughter and light from the moment drained away as she remembered what she'd have to face at the end of their journey.

"Go ahead and grab it," Jack said. "I forget something in the dressing room." He disappeared back inside the building.

Tegan sat on a boulder in the dusty truck stop parking lot and answered the call.

"Hey, T." Jamie's voice carried through the phone and, as always, just the sound of it comforted her. "How's it going?"

Tegan shook her head. Only Jamie would call to ask *How's it going* like everything was normal. "How are *you*, Jamie? How are you feeling?"

Jamie blew out a laugh. "I'm pretty much the same as I was when you asked me that yesterday. But we're here to talk about you. Are you back in that place you told me about? Copper Creek?"

"Canyon. Copper Canyon."

"So, you're there now?"

Tegan hesitated. She understood why he wanted her to go back there, why he'd want to see her settled somewhere she was happy. But Copper Canyon would never be home without Jamie. "No. I'm at a truck stop in Nebraska." Somewhere in the distance, thunder rumbled. She looked up at the sky, where dark gray clouds slowly rolled in overhead.

"Why?"

"Because the World's Largest Ball of Stamps is here," she said with forced cheer. "Although, let me tell you Jamie, it's highly overrated."

He sighed. "But why aren't you in Colorado? I thought we talked about this."

"Because," Tegan said, more subdued now, "Nebraska is on the way to Pittsburgh."

"Tegan, there's nothing in Pittsburgh for you." He sounded tired today, and she hated to think she was making things worse for him. She'd always listened to Jamie, and trusted that he knew best. But this time she wasn't sure he did.

"Don't say, that," she said, heart aching. "*You*'re in Pittsburgh."

"Like I said… there's nothing here for you. You said you love Copper Canyon, and you met great people there. Go back. I hate to think of you passing all that up to be alone."

Tegan gazed across the parking lot at Jack moving things around in the backseat of his car. She wasn't alone, but Jamie didn't know that. She hadn't told him about Jack, didn't want to worry him. But even more than that, she didn't want to raise his hopes that she'd have someone looking out for her after he was gone.

The last few days with Jack had been like a dream, traveling across Colorado, Wyoming, and Nebraska, stopping at every roadside attraction or beautiful overlook along the way. At night, they'd checked into cheap roadside motels, climbing into bed with boxes of pizza and bottles of gas-station wine, talking late into the night about her childhood, his family, or anything and everything that had brought them to that moment together. And when they'd grown exhausted with conversation, they'd stayed up even later, too occupied with each other to talk at all.

She'd never felt this way about someone before. She'd never let someone in before. It had always been her and Jamie on their own little island. People always left, or let her down. First their mother took off, then they lost their father to his addiction. Even their grandmother had sent them back home after that one magical summer.

And now, Jack had made his way into her heart, and she had absolutely no idea if he'd planned to stay there. With each mile they traveled together, she got to know him a little more, grew to care for him a little more. But as home drew nearer, she became increasingly torn between wanting to get to Jamie, and knowing it meant the clock was ticking for her and Jack.

But she couldn't tell any of this to Jamie. She'd burdened him enough, and he didn't need to worry more about her on top of his own problems.

A couple of fat raindrops hit the rocks around her, and a gust of wind blew her hair into her eyes. "I have to go." She wasn't going to change his mind, so she might as well get on the road before the storm blew in. She'd be home in a few days, and despite Jamie's urging to go back to Colorado, she knew he'd be happy to see her. "I'll call you again soon."

Tegan ran across the parking lot and got to Jack's car just as the sky opened up. He'd left a box on the seat so she pushed it to the floor to climb in before the rain soaked her. Jack flipped on the windshield wipers and eased the car onto the two-lane highway.

"Careful." He hitched his chin at the box by her feet, flashing her a quick smile before turning back to concentrate on the road. "That's a present for you."

"What?" Where could Jack have gotten her a present? Tegan picked it up, but it was wrapped in plain brown paper that didn't give anything away. She looked back and forth between the box and Jack.

"Open it."

Tegan slowly pulled off the paper and flipped open the lid.

"Oh!" she gasped. *The cowboy boots.*

He'd said he'd forgotten something, and had gone back to buy those boots while she was on the phone with Jamie. "I can't believe you bought them…" She trailed off.

"You had to have them." He flashed her another grin. "It didn't feel right, otherwise."

Tegan stroked the pattern on the side of the boots with her finger. She loved those boots, loved the romantic small-town notion of wearing them. But even more than that, she loved that Jack had been so thoughtful. "Thank you, Jack," she whispered, as the back of her throat began to burn and her eyes pricked with tears.

"You're all set for the next bicentennial festival," Jack murmured, swerving to avoid a giant puddle on the road in front of them.

She was saved from having to answer by the sound of the rain picking up and the steady beat of Jack's windshield wipers on double-time. They flipped back and forth like a high-speed metronome, but the rain continued to stream, practically opaque, down the windows. Jack squinted, ducking his head to try to see through the deluge, and Tegan quickly swiped at her wet cheeks with the palm of her hand.

He could break my heart.

With that thought came a rush of tears that rivaled the storm outside. She pressed her palms to her face to try to hold them at bay, and at that moment Jack glanced over. "Hey, are you crying?"

His eyes darted back to the road, now completely obscured by the river rushing down the windshield. Swearing, he swerved to the side of the road and hit the brake, bringing the car to an abrupt stop. "Tegan, hey. I didn't mean to make you cry..." He reached a hand out, holding it to her wet cheek, but she shook her head.

"No, you didn't. It's not you. It's—" She'd been walking a tightrope of emotions since the day she'd met Jack and, suddenly, it felt as if it had been raised a hundred feet off the ground. She could slip and fall, and for the first time in her life, nobody would be there to catch her.

"What is it then?"

Water pounded on the roof and the windows fogged up, leaving the interior of the car steamy and damp. He'd cranked up the heat, and suddenly Tegan felt hot and suffocated with Jack and the artifacts of a life she wasn't a part of in those boxes in the back.

She groped for the handle to her right and pulled. The door swung open, and in the next breath, Tegan jumped from the car into the pouring rain.

CHAPTER TWENTY-SIX

Jack

"Tegan, wait!" Jack grabbed for her arm as she leaped from the car, but Tegan was already outside. She slammed the door behind her, and through the stream of water flowing down his windshield, he could make out the shape of her leaning against the car.

He hesitated for only a second, and then he followed her out into the downpour. It immediately soaked through his clothes, leaving them plastered to his cold, wet skin.

"Tegan, what are you doing?" He was yelling to be heard over the beat of raindrops ricocheting off the ground. Her eyes were red, and he suspected she was crying, but her tears mingled with the water falling all around them.

"I don't know."

He stared at her, totally confused. Did something happen on the call with her brother? Why didn't she tell him? "Is Jamie okay?"

She shoved a dripping curl from her face. "He's fine. The same."

"So…" Had he done something to upset her? They'd been having fun in the western shop. And then… "Are you upset about the boots?" Was this about him paying for things again?

"No… Yes." She shivered, scrunching up her shoulders and rubbing her bare forearms with her hands. "*I don't know.*"

A gust of wind picked up, blowing right through him. "Well, can we at least go somewhere dry to discuss this?" He reached for her hand, but she pulled it out of his reach.

Tegan walked along the narrow white strip that marked the road, away from him, and then all of a sudden, she swung back around to face him. "I'm falling for you, Jack," she yelled.

For a moment, he wasn't sure if the vibration that shot through him was thunder in the distance or his heart banging out of his chest.

Stopping in front of him, she continued, her voice urgent. "I didn't come on this trip looking for this, and I know you didn't either. This is the worst possible timing, and I don't know how any of this is going to work. But..." Tegan shook her head, water droplets flying. "I don't care. I don't care that you live in New York, and I don't care that I've only known you for a few weeks, and I don't care that on paper we're completely wrong for each other. I'm falling for you, and I need to know if you're really in this with me or not."

She stood perfectly still now, right in front of him, waiting for an answer.

The rain fell harder, hitting the car like the barrage of a thousand bullets, and Jack's gaze swept over Tegan, soaked to the bone on the side of a Nebraskan highway in the middle of a rainstorm.

No, he hadn't come on this trip looking for this. In fact, if someone had told him the direction this trip would take when he was setting out, he probably would've hit the brakes and turned the car around. But here he was, his map crumpled in the backseat and his carefully laid plans crossed out so many times he barely knew which way was up.

He had no idea how they'd make this work. How she'd fit into his life, or how he'd fit into hers. If he were a better man, he'd end it before he broke her heart. If he were smarter, he'd stop this before she broke his.

But he couldn't. Because, despite his misgivings and doubts, and the mountain of obstacles blocking their way, he was exactly where he wanted to be.

There was a very good chance he was going to get hypothermia, coaxing this free-spirited hippie woman back into the car. Or a truck was going to barrel down that rain-soaked highway and plow right into them. He was so cold he could barely feel his hands. But he wouldn't change a thing.

And if that tiny voice whispered in his ear, reminding him that the anniversary of Charlotte's death was approaching, and pointing out the crack that still snaked across his heart… Well, the thunder drowned it out.

"Tegan," he said, taking a step toward her. "*I am in this with you.*"

This time when he reached out a hand, Tegan took it, and then she was in his arms. Her mouth found his, and she fisted her hands into his shirt, pulling him closer.

He would have stayed like that, kissing her in the rain forever, but he felt her shiver against him. He reluctantly took a step back, framing her face with his hands. "You're going to freeze to death out here. Come on."

They climbed back into the car. While she adjusted the heating vents, he grabbed her backpack from the back. "Here, you should change into something dry."

"Okay," Tegan said, through chattering teeth. "What about you? You're soaking, too."

Jack leaned into the backseat to dig through his own bag for dry clothes, and when he turned back around, she'd stripped down to her bra and underwear. She was so beautiful, he'd never get tired of the sight of her. Tegan caught him looking and smiled. And then, instead of pulling on her dry shirt, she tossed it on the dashboard and climbed over the center console right into his lap.

"Let's get you out of these wet clothes," she murmured, reaching down to pull his shirt over his head.

"We're in a public place," he protested, but his heart wasn't in it. Because even as he said the words, he was wrapping his arms around her, pulling her mouth to his, picking up where they'd left off out in the rain.

Thunder crashed, and water poured down the windows, obscuring them from the outside world as if they were alone together underneath the ocean. But though he felt like he was drowning, he knew it was Tegan keeping him afloat.

*

Over the next few days, they wound their way through Iowa and Illinois, finally pulling into Chicago late one afternoon. Jack had arranged to stay at his parents' empty condo for a couple of days, and he found he was looking forward to sleeping in a comfortable bed and maybe eating a meal that wasn't cooked on a griddle.

Tegan didn't seem completely happy about the Chicago plan, but she'd agreed to go along with it. He knew she was apprehensive about coming face to face with his normal way of life, but they couldn't ignore it forever. They couldn't always stay in cheap motels, and this was a low-stakes way to ease her into a small part of his world.

And he wanted her in his world.

Somehow, standing in out there in the pouring rain, with Tegan asking him if he was in this with her, had brought it all into sharp focus. And now, as they drew nearer to their separate destinations back east, Jack found himself going around and around in his head for a solution that would turn their temporary situation into something more permanent. Could he take another leave and stay in Pittsburgh with Tegan for a while? Or if the firm insisted on having him back at work in New York, maybe he could he fly back and forth each weekend? It was really only a short flight between the two cities. And then long-term, would Tegan ever be willing to compromise on her small-town dream and move to New York? Jack had plans to use these days in Chicago to show her that not all cities were like the gritty alleyways where she'd grown up. Maybe New York would grow on her someday.

Jack hadn't been anticipating his own nerves as they parked in the garage under the building and took the elevator to his parents' apartment on the twenty-fourth floor. He knew he was being quieter than usual as they followed the hallway to the door at one end, but he couldn't help it. That cold marble flooring and stately mahogany archway commanded the same silent respect as an imposing old library or courthouse. This wasn't the sort of place you ran through, hand-in-hand, stopping to make out against the vending machine because you couldn't possibly wait until you got to the room to kiss each other.

In fact, with each step that brought them closer to the condo door, those motel room adventures with Tegan began to feel farther and farther away. The last time he'd been in this hallway was with Charlotte. The last time he'd slept in the guest bedroom of his parents' condo was with Charlotte.

Jack reached for the keys in his pocket, and realized his hands were shaking. He stopped abruptly, and took Tegan by the arm. "You know what? I'd love some coffee."

"Do you think your parents will have the place stocked with some?" she asked.

Jack eyed the door to his parents' condo, looming at the end of the hall. He needed a few minutes to process these unexpected memories of Charlotte and prepare himself before he took Tegan in there. "Let's go to the place down the street." He spun on his heel and headed back toward the elevator. A hint of confusion flashed across Tegan's face as he walked past, but she trailed him down the hall.

*

As soon as he settled into his chair across the table from Tegan, steaming mug in front of him, Jack began to breathe easier. They'd talked about where they'd go to dinner on the walk to the coffee shop, and he'd teased her about how much sugar she'd dumped into the latte the barista had handed her. These easy interactions with Tegan felt comfortable, normal again. That panic back in the hallway was only momentary shock at being confronted by a place where he'd used to be with Charlotte. But now that the first rush of memories was behind him, he could move on and start making new memories with Tegan.

"So, I was thinking," Jack said, focusing his attention on the woman in front of him. "I could use my dad's office to print out a couple of your published stories while we're here." He said it lightly, because even a week or two ago, she'd seemed nervous about sharing her work with him. From the way he'd mocked her over her writing when they'd first met, he couldn't completely blame her. "I really want to read the one that inspired the book you're writing." He still didn't know very much about it.

Tegan met his gaze. "I'd love that, Jack," she said, an intimate smile tugging at her lips.

It should have pleased him to see the happiness in her eyes, and the trust that had been growing ever since that moment in the rain when they'd made a bigger commitment to each other. But the erratic beat of his heart didn't feel quite so exhilarating as it had back then. In fact, it was making him a little nauseous.

He gazed past her out the window, and they mostly made small talk as they finished their coffee.

Back in the hallway in front of his parents' condo, Jack turned the key in the lock and pushed the door open. He motioned for Tegan to go first, and she took a tentative step inside. "Oh, it's very pretty," she remarked, turning to look around the room. But Jack could only spare a cursory glance at the gleaming hardwood floor stretching across the open living room to a wall of windows overlooking downtown Chicago. He seemed to be stuck in the doorway, his gaze glued to the space over the fireplace. To the spot where his engagement photo with Charlotte sat on the mantel.

Why hadn't he considered what it would feel like to bring Tegan to a place where he'd spent so much time with Charlotte? Considered what it would feel like for these two worlds to collide? He'd made promises to Tegan. Promises he'd meant. Standing in the rain somewhere in the middle of nowhere, telling her they were in this together, it had all felt so simple at the time. But nothing about this was simple.

Another wave of nausea washed over him.

"Jack?" Tegan murmured, and he blinked, finally snapping out of it. She stared at him with wide eyes clouded with worry.

"Sorry, I spaced out for a minute there," he said, stepping into the room and placing his bag on the floor. *Get it together.*

Tegan kicked off her shoes and padded across the smooth floor, making her way to a gleaming white marble bar separating the living room from the kitchen. Four chrome and wood bar stools stood neatly in a line in front of it, and she hooked the strap of her dusty bag over the back of one of them. She'd obviously miscalculated the weight because the bar stool tipped backward, landing with a crash.

"Oops! Sorry," Tegan said with a rueful smile in his direction.

He walked over and grabbed her backpack, handing it to her, and righted the stool. He'd also forgotten to consider what her propensity for spilling things and knocking them over might do to his parents' place.

At that moment, footsteps echoed from down the hall on the other side of the living room, and a woman's steely voice called out, "My goodness, what is all that racket?"

Tegan's wide-eyed gaze swung to his. "I didn't know anyone would be here. Is that the house cleaner you said was coming?"

Jack froze, staring as a late middle-aged woman appeared in the doorway, tall and rail-thin, with the chiseled cheekbones and smooth, unlined forehead of someone who wasn't planning to age without a fight. There was no way this woman was cleaning for anyone.

Jack sucked in a breath. Finally, he managed to choke out, "Mom? What are you doing here?"

CHAPTER TWENTY-SEVEN

Tegan

Tegan tried to hide behind the bar stool as best as she could. Since they'd committed to making this work between them, she and Jack had talked about her meeting his family, but they'd never moved past the 'someday' time frame. She thought she'd have some warning, some time to prepare. At least some time to smooth down her hair and put on a clean shirt.

"Oh, Jack, it's so good to see you!" Jack's mother strode over to where he stood rooted to the spot. She put her hands on his shoulders, holding him at arm's length and looking him up and down before crushing him against her. Still appearing dazed, Jack gave her a lame pat on the back in return.

His mother let go, and he stumbled backward, running his hand through his hair. "Seriously, Mom. What are you *doing* here?"

"What kind of greeting is that for your mother?" She shook her head and her sleek blond bob swished. "I have a colleague at the University of Chicago that I've been trying to meet with for a while now. And then you had that dreadful accident, and your trip was delayed. So, when you texted that you'd be here, I thought this would be the perfect time for a trip." She pressed her hand against Jack's cheek. "I've been so worried about you."

Jack ducked away from her like a toddler who didn't want his face wiped. "Why didn't you tell me?"

"I thought it would be fun to surprise you." His mother flashed him a smile that didn't reach her eyes. Or maybe they'd frozen from the Botox.

Tegan had only known Jack for a few weeks, and she knew he hated surprises. So, his mother had to be incredibly dense, which didn't seem possible, given her PhD in psychology or, more likely, she'd known he wouldn't be thrilled that she was planning to come, and she'd decided to show up unannounced.

"Are you staying here?" He pinched the back of his neck, wincing slightly.

Tegan stood by the kitchen island, shifting her weight from one foot to the other. She was still holding her backpack, so she slowly lowered it to the floor. Had his mother even noticed her standing there? Jack hadn't introduced her, and the more she hovered silently, the more awkward this was going to get.

"Yes, of course. Where else would I stay?" Jack's mother's eyes finally darted to Tegan, giving just the slightest flicker down to her feet and then back to her head.

Tegan stood up straighter and resisted the urge to smooth the wrinkles from her embroidered peasant shirt. They'd been driving all day with the windows down. She hadn't seen a mirror in hours, but her hair had to look like it had survived a tornado, and her cheeks must be pink and wind-burned. Why was his mother here *now*?

Jack's mother blinked and then turned back to Jack. "I've set up in the master bedroom, and your friend can have the guest room. I'll make you a bed on the couch."

Tegan waited for Jack's response to that, right along with his mother. Who did his mother think Tegan was? Had Jack mentioned her at all? They hadn't talked about any of this, but they really should have.

Jack finally seemed to remember that she was there. "Mom, I'd like you to meet Tegan."

Tegan walked into the center of the room, clutching the thigh of her jeans to discreetly wipe the sweat from her palm before holding it out to his mother. "It's nice to meet you, Doctor—" She abruptly stopped talking. Because she didn't know Jack's mother's last name. A flush crept across her, the kind that turned her cheeks bright red and left pink splotches across her chest and pale arms. *I don't know Jack's last name.* In all their late-night conversations, it never came up. Why hadn't she glanced at his ID when he was checking into a hotel? Why hadn't she asked?

What would his mother think of her? Sleeping with a man whose last name she didn't even know. And he didn't know hers, either. What did that say about their relationship?

"Bennett. Kathleen Bennett." Jack's mother reached out and returned the handshake. Her skin felt cool and dry. "Please, call me Kathleen."

"It's nice to meet you, Kathleen."

"You too, Tegan. I understand from my daughter, Olivia, that Jack has been traveling with you?"

"Yeah—I mean, yes." Tegan said. "He has. Been traveling with me. Or I guess I've been traveling with him, since it's his car…" Tegan cleared her throat. "Um. It's kind of a funny story, actually. We were in a diner in Arizona, and Jack tried to pay with his credit card. They only took cash, so they were giving him kind of a hard time. I think it was just a joke—they weren't really going to make him walk all the way to Diablo to use the ATM. But anyway, I paid for his lunch and he offered me a ride."

Kathleen's frozen eyebrows managed to raise a fraction of an inch. "My goodness. That doesn't sound very funny. How far was Diablo?"

Of course, his mother wouldn't think her son getting harassed was funny. "Oh, um, just a few miles. But like I said, they were just kidding…" *Shut up, shut up.* Tegan glanced at Jack for help, but he just stood there with his back as stick-straight as the floor lamp in the corner. And contributing about as much to the conversation.

Tegan tried to shake it off. People always liked to talk about themselves. She just had to turn this around and get Kathleen talking. "So, Jack said that you're a psychologist?"

"Yes, that's correct. I have a private practice in New York, and occasionally I teach a class at Columbia. What do you do, Tegan?"

"Um. I'm a writer. I've been published in a couple of literary journals and magazines…"

Kathleen nodded and remained silent. Tegan rubbed her palms on her jeans again. "I'm, uh, I'm working on a novel right now. That's partly why I've been traveling… to work on my novel." Damn it, this woman was a professional at getting people to talk. She knew all the tricks. Tegan coughed, just to fill the silence, and the sound seemed to drag Jack back into the room.

"Well, it's great to see you, Mom. And it certainly was a surprise. I think I'll show Tegan to the guest room." He moved toward the kitchen and lifted her backpack. Somehow it looked even grubbier up against his pressed khakis and polo shirt. She had yet to solve the mystery of how he managed to sit in a car for eight hours and not end up all wrinkled.

"That's a good idea." Kathleen eyed the creases on Tegan's blouse. "I'm sure she'd like to clean up a little. We can all have dinner tonight. I'll make a reservation at Jean Marc's."

Jack had been planning to take her to a Mexican restaurant he said she'd love. She'd been picturing someplace dark and loud with colorful margaritas and salsa music playing in the background. She'd also pictured them coming home later, happy and tipsy and barely able to keep their hands off each other.

Jean Marc's, whatever that was, wasn't going to serve tacos and margaritas, and at this point, she wasn't sure if Jack would be sleeping with her or on the couch.

She trailed behind Jack down the hall, to a guest room with views of the city and the same understated, elegant décor as the living room. It was easily the most beautiful, luxurious room she'd ever stayed in, and damn how she wished with all her heart to be back in a shitty motel on the side of the highway. A room with rough, worn carpeting, a creaky double bed covered in a chenille bedspread, and the sound of tractor trailers zooming past the cheap vinyl window.

Jack set her backpack on a chair in the corner and gestured to a door across the room. "That's the bathroom over there, if you want to shower. My mom will probably make a reservation for seven." He turned to leave, but she reached out and grabbed his arm.

"Jack, wait."

He stopped and looked at her.

Why are you acting so cold? I thought you said your mom would like me. Are you sleeping on the couch tonight? How had she felt so close to him less than an hour ago, and now she couldn't even say what she was thinking? She finally settled on, "Is everything okay?"

"Yes. I'm sorry." His expression softened. "I'm surprised to find my mother here, and not really prepared to see her."

"She doesn't know about us."

He rubbed at the stubble on his jaw. "Well, I think she suspects."

Tegan took a page from his mother's book and remained silent.

After a moment he sighed and raked his hand through his hair. "She knows I've been traveling with someone. I planned to tell her about you—*us*, after I was back in New York. I never would have thrown you in like this."

"And here I thought she'd like me. You seemed to think so a few days ago."

"She *will* like you. This is not about you. This is about her being overprotective of me, because she's worried that…"

"What?"

He winced and looked away from her. "That… I'm not over Charlotte."

Are you over Charlotte? But she couldn't ask. She knew the answer.

"I'll talk to her, okay?" He finally met her gaze. "She's going to love you once she gets to know you better."

Tegan looked up into his familiar blue eyes. He'd given her a ride when he didn't have to. He'd come back for her in the biker bar in Colorado, even when she was acting like a brat. He'd held her and comforted her when she found out her brother was dying. He'd spent the last few weeks making her smile, making her happy, making her feel things she never felt before.

And, most of all, he'd promised her he was in this with her. She trusted him. She had to believe that they were going to be okay.

CHAPTER TWENTY-EIGHT

Jack

Jack closed the bedroom door and stood in the hall taking slow, deep breaths. He needed to get a hold of himself. Ever since he'd walked into the apartment, he'd felt like an ambulance siren was wailing inside his head, growing closer with each passing minute.

How could he have forgotten that the last time he stayed here was with Charlotte? Now he couldn't help seeing her everywhere he looked. On the couch where they'd shared a bottle of wine, in the kitchen where they'd cooked dinner together. In that same guest bed where they'd…

What had he been thinking, bringing Tegan to this apartment?

He closed his eyes and shook his head. He'd been thinking that he was finally getting over Charlotte, and that the past few weeks with Tegan had been amazing. He'd brought her here because if they were going to have any kind of a future, he couldn't avoid his life any longer. They couldn't stay on the road in their own little world forever.

Jack sighed as he heard the clink of a glass on the coffee table in the living room, reminding him that, to complicate things even more, his mother was out there waiting for him. He found her in the living room, flipping through a magazine and sipping a glass of white wine. When she saw him, she smiled and set the magazine on the coffee table.

"I can't tell you how happy I am to see you." She patted the couch next to her.

He perched on the edge of the cushion and turned to face her. It wasn't like him to be so abrupt with his mother, and he owed her an apology for how he'd acted earlier. "It's good to see you, too. I'm sorry about how I spoke to you when I arrived. I wasn't expecting to see you."

She waved off his apologies. "I should have told you I was coming. I was excited to see you, but I should've remembered that you don't really like surprises."

No, he didn't. Never had. He liked plans, and itineraries, and to think through his next move. Since Charlotte died, those impulses for control had grown stronger. He had a routine and he never strayed from it.

But then he met Tegan.

Still, he'd had a plan for how to introduce her to his family. His mother had already heard a little about Tegan on the phone, but that was different. That was before he'd realized what he really felt about her. He would've told them all about her and their relationship when he got back to New York, and shared her story of how much she'd been through. Given them a chance to slowly adjust to the idea that their son had feelings for a free-spirited writer from Pittsburgh. And then he would've introduced them. Probably starting with Liv first.

It was too late for that now. All he could do now was manage the situation.

"So, about Tegan."

"Yes." His mother's voice was clipped. "Tegan. She seems like a nice young woman."

Jack studied his mother as she took a sip of wine. He knew from almost thirty years in the orbit of wealthy Upper East Side women that sometimes calling a person "nice" was the equivalent of saying "bless her heart" to well-bred Southern ladies: an insult wrapped in a kind phrase.

"Yes. She *is* nice. And smart, and funny, and talented."

His mother blinked at him from over the rim of her wine glass, and then slowly lowered it to the coffee table. "So, you *are* involved with her."

He stared past her out the window.

"Jack."

He sighed. "Yes. I am."

"Mmm hmm."

She was doing that psychologist thing, making vague noises and waiting for him to say more. At least she wasn't reflecting his feelings back to him, or quoting from a textbook. That would come later, if past experience had taught him anything.

"I didn't plan it. But, yes. I have feelings for her. And if you get to know her, I think you'll really like her. When you hear about her childhood, and what she's been through, you'll be amazed. Her mom left, her dad was an alcoholic. She and her brother were entirely on their own. But she doesn't let it define her. She has such a positive way of looking at the world…" He trailed off, aware that he was babbling, which was not like him. He snuck a glance at his mother, whose spine had grown straighter as he talked.

"You sound quite taken with her."

"Yes. I guess I am."

She nodded, but her face remained expressionless. "And I assume she feels the same way about you?"

"I—" He remembered rain mingling with the tears on her cheeks. *I'm falling for you, Jack.* "Yes, she does."

His mother picked up her glass of wine again. Was he imagining that she took an extra-large gulp? "And have you talked about what you'll do after you go back to New York?"

He hesitated. She wasn't going to be happy about this. "I don't know when I'll be back in New York. Her brother is in Pittsburgh.

He's sick, and I don't think he has much time. I need to get her there, to be there for her when she's going through that. Then we'll figure it out."

"You're going to Pittsburgh?" Her voice raised an octave. "For how long?"

"I—well—it depends on her brother. I've been thinking that I may take a longer leave from work to be there with her if he's... near the end."

His mother inhaled a breath and set her spine even straighter, if that was possible. "You're not serious, Jack. You're actually thinking of taking leave from the law firm to be with a girl you met in a diner a few weeks ago?"

When she phrased it like that, he did sound unhinged. He closed his eyes, remembering the nights in the motels. The conversations in the car. How Tegan made him laugh for the first time in way too long. He couldn't possibly explain it to his mother. The way he'd been going through the motions, but not really living. Until Tegan came along. Not only did she make him want to get back to his former self, she made him want to be a better person.

"Jack, are you under the illusion that you're in love with Tegan?"

He couldn't discuss his feelings for Tegan with his mother like this. They were too new, too uncertain.

"Look, honey." She leaned in, patting his leg, her body language shifting from disapproving mother to sympathetic therapist. "I understand. She's very pretty, and outgoing, and she's going through a difficult time. You've been through a trauma that nobody should ever have to experience. I can see how you would feel a certain responsibility for her."

"A responsibility?" he echoed. "What are you *talking* about?"

"Just that I know you have a lot of guilt over Charlotte. That you feel like you weren't there for her the way you should have been. Am I wrong about that?"

Jack pressed his lips together, shaking his head. "What does this have to do with anything?"

His mother reached over to stroke his hair off his forehead, and he arched away from her. "Well, here is this young woman with a very hard life, going through a difficult time. And maybe you see a chance to help her the way you couldn't help Charlotte."

He shook his head slowly. He cared about Tegan, so of course he wanted to be there for her while her brother was dying. But getting Tegan back to Jamie wasn't some messed up way of absolving his guilt over Charlotte.

Was it?

He remembered the anxiety that had washed over him when she said Jamie wanted her to go back to Copper Canyon. That absolute certainty that he couldn't let her make a huge mistake. He rubbed his hand over his eyes and looked up to find his mother watching him.

"Jack, it's understandable that you're confused about your feelings for Tegan. It's only been nine or ten months since Charlotte passed and—"

"Eleven and a half months. It will be a year on April nineteenth."

She shook her head. "Well, Jack. That's my point. You're counting down the days until the anniversary, aren't you?"

Not intentionally, but it was always in the back of his mind. When he woke up a few days ago, and the date on his phone flashed April first, it had been like a knife twisting in his gut. Every day since then, it was the first thing he thought about. April second. April third. *April nineteenth.* He couldn't wait until it was finally behind him.

"Jack, you've been through a terrible trauma. It's not the sort of thing you can move past in a couple of months, or even years, especially without extensive therapy."

She'd been pushing therapy since he collapsed at Charlotte's funeral, and he'd been deleting her emails with the names and phone numbers of therapists she recommended. He opened his mouth to argue with her, but she cut him off.

"When someone passes away like Charlotte did—violently and suddenly—it's a much different experience than, for example, when your grandfather died at the end of a long life. You're mourning not just the loss of the person you loved, but of the whole life you planned together."

He knew this already. Had felt it a million times over the last year. The wedding they would have had with their whole group of friends in the wedding party. Charlotte's brother as his best man, and Liv as her maid of honor. The trips they would have taken; all the places they wanted to travel together. The children they might have had. They'd both wanted at least two, close in age.

His hands shook. He knew this. Why was his mother scratching at these old wounds, making them bleed again, when he was finally starting to heal?

She squeezed his hand. "Having been there on your way to the marathon, and then rushing to get to the hospital, not knowing. The trauma from that isn't insignificant, Jack. You're suffering from a chronic stress disorder."

Her voice was gentle, kind, but it didn't matter. The memories of that day rushed back, suffocating him.

"And then there's the way you've hidden away in your apartment, cutting off all your friends, barely going outside other than to work. All those are clear indications of complicated grief, which again, doesn't just go away because you met someone new. And there's no doubt it's exacerbated by these feelings of guilt you've been carrying."

He pressed his shaking hands to his temples, wishing she'd stop talking.

"Jack, I'm not trying to discourage you. But I worry that you're substituting your relationship with this young woman for the real work of healing from the trauma you suffered. I'm not sure if you'll ever really be able to move on unless you spend some time coming to grips with what happened to Charlotte."

Was she right? He didn't know. He couldn't think. His chest felt like someone had parked a truck on it. Had he been fooling himself into believing he had feelings for Tegan, when really, he'd been trying to escape the pain and grief of losing Charlotte? *Was* he atoning for his failure to stand up for Charlotte by thinking he could save Tegan?

Sitting there in his parents' apartment, where he and Charlotte had shared the guest room just last year, with the photos of his family on the mantel, the doubts seeped in. His old life came into sharp focus, while motel rooms and silly tourist attractions felt as scratched and vague as an old home movie.

Tegan was the first woman he'd been attracted to since Charlotte died. Maybe he'd convinced himself it meant more than it did.

At that moment, Tegan walked into the living room, and his gaze roamed over her, waiting for that kick in his gut that would show his feelings for her and prove his mother wrong. She was pretty—beautiful even—with her long, reddish hair flowing down her back and her cheeks flushed pink. But something was wrong with him. It was like his heart had frozen over—because he couldn't feel anything at all.

He rubbed his forehead, his head pounding, and wished he could lie down in the guest room and skip the rest of the night. He avoided Tegan's eyes, and the hopeful, wary expression on her face. Instead, he stared at Charlotte, whose photo smiled down at him from the mantel. Charlotte, who should still be here.

Tegan took a step toward him and then stopped. Her head swiveled to the photo of Charlotte and then back to his face. Something in her expression seemed to shut down, to fold in on itself. An avalanche of self-hatred rolled over him. He was horrible and broken and he didn't deserve Tegan.

His mother flashed her a thin smile. "I hope you found everything you need in the guest room."

Tegan smiled in return, friendly, appreciative, but he'd seen her smile a hundred times before and he knew this one wasn't real.

"Yes, thank you." She perched on the leather chair across the coffee table. "The room is lovely."

"I'm glad to hear it." His mother pressed her hands together. "Well, unfortunately, I was unable to get a reservation at Jean Marc's. But there's a very nice sushi restaurant just down the street. How does that sound for dinner?"

Jack studied his mother's face. She had to be lying. His parents were good friends with Jean Marc and his wife, and they were never "unable to get a reservation" at his restaurant. She must have realized that Tegan would never fit in there. But sushi? He thought about Tegan's diet of spray cheese, Twizzlers, and pie. Had Tegan ever had sushi?

"Oh, I don't know if Tegan—" he began.

She cut him off. "Sushi is fine. I love sushi."

CHAPTER TWENTY-NINE

Tegan

Tegan sipped her cup of sake and counted the minutes until this horrible meal could be over. It wasn't just that she hated sushi—did people really like eating slimy, uncooked fish?—it was that Jack had somehow morphed back into the guy she'd met in that diner back in Arizona. Or worse. At least in Arizona, he'd shown some emotion for her, even if it was annoyance. Now, he sat next to her with his shoulders square and his back as straight as a board. When he described their trip to his mother, it was like he was reciting facts from the guidebook. There was no fun or adventure in it, no hint that he was the same person who took silly pictures of her in front of the world's largest frying pan or pulled the car over just to kiss her.

She knew Jack well enough to know that he'd probably never be overly affectionate in front of his mother. But a smile would've been nice. A hand squeeze, or something to let her know that they were still in it together. But he sat in the next chair and barely even looked at her. When he finished talking to his mother in stilted tones about their trip, he went silent, gazing out across the restaurant.

She knew his mother barging in on them unannounced had upset him. Jack liked to plan things out, and this wasn't the way he wanted her to meet his family. But just sitting there not saying a word wasn't helping the situation.

Tegan fiddled with her chopsticks, fighting the urge to drum them on the table, just to fill the awkward silence. "So…" Tegan began, not even really sure where she was going with this. Talking to Jack was useless, but Kathleen was actually making attempts at civilized conversation, and Tegan felt obligated to play along. "I, um, I saw some books on the coffee table back at your apartment. Are you reading anything good?"

Kathleen's face lit up into a genuine smile. "Yes, I just finished a wonderful book. I can't stop thinking about it." She named the title of a recent bestseller.

Tegan blinked in surprise. Not only had she read it, she'd loved it too. The book was a sweet, quirky story about a socially awkward young woman. It had a been a huge commercial success, but there was nothing particularly highbrow about it. She'd expected Kathleen to say she was reading one of the classics. Or maybe Freud or Carl Jung or something.

"I read it for my book club last month," Kathleen said. "Next month is my turn to choose, but I'm afraid that one will be hard to beat."

"I loved that book, too," Tegan said, shyly. "Maybe I could recommend a couple others that you might like. I do a lot of reading."

"Yes, I'd think you would, in your profession." Kathleen reached for her purse and pulled out a little notebook and pen. "That would be wonderful. Thank you."

Tegan scribbled down a list of titles and authors while they chatted about other books they had in common and, for a few moments, she almost forgot that this whole situation was painfully awkward. But then Jack excused himself to go to the bathroom, and Kathleen tucked the notebook back into her purse.

As soon as Jack disappeared across the restaurant, Kathleen straightened her shoulders and crossed her hands in front of her, staring intently across the table. "Jack told me about your brother. I'm so very sorry."

Tegan traced her finger along the design on her chopstick. "Thank you."

"I get the impression that you and my son formed an intense bond pretty quickly."

Tegan raised her eyebrows in surprise. Kathleen was cutting right to the chase, wasn't she? "I guess you could say that. We haven't known each other that long, but we've basically spent every minute together. So, you know, it hasn't really been like a normal couple of weeks."

Kathleen nodded. "And I suppose that Jack told you all about Charlotte and the tragic way that she passed?"

Was Kathleen worried that Tegan didn't understand what Jack had been through? With all those long car rides and late nights in hotels, they'd talked about everything. He was still mourning Charlotte and, in some ways, he probably always would be. She didn't expect him to get over it because he'd met someone new. But it didn't mean that what they had wasn't real or special. "Yes, we've talked a lot about her."

"So, you're aware that all those boxes in the back of Jack's car—those are Charlotte's things? Her clothes, jewelry, even her books from medical school."

Tegan blinked, momentarily speechless. All that stuff was Charlotte's? He'd kept everything she owned and was carrying it all across the country? This was one thing he hadn't shared.

Kathleen leaned in. "He refused to get rid of anything. He wouldn't even put it on the moving truck that took most of his own belongings."

Tegan did her best to brush it off. He hadn't told her about the boxes, but he hadn't lied to her, either. So what if it was painful for him to sort through Charlotte's things? Plus, some of that stuff was probably valuable, or things her family might want, like the jewelry. Maybe he didn't want to just throw it all away. "Well, I'm sure he'll deal with her stuff when he's ready."

Kathleen pressed her lips together and looked out across the restaurant as if she were considering her next words. Then she turned back to Tegan and took a deep, slow breath. "And did he tell you he—" Her voice caught. She paused and cleared her throat. "Did he tell you he tried to take his own life a week after Charlotte's death?"

Tegan's heart stopped beating, and her vision flashed like a strobe light. She gripped the table with shaking hands to keep from falling over in her seat. Shock and nausea churned a whirlpool in her gut. The phrase *take his own life* echoed in her head, over and over. For a crazy second, she actually thought that Kathleen was making it up. To be cruel. To drive her away. She couldn't be talking about Jack. *Not Jack.* But no. Nobody could fake that haunted look in Kathleen's eyes.

Kathleen reached a hand across the table. "Are you okay?"

God, no. How could she possibly be okay? She was going to throw up raw fish all over this nice table.

Tegan pressed her hands to her hot cheeks and nodded anyway. Kathleen seemed to take this as an invitation to tell her more details.

"The doctor had prescribed some sleeping pills, to help him get past the shock. One night, Jack got drunk and took the whole bottle." Kathleen closed her eyes, shaking her head slowly, as if she were trying to erase the image from her mind. "Thank God, he and Charlotte had given a neighbor a key to water their plants when they were out of town. Jack and Liv usually talked in the evenings, and when she couldn't get a hold of him, she called the neighbor, who found him in time."

The reality of Jack in that kind of pain hurt so badly she nearly doubled over. Jack had almost died, had tried to *take his own life.* It was unbearable. She knew that he'd gone into a depression, had broken down and hidden out. But she'd had no clue that he'd been suicidal.

"Tegan," Kathleen's voice cut in gently. "I'm not telling you this to imply that Jack doesn't have feelings for you. When he talks about you, I can see how much he cares about you. But I think you should know the whole picture. Jack has been through an enormous trauma, one that he's never really dealt with emotionally."

It was like she was sinking under water and Kathleen was yelling at her from the surface. Everything was faint and muted.

"He blames himself for Charlotte's death. He thinks he should have stepped in more when he saw her making what he felt were poor decisions. And now he's planning to put his whole life on hold to make sure you get to Pittsburgh and to help with your brother. He believes he failed Charlotte and he doesn't want to fail you, too. But that's no basis for a relationship."

Tegan nodded numbly as understanding washed over her. Jack wasn't slowly getting over Charlotte's death, and starting to build something with her. He believed that he hadn't been able to save Charlotte. Guilt overwhelmed him every day. So, he'd focused his energy on saving her instead.

It would be so easy to let Jack save her. To let him take charge and get her home to Pittsburgh. She could introduce him to Jamie, and maybe Jamie would feel better knowing that he wasn't leaving her alone. She could have Jack's strong arms around her when she finally said goodbye to the most important person in her world.

And then what would happen when it all fell apart? When Jack looked up from his guilt and grief and realized that she wasn't who he wanted her to be, that she was just a poor substitute? He'd leave, and she'd still be that woman who couldn't take care of herself.

And what if he got worse again—spiraled downward—and it was her fault? Her whole body shook, her head pounded, and her vision blurred.

But one thing came into sharp focus.

It was time to go.

CHAPTER THIRTY

Jack

Jack woke up feeling like he'd been in a bar brawl—and lost. Every muscle in his body ached. All he wanted to do was sleep for the next week, but he couldn't. He'd forgotten to close the blinds when they went to bed, and the sun streamed through the wall of windows like someone had flipped a spotlight right on his face.

And then there was Tegan. Sitting on a chair across the room, watching him. He sat up, and she leaned forward, propping her elbows on her knees, clutching one hand with the other.

"Hey," Jack said, warily. They hadn't spoken on the way home from dinner the night before. As soon as they got back to the apartment, she'd disappeared into the guest room, and by the time he'd said goodnight to his mother and went in after her—sleeping on the couch would have made the awkwardness so much worse—she was already asleep. Or pretending to be. He'd climbed into the bed next to her and she didn't move. While he laid there tossing and turning for the next three hours.

"You're up early," he said now.

"Yeah." She looked down at her hands. "I have to go."

For the first time, Jack noticed she was already dressed in jeans and her worn Beatles T-shirt. Her bag sat by her feet with her jacket on top.

"Go… Where?"

"Pittsburgh. Home."

Did something happen with Jamie? If she was in a hurry to get to Pittsburgh, he had to snap out of it and help her get there. "Yeah, okay. Let me take a quick shower." His feet dropped to the floor next to the bed. "I can be ready in twenty and we can head out. We'll probably make it to Ohio by this afternoon."

Surely once they were on the road again, all these doubts and feelings of uncertainty and sadness over Charlotte would evaporate. He had to believe that.

Tegan continued to stare at her hands, and something about her expression made him stop reaching for his T-shirt. "What is it?"

"I'm not going to make it to Ohio, Jack." She finally lifted her head, squinting as if it hurt her eyes to look at him. "I booked a flight to Pittsburgh. I have to be at O'Hare at 11:30 this morning."

"You're—" His head snapped back like she'd hit him. And that was pretty much what it felt like. "You're flying to Pittsburgh. This morning?"

"Yeah."

"Alone?"

"Yeah." Her chest hitched.

Jack moved in her direction, but then stopped a few feet in front of her, part of him wanting to reach for her, and the rest of him wary. Finally, he perched on the bottom of the bed, facing her. "If you were in a hurry to get there, why didn't you tell me before you booked it? I could have—"

"You could have… what?" Her voice was flat. She let out a small, skeptical laugh that knocked the wind right out of him. "Come with me?"

"Well, yes. I thought that was the plan."

She played with a silver ring on her finger, spinning it around. "You're a successful attorney with a new life to start in New York. And I'm a homeless vagabond with a book to write. These last few weeks have been—" Her voice caught and she took a breath. "They've been fun. But I think it's time we get on with getting on with it."

She echoed so many of the doubts that had been plaguing him since yesterday afternoon. He should be relieved that she was making this easy on him. So why did it feel like he was drowning? "You don't really want that."

Her eyes flickered to his, and for a moment she looked like she wanted to say no, but then she shook her head. "It's for the best."

For the best. He had no idea what that meant. The best for who? There was no scenario here that felt like it would be anything less than awful. But leaving it like this had to be the worst. "Tegan, I'm not going to let you go all by yourself. I'll get a ticket and come with you."

She pressed her lips together and looked at the ceiling. Finally, she took a deep breath and looked at him. "You can't get over Charlotte by fixing me, Jack." Her voice was a whisper. "You can only do it by fixing yourself."

He wanted to deny it. Wanted to tell her that she didn't know what she was talking about, but the last twenty-four hours had tossed him around like a tidal wave. He was shaken and battered, desperate for air, and he had no idea which way was up.

Before he could say anything, she got to her feet and threw her bag over her shoulder. "I should go."

He stood up and took a step toward her. And then stopped. "Give me a few minutes. I'll drive you to the airport."

She nodded. "I'll be in the living room," she whispered, grabbing her bag and slipping out the door.

On the 45-minute drive to the airport, Jack almost pulled the car over a hundred times. Turned in his seat and grabbed her and begged her not to go. But then the doubts crept in and the words stuck in his throat.

It was true. He wasn't over Charlotte. He probably was suffering from post-traumatic stress and complicated grief and whatever other psychobabble terms his mother used. And he had so much shame. For how he'd treated Tegan, how he'd used her. He was nothing but a thousand broken pieces, and he couldn't ask her to wait around while he tried to put them back together. Especially when he honestly didn't know if he'd ever be whole again.

When he pulled up at the departure gate, he finally turned and met her eyes. The turquoise shine was gone and she stared back at him—dull, gray, shuttered.

"I'm sorry," he said. The two most meaningless words in the English language.

"Me too," she whispered.

And before he could say anything else, she grabbed her bag and bolted from the car. He watched until she disappeared into the airport, her dusty black backpack the last sight of her as the glass doors slid shut.

He picked up his phone and fired off a text to his mother and Liv—*I'm fine. Don't worry. I'll see you in New York soon*—before shutting it down and tossing it in the glove compartment.

And then he pulled out onto the highway, and he drove away.

CHAPTER THIRTY-ONE

Tegan

Tegan pushed open the apartment door. Her gaze immediately snapped to the man sitting on the couch, an old quilt thrown across his lap and a book in his hand. The breath she felt like she'd been holding since she left Chicago finally rushed from her lungs.

Jamie.

He looked up, and a huge grin stretched across his face, smoothing out the hollows in his cheekbones and masking the dark circles under his eyes. God, it was good to see him. She launched herself at the couch, throwing her arms around him, a little surprised when she knocked him sideways.

Laughing, he groped for the back of the couch with one hand and shoved her hair out of his face with the other. "Easy there, T. I'm not at my best at the moment."

She sat up and scooted to the other couch cushion. "Oh, shit. Did I hurt you?"

Jamie slowly pulled himself to a sitting position. "Nah, I'm fine. It's going to take more than my wimpy little sister to cause permanent damage."

Her gaze swept over him, and the sight soothed her like a favorite blanket. His tall frame folded into the couch, his laughing brown eyes, the Pittsburgh Pirates hat he'd practically lived in since his hair started to fall out from the chemo. It was all so familiar and comforting. "I missed you, Jamie." She took a slow breath to smother the burning in her eyes and smooth out the barbs choking the back of her throat. "You have no idea how good it is to see you."

"You too, T."

Tegan leaned over, resting her head on his shoulder, noticing how thin and bony it felt against her temple. Almost a decade of working construction had sculpted Jamie until he was broad and beefy, the kind of guy you wouldn't want to go up against in a fight. But now he was skin and bones, and all that couldn't have happened in the few months she'd been gone. How had she missed that he was growing brittle and frail, like an old house where the walls were starting to give way?

Probably because in her mind, her big brother would always be a skyscraper. Strong and solid, larger than life. Cancer couldn't change that, nothing could ever change that.

She sat up so she could look him in the eye. "Jamie, I know you said you're done, but there could still be treatments that might work. One of those research trials. Something that could give you more time." She hated the tremor in her voice. She'd promised herself that she wouldn't do this; that for once, she'd be the strong one.

But she couldn't. She'd tried, and look where it got her. How was she supposed to go on alone? Jamie was her North Star, guiding her in which direction to go. Without him, she was lost.

He stared across the room at the opposite wall. "Tegan, you know I'd do anything for you."

She nodded. It was the only thing she knew for sure.

Anguish slashed across his normally sanguine face. "Don't ask me to do this. Because you know that I probably would. And—" He pressed a shaking hand to his forehead and finally looked at her. "Just please don't ask me."

A tear trickled down her cheek as she watched her big brother's head bow and his shoulders slump. Even after everything, somehow, he was still more torn up over letting her down than he was about his terminal diagnosis.

She stared down at her hands, humbled by all the he'd done for her. And aware of how little she'd given in return. And, in that moment, she knew that this was her chance. He'd spent his entire life caring for her, protecting her, and he would continue to sacrifice everything if she asked him to.

She could ask him to. Or she could make the biggest sacrifice of her life and let him go.

CHAPTER THIRTY-TWO

Jack

Jack drove for days. Blindly, and without a destination, he drove, unable to stop. It was as if the more miles he traveled, the more Charlotte and Tegan and the last terrible year of his life were finally behind him.

He headed through Wisconsin, Minnesota, North Dakota, only vaguely aware of his location by the signs announcing his entrance into a new state. When his gas light came on, he stopped at convenience stores to fill up the tank and buy crappy junk food that he ate while he drove, not even caring when he sloshed coffee on the floor mat or spilled potato chip crumbs on the passenger seat. When he grew too tired to drive, he stopped at roadside motels and collapsed on the cheap, sagging mattresses in a deep, dreamless sleep.

Eventually, he crossed the border from Oregon into California. From there, the expressway tapered into smaller back roads that zigzagged south and west through the forests near Mount Shasta. Late that afternoon, he took a fork in the road and found himself winding up a two-lane highway that hung high on the coast above the Pacific Ocean.

He slammed on his brakes as somewhere inside his head, the fog lifted.

The ocean.

He was on the west coast. He'd fled the Pacific a month ago. How did he end up back here?

His gaze turned westward as the sun begin its descent toward the sea and, for the first time in days, he pulled the car over and got out for something other than gas, food, or sleep. He hopped the guard rail and made his way down a rocky path until he came to a steep cliff. Near the edge, his Top-Siders slid in the gravel, sending a few stones tumbling over the side. His stomach rocked as he realized how far away the ocean lapped against the rocks.

He peered down at the water churning beneath him. If he were to slip over the side of the cliff, would he hit rock first, or plunge straight into the deep, dark water? What would that cold feel like, closing over him?

As Jack stood there, mesmerized by the ocean swirling below, the sun dropped a notch and the light slanted right into his eyes. He put his hand on his forehead to block the glare and for the first time, he saw the slashes of tangerine, red, and purple in the sky. They radiated out from the sun, burning their way deep into some dark place inside him. His breath caught, and he unconsciously took a step back from the edge of the cliff, sinking down to the ground.

He didn't know how long he sat there, watching the inferno pulse and blaze in the distance. Finally, as the last of the sun's rays shimmered on the water, he tore his eyes away and glanced at his watch, but he barely registered the time. Instead, his gaze zeroed in on the date.

April nineteenth.

The anniversary of Charlotte's death.

Somehow, he'd made it. There had been so many times when he almost hadn't.

At that moment, something pulled in his heart. A tiny thread, like the time he'd fallen off his bike and needed stitches in his chin. The pain of all that he'd lost hadn't healed, not even close, but the wound wasn't quite so gaping, so raw and exposed.

Jack watched the sky until the last ray of sun faded and the moon appeared over the water. Then he pulled himself up from the ground and slowly made his way back up the dirt path to his car. He opened his glove compartment and powered on his phone. Ignoring the dozens of messages from his family and work, he typed a quick text to his mother.

I'm okay, I promise. I'll be home in a week. Maybe you could email me that list of therapists you recommend.

Then he eased the car back onto the highway, pointing it east, away from the Pacific. Finally, with a destination in mind.

Home.

He'd come so far. Too far to turn back now.

CHAPTER THIRTY-THREE

Three months later

Tegan

When people ask what I want to be when I grow up, I tell them I want to be like Jamie.

Jamie never went to college, but that was okay. College was for people who didn't know things, and Jamie knew everything. Jamie knew how to pilot a spaceship to Mars, and he knew where all the best treasures were buried. When I had scary dreams, Jamie knew how to chase away the monsters.

Jamie could've been a hostage negotiator for how well he knew how to talk his way out of a situation. When other eighteen-year-olds were playing sports and hooking up with girls, Jamie was busy convincing a judge that he was responsible enough to take care of his little sister when our dad died of liver failure.

Jamie knew how to be a mother, and a father. A big brother, and a best friend. He helped me pick out my prom dress, and he put food on the table. He taught me how to drive, and held my hand when my first boyfriend dumped me.

Jamie knew how to love with his whole heart.

*In a childhood that could have been as dark and bleak
as a cave, Jamie was the firelight.
When I grow up, I want to be like Jamie.*

*

The moment Tegan got home from her shift at the diner, she knew something was wrong. The apartment was quiet, but that wasn't unusual on the mornings she worked the breakfast rush. Derek and Rebecca had day jobs, and Jamie usually took a late-morning nap before she came home to throw herself in the chair next to his bed and re-enact the diner drama of the day.

The living room looked the same: her sheet and pillow sat neatly next to the worn couch where she'd been sleeping for the past few weeks, and her backpack leaned in the corner. But a stillness hung in the air, heavy and thick, like the eerie moment of calm before a tornado rolls through.

She dropped her bag on the floor and ran for Jamie's room. She found him awake and sitting up, but his face was ghostly pale and he breathed in and out in slow, labored gasps. She raced to the bed and put her hand on his cold, clammy forehead.

"*Jamie.*" She slid her hand down to his cheek. "You aren't feeling well. I'll call the woman from the hospice for more medicine." It was just a bad spell, that's all it was. A little boost in his painkillers and he'd be fine.

He waved away her concern, weakly, with one hand. "No. I don't need anything."

She pulled her phone from her pocket. "But—" His skin was ashen, and he was trembling. She had to do something.

But Jamie shook his head, and something about the intensity of his expression stopped her. She put the phone on the side table and slowly sank down on the chair next to the bed. "Are you in pain?"

Please God, just don't let him be in pain.

"No." But just that little bit of effort left his chest hitching for a breath. "No, I'm fine. Just sit here—with me."

She took his hand and pulled it to her heart, clutching it as if he'd fallen overboard into the ocean, and as long as she held on she could keep him from going under. She squeezed tightly, desperately. Willing him to hold on. She wasn't ready to let him go. There was so much she wanted to tell him. Still so much unsaid.

"Jamie," she choked out. "I hope you know you're the best big brother I could have ever asked for. I—"

She was a writer, but at that moment, words failed her. He'd given her everything. How could she express an entire lifetime of gratitude? A tear rolled down her cheek and she swiped it with her palm.

Jamie's face twisted and his eyes filled as he reached out and took her other hand. The warmth from it radiated up her arm, comforting and reassuring, even now.

"Tegan, I was a lonely kid with nothing but two checked-out parents until you came along. You were the best thing that ever happened to me. Never, ever doubt that."

"I love you, Jamie," she whispered as more tears spilled over. "I love you so much."

"I love you too, T. Promise me you'll be happy. That's all I want for you."

She sniffed, wiping her eyes with her sleeve. "Wherever you're going next, promise me you'll be happy too."

And then he gave her that grin that was vintage Jamie, wide and unrestrained, and it lit up even the darkest corners of her heart. "Well, you can bet I won't rest in peace. That sounds so fucking boring."

She laughed as the tears spilled over, dripping on his hand that was still clenched in hers.

His smile slowly faded and his eyes clouded over, and at that moment, he looked utterly exhausted. "I'm just going to take a little nap, okay?" he mumbled. "I'll see you on the other side."

Tegan nodded as he reclined back into the pillow and closed his eyes. A peace settled over his face as his gasping lessened and each breath grew long and slow. She watched the rise and fall of his chest, reassured by its steady cadence. Tightening her grip, she bent forward in her chair and rested her cheek on top of their joined hands. She had no idea how long she stayed there by her big brother's side, the same way she'd spent all the days of her childhood. Sometimes they were crammed into the front seats of a rundown station wagon, or sprawled out on the floor of a shitty studio apartment because they couldn't afford beds. But it never mattered where they were, because they had each other. Lulled by the sense of calm and safety she always felt when she was with Jamie, she drifted off to sleep.

*

When Tegan woke, she knew immediately that Jamie was gone. His body was in the room with her, but his spirit—that beautiful, indomitable spirit—had flown off somewhere far away. She hoped it was somewhere amazing, somewhere that he could follow his dreams, and find love, and have all the things that he never had in this life.

And in that moment, an overwhelming feeling of gratitude hit her. That she'd made it home in time and spent these past few weeks laughing with him over the silly little parts of their days and all of their shared stories.

That she'd had a chance to say goodbye.

For the first time in weeks, she allowed herself a fleeting thought of Jack. She'd tried to bury him in a dark hole where she didn't have to think about him, because she couldn't bear to waste one minute of her precious time with Jamie dwelling on all that she'd lost with Jack. But now, she realized fully, if it hadn't been for Jack, she might never have come back here. If she hadn't met him, and learned his own story of unbearable loss, she might still be out there on the road somewhere, searching for something that was here the whole time.

Jack was gone from her life, and the sharp edges of that fact might never dull. But it was worth every bit of pain, every second of heartbreak, to have been here with Jamie.

CHAPTER THIRTY-FOUR

Jack

Jack's phone buzzed in his pocket just as he was heading out of Liv's front door on his way to work. He dropped his briefcase on her entry table and, as he fished his phone out of his pocket, thought again about how it was time to find his own place. He'd been at Liv's for three months now, and knew he was overstaying his welcome. Liv hadn't even slept there the night before. She had a new boyfriend and was staying over at his place more often lately. She'd never say it out loud, but Jack was sure she'd like to have her space free of her older brother.

The problem was that none of the condos he'd looked at buying appealed to him. His mom's friend, a top real estate agent in the city, had shown him dozens of beautiful buildings with fantastic amenities and sweeping views of Central Park. But nothing felt right. He just kept hearing Tegan's voice telling him that she'd be happy sleeping in the back of the car as long as they were together. Asking him why he needed to stay someplace so fancy.

Jack's phone buzzed again and he saw the word *Mom* flash on the screen as he swiped to answer.

"Oh, Jack, I'm glad I caught you. Are you at work?"

He checked his watch. "On my way."

"Well, I won't keep you long. I just wanted to call because Angela Wallace told me that you RSVPed 'no' to the senator's annual fundraiser at the club next Saturday. I told her it was probably a mistake."

Jack sighed and stepped back in the apartment, dropping down in a high-backed chair by the door. "It's not a mistake. I did RSVP 'no'."

"But we always go to Senator Wallace's fundraisers."

He shrugged as if she could see him through the phone. "Well, *you* can still go."

"But what am I going to tell Angela about why you're not there?"

He shook his head, guessing *I don't give a damn* wasn't going to go over well with his mother. "Tell her I'm giving my money to a politician who supports a ban on assault weapons."

"Jack!" His mother's horror vibrated through the phone. "I'm not going to tell her *that.*"

"Well, tell her whatever you want. I'm not going."

"What will you do instead? You can't just hide out in Liv's apartment."

He didn't plan to hide out in Liv's apartment. In fact, he hadn't been hiding out since he came back to New York. He'd thrown himself into work, collaborating on a couple of interesting new cases, and even socializing with his colleagues after hours. He'd been out for drinks twice that week. It helped that most of his new co-workers hadn't met Charlotte, so while they all knew what happened, none of them looked at him with those uncomfortable, pitying expressions he'd gotten back in San Francisco.

"I'm going hiking." It just popped into his head, but the more he thought about it, the more he liked the idea. He'd get out of the city, drive upstate, and spend some time in nature. He hadn't been hiking since… Tegan.

He closed his eyes, remembering that day in Rocky Mountain National Park. Her blue eyes had shone with excitement when they'd crested a hill and the valley spread out before them with the snow-peaked mountains in the distance. No wonder the view of Central Park from an overpriced apartment wasn't doing it for him.

"Hiking?" His mother's astonished tone implied he was going dumpster diving. "Why would you want to go hiking?"

Jack laughed. "For exercise. Fresh air. It's a lot healthier than Senator Wallace's stuffy party. Someone is going to choke on one of those mini cheese puffs one of these days."

His mother was clearly not amused. "Fine," she murmured in a clipped tone. "I'll tell Angela that you were called away for work. But this is the third major event you've skipped since you've been back. I know that everyone understands what you've been though with Charlotte, but I'd hoped you'd consider getting back into the social scene a bit when you came back to New York. People are going to start to talk."

He leaned back in his chair. A year or two ago, the threat of the senator's wife gossiping about him would have had some sway over his decision. But now, it was all the more reason not to go to the party. "Mom, I think it's time you realize that I'm never going to settle back into my old life the way I was before. That life... it's gone. I've changed, and I'm not going to change back again. I can't help but think a lot of that stuff is a ridiculous waste of time now."

The phone went silent except for his mother's light breathing. Jack heard a clink that, at this hour, he hoped was the sound of a coffee cup and not a stiff drink. Finally, she sighed. "You know, Jack, I think this is the influence of that woman, Tegan. The one you met on your cross-country trip. You were never like this before."

Jack's spine straightened. "I never lost my fiancé before, either," he snapped. "Tegan has nothing to do with this." Except... he wasn't sure that was entirely true. Of course, losing Charlotte had changed him. But something had flipped inside him out there on the road, in truck stops and dairy farms and roadside motels. Something that made him unable to see the point of going along with social obligations for the sake of appearances.

That short time with Tegan had taught him to appreciate a simpler way of life.

"*Well,*" his mother said, in the same tone he imagined she used to gossip with the senator's wife. "I'm just glad Tegan had enough sense to realize that a man who'd been through what you had—with Charlotte, and… *everything*—was in no position to be getting involved with someone new. I admit I was surprised that she left so readily. I thought for sure she'd keep hanging on, dragging you to Pittsburgh to get involved with her sick brother and the whole sad ordeal."

Jack froze. He'd never talked to his mother about why Tegan left, and he'd told Liv only that they'd decided they weren't right for each other. So why would his mother assume that Charlotte's death had anything to do with it? Unless she knew something he didn't. "What do you mean that Tegan *left so readily?*" Jack asked with steel in his voice. "Readily, after *what happened?*"

"Oh!" His mother said in a falsely bright tone. "Oh, you know, I just meant that she probably realized that you were… anyway, it doesn't matter, does it? The point is that it was for the best."

A few years ago, he might have let that change in subject go, not wanting to rock the boat. But now, he didn't care if the whole damn vessel sank right to the bottom of the sea. "It sure as hell *does* matter. What did you do?"

"Nothing! I didn't do anything." She hesitated, and Jack let the uncomfortable silence echo through the phone. There wasn't a chance in hell that he was going to help her out here. After all, hadn't he learned from his psychologist mother that sometimes the way to get someone to talk was to say nothing at all? Finally, in a quieter voice, she said. "I may have mentioned that you were still struggling with Charlotte's death, and needed time to heal."

"Is that all?"

His mother took a sharp intake of breath, but didn't answer.

Jack lunged from his chair and paced across his sister's apartment. "You said Tegan knew about *everything*," he prompted. "Did you tell her about the thing with the pills?"

"I—well." For the first time in his life, his mother was speechless. And that told him all he needed to know.

Jack scrubbed a hand across his eyes. While he deeply, deeply regretted his suicide attempt, and would've given anything to go back and do it all differently, he wasn't ashamed of it. It had been the absolute lowest moment of his life. A black hole so dark, no light had shone through. At the time, he'd felt like it would be that way forever. But he'd clawed his way out and survived it. When he was ready, he *would* have shared it all with Tegan.

But it wasn't his mother's story to tell.

He paced across the apartment in silence, and finally, his mother managed to whisper, "I was only trying to protect you, Jack. Back then, you weren't in the right place emotionally to be involved with someone else. Were you?"

Jack stumbled to a stop in Liv's hallway. "No. I wasn't."

"Well, then," she said, more upbeat now. "Everything turned out for the—"

"No." He cut her off. "I wasn't in the right place to be with someone else. But it was *my decision to make*. On *my* terms. Not yours. It was up to *me* to decide if and when and how it ended."

After another pause, his mother finally said, "You're right." She cleared her throat. "You're right, and I'm sorry."

Jack sighed, flopping back into the chair he'd abandoned earlier. "Didn't they teach you about something called *boundaries* in your psychology classes?"

"Of course they did, Jack."

"Well, you might want to dig out that textbook and brush up a little. Because from now on, you and I are going to have a lot of practice with boundaries. No meddling. No telling me what to do." He paused. "No getting involved in my relationships."

"Are you *in* a—?" his mother said, and then abruptly stopped talking. "Um, I mean, never mind. Forget I asked."

Jack couldn't help but laugh.

"You know I love you, Jack," his mother said. "I just want you to be happy."

"I know. I've got to get to work."

He hung up the phone, feeling lighter. He still didn't have it all figured out, what happy meant for him. But he was slowly getting there.

*

A few days later, Jack left Liv as she got dressed for the senator's party and, relieved he wasn't spending this gorgeous Saturday inside the Harvard Club, headed two and a half hours north of the city. In a little town off the highway, he parked his car and connected with an eight-mile trail loop that meandered past a thirty-foot waterfall to a fire tower with a view of three states.

As he sank down on the bench at the top of the tower, Jack's thoughts drifted to Tegan again. He'd taken the rickety wooden stairs at a slow, careful pace, trying to avoid getting vertigo from glancing over the rail as the ground grew father away. But Tegan would have raced fearlessly to the top, her eyes flashing with laughter as she glanced behind her and called him a slowpoke.

What was Tegan doing at that moment? Was she with Jamie, holding his hand and helping him through his final days? Or had Jamie already passed?

A stab of regret hit him squarely in the chest. Regret that he wasn't there with her, that he had no idea what she was feeling now. A part of him knew they'd done the right thing by going their own ways. When she'd said that he'd only get over Charlotte's death by fixing himself, she'd been right. He still had a lot of work to do and wasn't ready to be in a relationship with anyone right now. But Tegan had dragged him out of the dark fog he'd been wrapped in, and as the sun began to seep through the haze, he could see just how much he cared about her. Just how much he missed her.

Jack slowly made his way back down the stairs and finished his hike just as the setting sun hit the tops of the trees and the shadows grew longer. He got in his car and headed for the city, but with every mile, he found himself easing his foot off the gas, trying to put off the moment when he'd leave the mountains behind and hit the Saturday evening traffic on the George Washington Bridge.

About thirty minutes into his drive, he noticed his gas gauge edging toward empty, so he turned off the highway at a little town at the base of the mountains. It was about two hours from New York—he could have easily made it to Liv's apartment in time to see if she wanted to grab dinner after the party—but after he filled the tank, he realized there was something about the place that drew him in and compelled him to stay for a while.

Maybe it was how it reminded him of a little town in Colorado. The mountains that rose up in the distance were the lush, rolling hills of the Catskills, not the hard granite of the Rockies. But unpretentious shops and restaurants lined the main street, and the locals he passed gave him welcoming smiles.

He stopped in the first diner he came to, and the waitress, an older woman with long, curling grey hair and an easy smile, led him to a table and handed him a menu. He only glanced at it for a second before looking up. "What do you recommend?"

The waitress tapped her pen on her notebook. "Well. The beer-can chicken is pretty good. It's the special today. But if you really want to know what I recommend, I'll tell you. The chef's blueberry pie won the New York State Fair pie contest three years in a row. One just came out of the oven and I suggest you don't miss your chance."

Jack's mouth twisted into a smile. "Pie for dinner, huh?"

"Life's short. Eat dessert first." She gave him a wide smile and an exaggerated wink.

He folded the menu with a slap and handed it to her. "I'll take a piece of the blueberry pie, and you can throw some ice cream on it, too."

"You got it, honey."

Jack settled back into the booth as the sounds of the diner drifted over him. When had places like this become familiar, comfortable even, instead of foreign and irritating?

The family at the next booth was celebrating a victory of the last little league game of the year. The kids were too loud, banging their forks on their plates and begging for chocolate milkshakes. But instead of the wave of annoyance that would have washed over him a few months ago, he found himself hoping the kids got their milkshakes. Life was too short to skip out on milkshakes.

The bell on the door jingled, and a middle-aged man in a flannel shirt wandered in. He waved at a couple of people in the corner booth and then sat at the counter, nodding at the waitress. "Hey, Dolores."

Dolores plunked a cup in front of him and filled it with coffee. The sounds of their conversation drifted over to Jack's booth.

"How ya doing, Hank?"

He shrugged. "Can't complain."

Jack smiled into his coffee, reminded of Gil Miller from back in Copper Canyon. He wondered how Linda and the kids were doing.

Hank tore the top off a packet of sugar. "You know anything about that sign I saw over at the Foley property? Did they finally put that old place up for sale?"

"Yep." Dolores handed him the creamer. "Phil Busbow from the realty was in here the other day. He said he's listed it."

Hank nodded slowly. "Pretty good spot right outside of town."

"Yeah, Phil says there are about seventy-five acres. The land goes all the way up the mountain. Great views. The house and barn need work, but they've got good bones."

"Well, maybe we'll get someone in there who'll fix it up. I hope it won't go to one of those developers who want to turn it into a subdivision."

From somewhere behind the counter in back, a voice called out, "Order up."

Dolores grabbed a plate off the pick-up window, and carried it over to Jack. "Here you are, honey. I hope you enjoy it. Can I get you anything else?"

Jack hesitated for a moment. His mother kept insisting that he not make any life-altering decisions when he was still going through a hard time. But that was before they'd established their new boundaries.

And, somehow, he knew this was exactly what he needed.

He turned to Dolores. "Actually, you can."

CHAPTER THIRTY-FIVE

Tegan

Derek and Rebecca invited Tegan to stay at their apartment for as long as she wanted, but the day after the funeral they held for Jamie with his small group of friends from the construction company, Tegan packed up her backpack and headed out. There was nothing left for her in Pittsburgh.

She stopped in the diner to pick up her last paycheck—$65.76. Added to the $58 she'd made in tips on her last shift, and the $308 in her checking account, it was just enough for a bag of snacks, a bus ticket, and four twenties stuffed in her bra for emergencies.

Three days later, she climbed the steps of an old white farmhouse and knocked on the door. It swung open and before she could say a word, she was yanked against a soft flannel shirt as a graying braid slapped her in the cheek.

"Oh, my goodness. Tegan!"

"Hi, Linda," Tegan whispered.

"What a wonderful surprise. Come in!" Linda pulled her into the house. "Let me just call Gil, and tell him you're here. He's out in the barn." She tugged at Tegan's backpack and dropped it on a chair, ushering her into the living room.

Tegan sat on the couch as Linda hurried out of the room. She could hear her talking excitedly in the next room. A few minutes later, Linda came back with a cup of tea and placed it on the coffee table in front of Tegan. "I want to hear everything.

What are you doing back here in Copper Canyon? How's Jack? Do you need a place to stay?"

Tegan's eyes welled up as Linda buzzed around her. She'd spent everything she had to get there because she literally had nowhere else to go. What would she have done if they'd turned her away? She nodded and managed to choke out, "I'd love a place to stay. Just for a little while."

Linda sat on the couch and placed a warm hand on her knee. "Oh, honey, why do you look so sad?"

All of a sudden, Tegan was spilling the whole story. About Jamie, and Jack, and her book, and the last dollars in her checking account.

"Well, now, you stop crying and don't worry about a thing," said a voice from across the room. "You can stay here as long as you like."

Tegan looked up to find Gil standing in the doorway, arms crossed over his broad chest. The sight of the warm smile on his weathered face had her crying all over again. Linda pulled her into her arms and Tegan breathed in the faint scent of fabric softener, and straw, and cinnamon, feeling her body relax for the first time since Jamie died.

Every morning, Tegan got up at dawn to help Gil with the cows. She shoveled manure and hauled bags of animal feed, her body growing weary from the physical labor, but her mind clearer than it had been in months. After her farm chores were finished, she sat at the kitchen table with Linda, drinking coffee and talking about Jamie. Telling stories that at first she could barely choke out without crying, but by the end she was inevitably laughing, because you couldn't help but laugh when talking about Jamie.

When it was time for Linda to disappear into the office to look through the weeks' orders and balance the books, Tegan took long walks through the pastures, discovering a spot next to a winding little creek with a view of the mountains. She sat there with the sun warming her shoulders, breathing in the earthy breeze blowing across the field, and scribbling memories into her journal.

In the late afternoon, she sat on Gil and Linda's front porch, and she wrote. All that summer and into the fall, she poured out her pain and sadness, her longing for Jamie and her heartbreak over Jack, onto the pages of her book.

And when the day came that she finally finished, she stayed up all night reading it by the light of the full moon shining across the clear Colorado sky. Just as the sun peeked its way up over the horizon and the rooster crowed out in the yard, her eyes swept over the final paragraph, and she snapped her laptop shut.

It was the best story she'd ever written. Jamie would have rolled his eyes and laughed, saying that he didn't know how she'd managed to make an ordinary guy like him sound so interesting. She'd taken some liberties with the plot, but Jamie's spirit shone through every page. The world was going to love him as much as she did.

That winter, she sent the book off to literary agents. And the agents responded. *It's a beautiful, heartbreaking story. It made me laugh and cry. I adored Jamie and his sister from the first page.*

By spring, Tegan had an agent and a two-book deal with a publisher. Her advance wasn't huge, but compared to what she started with, it was a fortune. If she lived simply, she wouldn't have to worry about money for a long time.

She'd made it. She'd accomplished the dream she'd hoped would lead to a new life for her and Jamie. Except that Jamie wasn't there to share it with her. But sometimes she could feel him in the wind blowing across the fields, and hear his voice in the gentle sway of the pines. Jamie would have been so thrilled at what she'd achieved.

As she sat at Linda and Gil's kitchen table looking over the list of cities where her publisher wanted to her to travel to when they launched her book, she thought about the other part of her dream: her wish to find a small town for her and Jamie to settle down and live a simple life.

She'd be leaving Copper Canyon soon, and she wasn't sure if she'd be back for more than a visit. Gil and Linda were like family now, and they would always be in her life. But Copper Canyon was so deeply marked by the pain of her past, and her grief over Jamie. This was *their* dream, not hers alone.

And then there was Jack.

Her heart ached every time she crossed Main Street at the spot where they'd danced at the bicentennial celebration. And the image of Jack standing in the barn, sweaty, dirty, and covered in straw would forever be etched in her memory.

She didn't know if she'd ever be able to forget Jack if she stayed in Copper Canyon, or to move on and be happy. And she owed it to Jamie to move on and be happy. Jack had gone back to his life in New York, and it was time for her to look toward her future instead of her past; to live in a way that would make Jamie proud, and make all of his sacrifices worth it.

CHAPTER THIRTY-SIX

Two years later

Jack

Jack stepped through the sliding glass doors of the downtown New York City building that housed the law firm of Townsend and Associates. A warm spring breeze ruffled his hair, reminding him that he should schedule a haircut while he was in the city. He'd grown more relaxed with his appearance since the view from his office had changed from glass and chrome skyscrapers to a vegetable garden and seventy-five acres of woods. But he still came to the city once a month to meet with clients and have dinner with his family.

The sun's early evening rays hit him as he walked down the sidewalk, and he shed his suit jacket and rolled up his shirtsleeves. The soprano trill of birds emerging from their hiding places after a long, frigid winter mingled with the cacophony of car horns and truck tires bumping through potholes.

April was a month of contradictions. In April, the world came alive again after months of dormancy. He loved sitting on his back deck, in the cool air laced with the promise of the spring, watching the deer emerge from the woods and the buds flower on the trees.

But April was a month of loss, too. Charlotte had died in April, three years earlier.

And April was the month he'd let Tegan walk out of his life. Looking back, he knew he'd needed this time on his own to get over Charlotte and figure out his future. But for the rest of his life, he'd regret how he hadn't been there for Tegan when Jamie was dying. And how he'd stupidly let her go without learning her last name or phone number. Now that his head was clearer, he couldn't help but wonder what could have been; if they might have at least stayed in touch, keeping open the possibility that someday they'd be ready for something more.

He'd tried to find her, had even hired a private investigator to track her down, but it was like looking for a flashlight in a sky full of stars. After an initial search, even the investigator hadn't been willing to take any more of his money with so little to go on.

The ache over that loss was always there, and somehow sharper at this time of year.

But it wasn't a day for sadness. He patted the messenger bag on his hip, and the box he'd tucked inside rattled. It was a day for moving on.

Twenty minutes later, he pushed open the door to a West Village café and slid into a chair across from Liv. She looked up from the menu and flashed him a smile so delighted, you would've thought she hadn't seen him in days, instead of earlier that afternoon when they'd discussed one of the cases they were working on.

"What?" he asked, as she continued to grin at him. "Why are you giving me that look?"

"Nothing." She shrugged innocently as she poured him a glass of wine from the bottle on the table. "I like having you around, working on cases together. And you look good lately. More relaxed or something."

Jack tugged a hand through his unruly hair and gave her a smile in return. He'd been taking on more of Liv's "bleeding heart" cases, as he liked to tease her, and he had to admit it had been rewarding. Not that he planned to give up his own clients anytime soon, but he was feeling more open-minded lately.

And speaking of open-minded, he had a couple of things that he wanted to discuss with Liv. "So. I've been thinking," he began, leaning back and taking a generous sip of his wine. "About your offer to fix me up with some of your friends."

Her eyes widened and her smile grew bigger, if that was even possible. "Yes?"

"Yeah. I, uh—" He'd decided to do this, but it still made him nervous to put it out there. "I think I'm ready."

Liv clasped her hands to her chest like a little girl who'd just found her Easter basket. "Oh, Jack! I'm so happy. I already have someone in mind and I really think you'll like her."

"Okay, but take it easy there, Liv. I just want to go on a couple of dates. Nothing serious yet."

Her smile vanished, but he could tell she was trying to hold it back. "Right, of course." She nodded over and over. "No pressure, just coffee or a drink the next time you're in the city. Just to start getting out there again."

He turned the idea over in his head. Getting out there again. Muddling through awkward first-date conversations in the hopes that someone might come along who he connected with. He couldn't imagine ever falling in love again. But he'd thought the same thing after Charlotte died. And then he met Tegan.

Tegan seemed to be in his head a lot today.

He shook his head to clear it. "So, in the spirit of moving on and getting out there again…" He dug in his bag and pulled out a small wooden box. "I want you to have this." He slid the box across the table.

Liv looked at him sideways as she lifted the lid. "What is it?" She looked down at the small pile of silk and velvet pouches. "Jewelry?"

Jack opened one of the pouches and spilled a pearl necklace out into his hand. "Charlotte's jewelry. She only had a brother, and she always thought of you like a sister. I think she would have wanted you to have it."

Liv took the necklace from him and ran a finger over the pearls. "Oh, Jack."

"If it feels too weird to wear it, you could keep it, and if you ever have a daughter, pass it down to her."

She smiled wistfully. "That's exactly what I'll do."

Jack packed up the jewelry and closed the lid. He felt a little pang of sadness handing it over to Liv, but at the same time, he felt lighter too.

"What did you do with the rest of her things?"

"Her parents took some jewelry and art that had been in the family for a long time. And I donated most of her clothes to one of those places that provides women in need with interview suits and outfits for work."

"Oh, that's perfect. Charlotte had beautiful clothes." Liv reached across the table and squeezed his hand. "Jack, this is really big deal. I'm so happy for you."

It *did* feel like a big deal. But one he was finally ready for.

After Jack had put Liv in a cab headed to the Upper East Side, he cut across Washington Square Park toward his place in the West Village. He'd bought a two-bedroom condo about a year ago so he'd have a place to stay when he was in the city. Otherwise, his parents would have wanted him to stay with them. While he had to admit that his mother had been working on backing off and accepting his life on his terms, a couple of dinners a month was more than enough togetherness for everybody.

On the other side of the park, Jack passed a small independent bookstore and, on a whim, decided to stop. Since he'd been taking the train upstate to avoid traffic, he had more time to read lately.

He walked in and almost crashed into a woman crouched in front of a display for a current bestseller. He veered to the left to avoid her, his gaze snapping automatically to the books she was unloading from a box on the floor.

The cover featured a photo taken from behind of a young woman with long blond hair sitting on the hood of a car. The desert stretched out in front of her and, in the distance, the sun set behind an outcropping of rocks.

Jack picked up a book, unable to tear his eyes away. Something about the image sparked a sense of déjà vu, as if he'd been there in that exact spot, with that exact woman.

"That's a really good one. Super popular."

Jack blinked and looked up.

The woman in front of him was wearing a T-shirt with the name of the bookstore splashed across the front. She laughed and gestured toward the table. "Hence the giant display."

Jack's gaze roamed across the pile of books to the cardboard cutout of the same photo from the cover, and a list of all the awards the book had won.

A Road Left Behind Me by Tegan Walker.

He gripped the table to keep his legs from giving out.

The woman looked at him sideways. "Are you okay?"

Jack turned the book over and opened to the back page where a photo of Tegan smiled at him. Her hair was shorter, cropped to chin-length, and something in her eyes suggested a wariness that hadn't been there before; as if she'd been through a lot in the past few years, and had come out just a little more guarded. But those freckles were still scattered across her cheeks, and they did all kinds of crazy things to his heart.

"She's coming here next week." The bookstore woman was talking to him again.

He looked up. "Excuse me?"

"Tegan Walker. The author. She's coming here for a book signing. I was just about to put up the sign." She paused and squinted at him. "Are you okay? You don't look very well."

Tegan would be here. In this bookstore. In one week.

He slammed the book shut and gripped it tightly against his chest. "Yes, I'm fine. I'm sorry. I'll take this." He fished his credit card out of his wallet.

As soon as she handed him his receipt, Jack bolted out of the store and stumbled across McDougal Street, back to the park. He flung himself on the first empty bench he came to and opened the book.

And then he saw the dedication on the first page and his heart, which had been pounding in his ears moments earlier, abruptly stopped beating.

For Jamie. May you find immeasurable joy in Heaven.
And Jack, may you find it here on Earth.

CHAPTER THIRTY-SEVEN

Tegan

New York City always left Tegan a little on edge. She'd visited the city a half a dozen times in the past year—both her agent and publisher were here—but all those pedestrians rushing around and cabs zipping by never failed to make her think of Jack. He was so close—maybe in the next building or just around the corner.

Most of the time, she focused on her career. Her first book had become a bestseller, racking up awards and landing on dozens of reading lists. And her second book would be published early next year.

Out on the road, she'd rarely let her mind drift to Jack, but somehow it always happened when she was in New York. There were 9 million people living here, but still, she searched every face for that one she could never completely get out of her head.

It was almost a relief to sit down for her book signing that afternoon. Jack probably lived in a high rise in the Upper East Side and worked at a fancy downtown law firm. The chances that he'd wander into an independent bookstore in the West Village on a Thursday at 4 p.m. seemed next to none. She could focus on talking to her readers without the temptation to search the back of the room in the hopes that the tall, sandy-haired man who'd just walked in was Jack.

Tegan signed autograph after autograph, humbled as always by the people who showed up to meet her and declare their love for her book. She was still smiling at a woman and her two daughters as they moved down the line when another copy of her book slid in front of her.

"Can you sign it to Neal Cassady, from Jacquelyn Kerouac?"

That voice.

Her head jerked up, and her heart slammed in her chest. Jack stood above her, his blue eyes crinkling and his dimple on full display.

"Jack," she whispered. "I—how did you—?"

"You're famous, Tegan." The dimple deepened.

He was here. Jack was here. A hurricane swirled in her brain, sweeping up her ability to think straight. "I never expected—" she stopped abruptly.

"To see me again?"

"Yes." And it had broken her heart.

His grin faded. Maybe he thought she never actually wanted to see him again. God knows, she was surprised *he* wanted to see *her* again.

She tried to smile, but her face seemed to be frozen.

"Congratulations on all of this." He swept his arm around the room, but his eyes didn't leave hers.

Something was wrong with her voice, because she couldn't speak, especially with those Colorado-blue-sky eyes staring her down. She twisted her Sharpie marker in shaking hands. Then the next person in line stepped forward, and Jack's gaze wrenched away from her.

"I'm holding up your line."

"Yes," she managed to choke out.

"I should go."

No.

Tegan grabbed his book and scribbled, *Jack, Thanks for the adventure of a lifetime.* Her pen stilled, and then she added, *Love, Tegan.*

He took the book and glanced at the two women in line behind him, who were both watching their exchange with open curiosity.

He turned back to Tegan. "Can you meet for coffee later? Or dinner tonight?"

Oh, God, she wanted to. But they had to leave for Philly the second she was done here. She glanced at her publicist who tapped her watch and circled her hand in a "move this along" gesture.

"I—I'm sorry. I can't." She was leaving town, and had book signings, readings, and interviews scheduled in cities all over the east coast until the end of the month.

"What about right after this? Just for a few minutes."

Her mind whirled. Could she squeeze in ten minutes before they had to get on the road? She shook her head. Her publicist had already told her that the New York crowd was bigger than expected, and they'd be cutting it close trying to get to Philly on time.

Jack glanced back at the line of people waiting to talk to her and then he nodded. "I know you're busy." He paused, opening his mouth as if he was going to say something and then changed his mind. He gave a slight shake of his head. "I'll let you get back to it. Sorry to just show up here like this. I know it's been a long time, and I'm sure you've—you've probably moved on." He tapped the book in his hand. "Congratulations again. It's a beautiful tribute to Jamie." And before she could say a word, he turned and headed across the bookstore.

Had he taken her hesitation as a sign that she didn't want to see him? Damn it, she should have said something, but she'd been too frozen with shock. Jack pushed the door open and stepped out onto the sidewalk.

No. He couldn't leave. She had no way of finding him again.

Tegan lurched to her feet. "I need five minutes," she hissed to her publicist as she darted around the table. Shoving the front door open, she stumbled out onto the street and looked around wildly.

She spotted Jack just as he rounded the corner and disappeared from sight.

"Jack!" she called, taking off running. She flew around the corner and nearly plowed into a woman stopped on the sidewalk so her dog could do its business. Tegan hopped over the leash and kept going. "Jack!"

He swung around. Confusion crossed his face for a second, and then something that she couldn't identify.

She slid to a stop in front of him.

"I looked for you, you know." Her chest hitched as she struggled to catch her breath. "A while after I left. I tried to find you."

"You—" He blinked. "Really?"

She took another deep breath in and out. "You know how many guys named Jack Bennett work at law firms in New York City? And if Google Images is accurate, most of them are balding and sixty."

His lips quirked. "You always thought I resembled a stodgy old man."

"I knew you said you worked at the family business, but I couldn't find any firm named Bennett in New York or San Francisco." He didn't need to know that she'd even googled Charlotte, but there was no mention of Charlotte's fiancé's name or contact information in any of the articles about the foundation he'd funded. Only that he wanted to remain private, which sounded like the Jack she knew.

"It's Jonathan Townsend," he said with a grin.

"What?"

"My name. Jonathan Townsend the Third."

"What?" She was like a record on repeat, trying to process this. "Jonathan?"

"My dad and grandfather go by John Townsend. So, I got Jack. And only my mom's last name is Bennett. She was already established professionally when she married my dad, so she never changed it." He smiled. "Try googling Jonathan or Jack Townsend next time."

"Jack Townsend." She liked how it sounded. It suited him.

"So, Tegan Walker, did you chase me down the street to tell me that I need to work on my internet presence?"

She shook her head. "We have to be in Philly for a reading tonight. And then I have to go to something like thirteen different cities in eighteen days." She took a baby step toward him. "That's why I can't see you later. It's not because—it's not that I don't want to meet you for coffee."

"So, you're still a nomad?" He shoved his hands in the pockets of his jeans, and something about that familiar gesture pricked at her eyes.

"Yeah, but now my trips are a little less spontaneous. I'm pretty much scheduled down to the minute." She laughed. "You'd love it."

His dimple flashed again. "You'd be surprised by how spontaneous I am lately."

She took a step back to take all of him in. His hair was longer, less styled, and streaked with blond, as if he'd been spending time in the sun. The blue button-up shirt was classic Jack, but he'd rolled the sleeves to his elbows and paired it with jeans and sneakers. She did a double take. Jack was wearing sneakers? Of course, they were leather, and probably expensive, but still.

It wasn't just the physical changes that struck her, though. She squinted at him, trying to figure out what was different. And then it came to her. The exhausted, haunted look in his eyes was gone. He seemed relaxed, peaceful even, instead of tightly wound and slightly on edge.

He cocked his head and gazed across the space between them. "So, do you ever think you'll settle down? Hang out in one place for a while?"

She thought about it all the time. But the small town of her little-girl dreams still hadn't materialized. She'd traveled all over the country, and it had only made her more restless. Longing for something she couldn't name.

Tegan glanced around at the New York sidewalk during rush hour, where an endless stream of people swarmed past like the migration of the wildebeest. A cab sped past, swerving into the right lane as at least three other drivers laid on their horns in protest.

This was Jack's world. He might seem more at peace than when she knew him two years ago, but he was still a wealthy New York lawyer, and she was still a vagabond writer. Suddenly, all the reasons why they would never have worked out came back to her.

"Sometimes. But you know me." She flashed him a rueful smile. "I couldn't live in a place like this. I need to see the stars. And sunsets."

"I remember the sunsets." He took a step closer. "So, you never said why you were looking for me."

Tegan studied her feet. "Oh, I don't know…" She'd basically admitted that she'd stalked him. But what could she say?

Because I never stopped thinking about you.

Suddenly, she was overwhelmed. Jack stood there, so appealing, and the memory of her feelings for him rolled back over her. She turned and looked in the direction of the bookstore. That was her life now, and she'd left a line of fans waiting for her back there.

"I have to go."

"I know."

She wrapped her arms around herself. "I don't know what to say to you. I'm not even sure why you're here. And I'm leaving for Philly in an hour."

"I know."

"And then I'll be on the road for weeks." Tegan paused. "I think about that trip all the time, Jack. But it wasn't real life, you know?" How could this still hurt so much, all these years later?

Jack took another step toward her, patting the pockets of his jeans. "Do you have a pen?"

Tegan looked at him sideways and then pulled the Sharpie she'd been using to sign books out of her back pocket. He took it and uncapped it with his teeth.

"When is this section of your book tour over?" He talked around the pen cap in his mouth as he took hold of her arm.

"May second, back here in New York. Then I have a week off. What are you doing?"

He scribbled something across her wrist. A name of a town? *Falls Creek, New York.*

"There's a train that leaves Penn Station every day at 8:30 a.m., going north. It gets into Falls Creek at 11:15. Can you meet me there on May third?"

"What's in Falls Creek?"

"Come, and I'll show you."

"But—"

"Please?" He was still holding her arm, and that same zap of electricity that had always pulsed between them hit her right in the abdomen.

Was there any real point to this, or would it just set her up for more heartache? "I don't know, Jack."

"Just think about it, okay?" He said. "May third. I'll be there waiting for you."

CHAPTER THIRTY-EIGHT

Tegan

"We have time for one more question," Tegan's publicist announced to the crowd lined up in rows of folding chairs and holding copies of her recently signed book.

Finally, it was the last night of Tegan's book tour. The past three weeks had moved at a glacial pace, with Jack on the edge of her mind for pretty much all of it. One more question to go, and then…Well, and then she had no idea.

A young woman near the front raised her hand, and Tegan nodded in her direction. The woman stood up, smoothing her skirt nervously. "I loved your book so much," she began, slightly breathless.

Tegan gave her a smile. "Thank you. It never gets old to hear that."

The woman shifted the book in her hand. "So, my question is—what would Jamie say if he could see you now?"

Tegan opened her mouth and then closed it. She was used to talking about Jamie—he was the subject of her book, after all—but she hadn't been expecting that question. What *would* Jamie say if he could see her now?

Jamie would say… that he was beyond proud of her success.

And he'd say that he was worried as hell.

Lately, most of Tegan's time was spent shuttling around the country on book tours and, when she had a few weeks off, she'd rent a cabin or AirBNB to hide out and work on her next project. As Tegan looked out at the dozens of faces at this latest book event, it occurred to her that she vacillated between talking to crowds of complete strangers and talking to nobody at all. It wasn't exactly the life she and Jamie had imagined: one where they'd drop off casseroles for sick neighbors and volunteer at the local church carnival. One where they had friends, family, and a community surrounding them.

If Jamie could see her now, he'd say… that she should go meet Jack in Falls Creek.

Tegan's heart gave a tiny flip. She couldn't imagine why Jack had invited her to this town in upstate New York instead of suggesting they meet for coffee somewhere in the city. She'd googled Falls Creek, of course, but the town's website touting its bike trails and breweries didn't offer any clues. And as for why he'd shown up at her book signing and wanted to see her again… Tegan didn't know that either. But she'd had plenty of time on the car rides between different cities to remember long drives with Jack. How good it had been between them for those days—and nights—before it had all fallen apart.

Tegan looked at the woman in front of her, still eagerly awaiting an answer to her question. She flashed a grin at the crowd. "Jamie would say… just because I'm a successful author now, it doesn't mean I can get out of doing the dishes."

The crowd broke up laughing, and Tegan's publicist took the opportunity to wrap things up. As people filtered out of the bookshop onto the street, Tegan helped pack up the leftover books.

"Have you booked an AirBNB where you'll be staying on the break?" her publicist asked as they loaded everything into the van outside.

Tegan glanced around at the people laughing, talking, and making plans to grab dinner together. "No," she said. "Can you drop me at a hotel near Penn Station? I have a train I need to catch in the morning."

*

The moment the train pulled into the station, Tegan spotted Jack leaning against a stone wall with his hands shoved in the pockets of his jeans and one hiking boot crossed over the other. Her pulse kicked up at the sight of him and, suddenly, she couldn't get off the train fast enough.

Jack's gaze roamed across the passengers as they disembarked from the train. She forced herself to slow her pace as she crossed the tracks to where he stood. When his eyes settled on her, something flashed across his face that resembled relief.

Had he been worried that she wouldn't come?

"Hi," she said, stopping in front of him.

His face broke out into a smile. "Hi." He took the strap of her backpack from her shoulder and slid it onto his own. "I'm glad to see that your book sales are robust enough to allow you to afford more duct tape for you backpack."

She smiled ruefully. She couldn't tell him that her book sales were more than robust, but she still hadn't replaced her ratty old backpack because it reminded her of their trip together. "So, where am I, anyway?"

"Falls Creek, New York."

"Yeah, I figured out that part. But, you know, like on a metaphysical level. *Where am I?*"

He laughed. "It will all become clear, Jacqueline Kerouac." He tucked her hand into the crook of his arm. "Come on, I parked a few blocks down Main Street. You can tell me what you think of the town."

They strolled out of the historic old train station into the May sunshine. As Jack steered them down the steps and out the gate,

Tegan's eyes widened. Stretched out before them was a street lined with old maple trees and rows of colorful, impeccably restored Victorian buildings. In front of the buildings, menu boards and signs stitched on awnings announced the names of a bookstore, several cafes, and an old-fashioned hardware store. If the Rocky Mountains had loomed in the distance, she would have believed she was back in Copper Canyon.

"Hey, Jack."

A thirty-something guy in a tight-fitting flannel shirt and hipster beard waved in their direction from where he was sweeping the sidewalk in front of an antiques store. Jack smiled and tugged her in the man's direction. "Hey, David, how are you?" They shook hands like old friends.

"Good. Hey, how'd those door handles work out for you?"

"Perfect. Thanks. I still can't believe you found a match for the ones that were already in the house."

"It was no problem. Let me know if you need anything else."

David went back to sweeping, and she and Jack continued down the block. For about the hundredth time, Tegan wondered about Jack's connection to this town. Had he taken a trip out of the city one weekend, maybe looking for antiques for his apartment, and stumbled on Falls Creek? He knew about her romantic notion of living in small towns; maybe he wanted to show it to her.

She had to admit he'd gotten it exactly right. She'd only been in Falls Creek for ten minutes but she was already charmed by the shops and friendly people, who all seemed to know each other. Quite a few of them seemed to know Jack, too. Just how much time did he spend here?

She only had a short time to wonder about it, though, because in the next minute they arrived at his car and the memories almost knocked her over. Jack still drove the black Mercedes SUV and, except for the boxes missing from the backseat, it was exactly the same. The radio they'd argued over, the floor mat that she'd been pathologically unable to keep clean, the center console she'd climbed over into his lap while a storm raged outside. As she slid into the passenger seat, it was like entering a time machine.

She looked at Jack sideways as he drove the car out of town and turned off the main highway onto a smaller road that wound up into the mountains, still with no explanation of their destination. "Are you kidnapping me?"

He chuckled. "Absolutely."

A few minutes later, Jack slowed the car as they drove up next to a crumbling old stone wall that ran alongside the road. He made a right past a red-painted mailbox and onto a driveway that curved into the woods. Around the next bend, he pulled the car to a stop in a clearing and glanced in her direction.

Tegan looked from Jack to the three-story Victorian-era farmhouse in front of her, and then her eyes skated across a field of wildflowers to a wooden barn at the edge of the woods. Her gaze flew back to Jack. "Okay, I give up. Where am I?"

He hesitated, pressing his lips together, and then his mouth curved in a tentative smile. "My house."

"Your—" She shifted her body forward again. The house looked like it had been recently renovated, with celadon-painted cedar siding, eggplant-colored trim around the dormers and roof gables, and a giant porch that wrapped around three sides. The colors of the house fit in perfectly with the woods, and there were a bunch of charming little touches, like the stained-glass transom window, the white-painted porch swing, and the window boxes stuffed with flowers. "Your house? What, like a weekend home?"

"Nope." He shrugged. "Not a weekend home. Just my home. I have a small place in the city but I only stay there when I have meetings at the office, maybe once a month. Most of the time I'm able to work from here. This is where I live."

Her mouth dropped open. "I—wow. I wasn't expecting that."

He grinned. "Come see the inside."

The interior was as charming and impeccably restored as the exterior, with airy whites and creams contrasting with dark wood accents, and comfortable modern furniture mixed in with quirky antiques. "It's gorgeous, Jack."

"You really like it?" He tapped a hand against his thigh and Tegan wondered if he was nervous.

She knew Jack well enough to know that he didn't bring her here just to show off, and he seemed concerned that she liked the house. He led her through the kitchen to a pair of French doors that opened to an enormous deck off the back. Past the deck was a small lawn with a fenced-in vegetable garden and a shed painted to match the house. And then beyond that, the cliff dropped off, revealing the expansive mountain range, lush with blooming trees and May wildflowers, stretching all the way to the patchwork farmlands of the Hudson Valley. It was so beautiful that for a moment she was speechless.

Jack laid her backpack on a deck chair. "Do you have hiking boots in here? There are trails that go all through these mountains. I thought we could take a little hike, and—" He flashed that uncertain look again. "—catch up a bit."

Tegan's heart did a backflip. It was a sunny spring afternoon, she was in one of the most beautiful places she'd been in a long time, and she still couldn't believe that after two years of thinking that she'd never see Jack again, he was standing in front of her. She wanted more time with him. If this was just about making amends or getting closure before they went their separate ways again, she wanted to put that off for just a little bit longer.

Jack filled a backpack with snacks and water, and they headed out into the woods, wandering along a path that zigzagged down the mountain. They hopped over a crumbling stone wall that Jack said had been there since the 1700s, and followed the trail along the bank of a creek. They chatted about his work, and her book tour, and everything but their past relationship, or how it had imploded.

On their way back to Jack's house, he asked about Jamie, and she told him about their last few weeks together. When her voice trembled, he stopped in the middle of the path and pulled her into his arms. She leaned into him, feeling his heartbeat and breathing in that scent that was still so familiar, even after two years.

When they got back to Jack's house, he led her into the living room. As they settled on the couch Tegan turned to face him.

"This is amazing, Jack. I wouldn't have expected to find you living in a place like this."

"Why not?"

"I don't know. I thought you'd go back to your city life. Corporate attorney job, fancy parties and social events." She'd been sure she wouldn't fit into that life. But that wasn't the real reason she'd left him.

Three years had passed since Charlotte died. Was he still grieving her?

That was a stupid question, though. She was still grieving Jamie. You didn't get over losing someone you loved like that.

Jack gazed across the living room, and she turned to see what he was looking at. Framed over the fireplace mantel hung a beat-up, wrinkled map with torn edges and a water stain in one corner. A map of the United States with colorful pen lines criss-crossing the country, and hand-drawn circles and notes marking various towns. She gasped and jumped to her feet to move closer.

Her eyes automatically snapped to a little spot in the middle of Nowhere, Arizona. There was a red star near Diablo that hadn't been there before. Jack appeared next to her, and she turned to face him. "I'm surprised it's not painful for you to look at this," she said. "After... everything that happened."

He stared at the map for a moment, and then turned back to her. "When I have those moments where everything feels hard, I come in here and remember that you have to keep going because you never know what unexpected turn you'll end up taking. That trip changed my life."

Her heart ached at the sorrow that flashed in his eyes. Did everything still feel hard for him? "I bet you miss Charlotte every day."

"I miss Charlotte." He paused, shoving his hands in his pockets. "Part of me will always miss Charlotte." Jack gazed past her, out the window. "You asked why I didn't move back to the city. I had a good life with Charlotte, but it's over. I was going through the motions, just trying to keep moving forward, and New York seemed like the obvious destination. And then right about here—" He gestured toward the star in Arizona. "I changed direction."

Tegan looked at that spot on the map. She'd been so lost, even though she hadn't known it at the time. In the past two years, she'd grown up, faced the worst thing that ever happened to her, and survived it. And she'd finally made it on her own.

Suddenly, it became clear that she was never going to find the perfect small town of her childhood dreams. There was no magical place on Earth that could give her a happy ending if the people she loved weren't there with her. That magical place was next to Jamie while he was hopped up on drugs to mute his pain, but still able to laugh so hard he nearly fell off the bed. It was in a roadside motel with Jack, drinking a bottle of cheap wine and talking until dawn. And it was this beautiful day with him, remembering all the reasons why she fell in love with him two years ago.

She'd walked out of his life once, but she was wiser now.

"Jack, I know this doesn't make a lot of sense." She took a step toward him. "Really, I've only known you for a few weeks, and I haven't seen you in two years. But, I've never been able to get you out of my head."

He looked at her, his expression unreadable. Then he reached out and took her by the shoulders, pulling her closer. The heat from his hands burned a path right to her heart. "Tegan, when

Charlotte died, I felt like I'd died too." He looked down at her, his eyes naked with emotion. "You brought me back to life."

All the breath rushed from her lungs.

And then he slid his hand behind her head and pressed his mouth to hers. She pushed herself up on her tiptoes and kissed him back, clutching the fabric of his shirt, holding on for dear life and vowing to never, ever, let him go again.

When they broke apart, he took her face in his hands, brushing her hair off her cheek. "Tegan, stay here with me. I know you're a vagabond writer and you have to go back on your book tour next week. But when it's done, I'll be waiting for you. I'll always be waiting for you."

The tears that had been pricking the back of her eyes spilled over. She laughed as she brushed them away with her sleeve. "But, Jack, this house is so beautiful. What happens when I drop pretzel crumbs on the rug or spill my coffee all over the couch?"

"Tegan, I will be so happy to see crumbs in the rug and stains on the couch, because it means you're here with me." He took her hand and flashed her a grin. "You haven't seen the rest of the house yet."

She followed him up the staircase, barely noticing the photo of a desert sunset hanging in the landing because that's where Jack stopped to kiss her. And as he tugged her down the hall, a wonderful thought flashed into her mind.

She was home.

A LETTER FROM MELISSA

Dear reader,

I want to say a huge thank you for choosing to read *The Girl in the Picture*. I hope you enjoyed it! If you'd like to keep up to date with all my latest releases, just sign up at the following link. Your email address will never be shared and you can unsubscribe at any time.

www.bookouture.com/melissa-wiesner

It may surprise you to learn that this book was almost two decades in the making! Jack and Tegan's story first began on a road trip I took across the US while in college. A friend and I traversed the country from east to west and back again, listening to NPR and country music on the radio, and stopping at every roadside attraction we could find. Unlike Tegan, I didn't end up in any strangers' cars, but I did end up with an abundant supply of inspiration that eventually culminated in this book.

If you enjoyed Jack and Tegan's adventure, I would be very grateful if you could write a review. I'd love to hear what you think, and it makes such a difference helping new readers to discover my books for the first time.

Please be in touch! You can reach me on my Facebook page, through Twitter, Goodreads or my website.

Thanks,
Melissa Wiesner

MelissaWiesnerAuthor

@Melissa-Wiesner

www.melissawiesner.com

ACKNOWLEDGMENTS

I'd like to thank the talented team at Bookouture for all your hard work in helping me bring this novel into the world. I was so fortunate to have the opportunity to collaborate with two wonderful editors this time around! Thank you to Caolinn Douglas for falling in love with this book, pulling it out of the slush pile, and launching my career as a published author. And thank you to Ellen Gleeson for making the editing process seem effortless. It was amazing to work with you both.

Thank you to Julie Dinneen and Bob Diforio at the D4EO Literary Agency. It's been an honor to be represented by you.

Thank you to my fellow writers who critiqued this novel and helped shape it into something wonderful. In particular, thank you to Meg Ripley, Becky Fettig, Daniele Arndt, and Keely Bowers and the *Madwomen in the Attic*.

To Amy DeGurian—I don't know if this book would be the same without the knowledge I absorbed from sitting in on your many grief and loss lectures. The idea that grief is not a straight line from denial to acceptance, but a wild, squiggly scribble helped to shape Jack's story of loss, and of moving on. Thank you for double clicking on that, Steve-o.

To my family, thank you for your unending support and encouragement.

And finally, my most sincere gratitude to my readers. It's an absolute honor to write for you.

Made in United States
North Haven, CT
04 August 2023

39916005R00182